THE
CHOCOLATE
TOUCH

ALSO BY LAURA FLORAND

The Chocolate Thief

The Chocolate Kiss

THE
CHOCOLATE
TOUCH

LAURA
FLORAND

KENSINGTON PUBLISHING CORP.
www.kensingtonbooks.com

KENSINGTON BOOKS are published by

Kensington Publishing Corp.
119 West 40th Street
New York, NY 10018

All Kensington titles, imprints, and distributed lines are available at special quantity discounts for bulk purchases for sales promotions, premiums, fund-raising, educational, or institutional use.

Special book excerpts or customized printings can also be created to fit specific needs. For details, write or phone the office of the Kensington special sales manager: Kensington Publishing Corp., 119 West 40th Street, New York, NY 10018, attn: Special Sales Department; phone: 1-800-221-2647.

KENSINGTON and the k logo are Reg. U.S. Pat. & TM Off.

ISBN-13: 978-0-7582-8632-1
ISBN-10: 0-7582-8632-5

First Kensington Trade Paperback Printing: August 2013

10 9 8 7 6 5 4 3 2

Printed in the United States of America

First electronic edition: August 2013

ISBN-13: 978-0-7582-8633-8
ISBN-10: 0-7582-8633-3

CHAPTER 1

"She's back."

Dom straightened from the enormous block of chocolate he was creating, gave his *maîtresse de salle,* Guillemette, a disgruntled look for having realized he would want to know that, and slipped around to the spot in the glass walls where he could get the best view of the *salle* below. He curled his fingers into his palms so he wouldn't press his chocolaty hands to the glass and leave a stain like a kid outside a candy shop.

She sat alone as she always did, at one of the small tables. For a week now, she had come twice a day. Once in the morning, once in the afternoon. She was probably a tourist, soaking up as much French artisanal chocolate as she could in her short stay in Paris, as they liked to do. But even he admitted it was strange that her soaking up should be only of him. Most wandered: him in the morning, Philippe Lyonnais in the afternoon, Sylvain Marquis the next day. Tourists read guidebooks and visited the top ten; they didn't have the informed taste to know that Sylvain Marquis was boring and Dominique Richard was the only man a woman's tongue could get truly excited about.

This woman—looked hard to excite. She seemed so pulled in on herself, so utterly quiet and contained. She had a wide, soft poet's mouth and long-lashed eyes whose color he couldn't tell from that far away. Hair that was always hidden by a hood, or occasionally a fashionable hat and a loosely tied scarf, like Audrey Hepburn. High cheekbones that needed more flesh on them. A dust-powder of freckles covered her face, so many they blurred together.

The first day, she had looked all skin and bones. Like a model, but she was too small and too freckled, so maybe just another city anorexic. When she had ordered a cup of *chocolat chaud* and a chocolate éclair, he had expected to see her dashing to the *toilettes* soon after, to throw it up before the binge of calories could infect her, and it had pissed him off, because he loathed having his chocolate treated that way.

But she had just sat there, her eyes half closed, her hands curling around the hot cup of chocolate caressingly. She had sat there a long time, working her way through both éclair and *chocolat chaud* bit by little bit. And never once had she pulled out a journal or a phone or done anything except sit quite still, absorbing.

When she had left, he had been surprised to feel part of himself walk out with her. From the long casement windows, he had watched her disappear down the street, walking carefully, as if the sidewalk might rise up and bite her if she didn't.

That afternoon, she was back, her hands curling once again around a cup of his *chocolat chaud,* and this time she tried a slice of his most famous *gâteau.* Taking slow, tiny mouthfuls, absorbing everything around her.

Absorbing him. Everything in this place was him. The rough, revealed stone of the archways and three of the walls. The heavy red velvet curtains that satisfied a hunger in him with their rich, passionate opulence. The rosebud-embossed white wall that formed a backdrop to her, although no one could understand what part of him it came from. The gleaming, severe, cutting-edge displays. The flats of minuscule square chocolates, dark and rich and printed with whimsical elusive designs, displayed in frames of metal; the select collection of pastries, his *gâteaux au chocolat,* his éclairs, his *tartes*; clear columns of his caramels. Even the people around her at other tables were his. While they were in his shop, he owned them, although they thought they were buying him.

The third afternoon, when the waiter came upstairs with her order, Dom shook his head suddenly. "Give her this." He handed Thierry the lemon-thyme-chocolate éclair he had been inventing that morning.

He watched the waiter murmur to her when he brought it, watched her head lift as she looked around. But she didn't know to look up for him and maybe didn't know what he looked like, even if she did catch sight of him.

When she left, Thierry, the waiter, brought him the receipt she had left on the table. On the back she had written, *Merci beaucoup,* and signed it with a scrawled initial. L? J? S? It could be anything.

A sudden dread seized him that *Merci* meant *Adieu* and he wouldn't see her again, her flight was leaving, she was packing her bags full of souvenirs. She had even left with a box of his chocolates. For the plane ride. It left a hole in him all night, the thought of how his *salon* would be without her.

But the next morning, she was back, sitting quietly, as if being there brought repose to her very soul.

He felt hard-edged just looking at her restfulness, the bones showing in her wrists. He felt if he got too close to her, he would bump into her and break her. What the hell business did he have to stand up there and look at her? She needed to be in Sylvain's place, somewhere glossy and sweet, not in his, where his chocolate was so dark you felt the edge of it on your tongue.

She needed, almost certainly, a prince, not someone who had spent the first six years of his working life, from twelve to eighteen, in a ghastly abattoir, hacking great bloody hunks of meat off bones with hands that had grown massive and ugly from the work, his soul that had grown ugly from it, too. He had mastered the dark space in his life, but he most surely did not need to let her anywhere near it or to think what might happen if he ever let it slip its leash.

"She certainly has a thing for you, doesn't she?" his short, spiky-haired chocolatier Célie said, squeezing her boss into the corner so she could get a better look. Dom sent a dark glance down at the tufted brown head. He didn't know why his team persisted in treating him like their big brother or perhaps even their indulgent father, when he was only a few years older than they were and would be lousy at both roles. No other top chef in the whole city had a team that treated him that way. Maybe he had a knack for hiring idiots.

Maybe he needed to train them to be in abject terror of him or at least respect him, instead of just training them how to do a damn good job. He only liked his equals to be terrified of him, though. The thought of someone vulnerable to him being terrified made him sick to his stomach.

"She must be in a hotel nearby," he said. That was all. Right?

"Well, she's not eating much else in Paris, not as thin as she is." Célie wasn't fat by any means, but she was slightly more rounded than the Parisian ideal, and judgmental of women who starved themselves for fashion. "She's stuck on you."

Dom struggled manfully to subdue a flush. He couldn't say why, but he liked, quite extraordinarily, the idea of Freckled Would-be Audrey Hepburn being stuck on him.

"You haven't seen her run and throw anything up?" Célie checked doubtfully.

"*No*, she doesn't—*non*. She *likes* having me inside her."

Célie made an odd gurgling sound and looked up at him with her eyes alight, and Dom replayed what he had just said. "Will you get out of my space? Don't you have work to do?"

"Probably about as much as you." Célie grinned smugly, not budging.

Hardly. Nobody worked as hard as the owner. What the hell did Sylvain Marquis and Philippe Lyonnais do with employees who persisted in walking all over them? How did this happen to him? *He* was the biggest, ugliest customer in the whole world of Parisian chocolate, and yet in his own *laboratoire*—this was what he had to put up with.

Célie waggled her eyebrows at him. "So what's wrong with you? Are you sick? Why haven't you gone up with your—" She braced her shoulders and swung them back and forth, apparently trying to look macho and aggressive. She looked ridiculous. "We could cover for you for a couple of hours."

She tried to treat it like a joke, the way Dom could walk up to a woman, his aggression coming off him in hard edges all over the place, and have that woman get up and disappear with him for a couple of hours. But a profound disapproval lurked in her brown eyes.

Dom set his jaw. His sex life was really *nobody's* business, even if it was infamous, and, well—"*No*. Go start on the *pralinés* before I make you come in at three a.m. tomorrow to do them."

For a wonder, Célie actually started to move. She got three steps away before she turned back. "You haven't had sex with her already, have you? Finally broken someone's heart, and now she's lurking here like a ghost, snatching at your crumbs?"

Dominique stared at her. "Broken her—ghost—crumbs—what the *hell* do you guys make up about me when I'm not in earshot?" He never had sex with women who had hearts. Not ones that beat for him, anyway.

"Nothing. We contemplate possible outcomes of your actions, *chef,* but I think we're pretty realistic about it." Célie gave him her puckish grin and strolled a couple more paces away. Naturally, his breath of relief was premature, and she turned back for one last shot. "Now if we were *creative,* we might have come up with this scenario." She waved a hand at Dom, wedged in a corner between glass and stone, gazing down into his *salle* below.

Whatever the hell that meant.

He blocked Célie's face from the edge of his vision with a shift of one muscled shoulder and focused back on the freckled *inconnue's* table.

Putain, she had left.

Cancer, he thought that night, with a chill of fear. Maybe that explained the hats or hoods or scarves that always hid her hair. Maybe that explained the thinness, and the way she seemed able to just sit still forever, soaking up his life.

He started preparing her plates himself, arranging whatever she had ordered to his satisfaction and then adding in little surprise presents: a miniature tower of three of his square *bonbons,* for example, fresh from the ganache room where trays of them were scattered on wire shelves, waiting to replenish the displays below.

He went to his secret spot, in the corner of the glass walls above the *salle,* to see her reaction. She didn't smile. But she bit into them slowly, taking her time, eating the tiny morsels in two, sometimes even three bites, as if she wanted to savor every aspect of his flavor. The texture of him on her tongue.

And when she was done with him—with *them,* with the chocolates—she always left. Rising. Brushing crumbs off her lap if she had had one of his famous chocolate *mille-*

feuilles. Laying down cash, never once paying with a card so he could know her name.

Was it just his imagination, or was her boniness softening, from the week of absorbing him?

The sixth day, he broke cover, moving suddenly out of his observation post when he saw her rise. His feet sounded too loud, too violent on the polished metal spiral that descended into the room. He was only halfway down by the time she reached the door. She didn't look back toward the sound. She stood as the glass doors slid open for her, and her shoulders shifted in a sigh. And then she was gone, out on the street.

Guillemette and both waiters were eyeing him, eyebrows raised. He turned abruptly on his heel and went back up into his *laboratoire.*

The seventh day, he almost wanted to open the shop, even though they never opened on Monday, because— what would she do? Where would she go without him?

He resisted his own foolishness and then spent the entire day off roaming restlessly around Paris, sometimes on his motorcycle, sometimes on foot, visiting all the tourist spots, which was ridiculous. Sure, a man should take the time to appreciate his city and not leave it all to tourists, but the odds of spotting someone in the Louvre when you didn't even know if she was there were . . . pretty nearly none. Standing looking up at *La Victoire de Samothrace* and as she soared above the crowds in the Richelieu wing of the Louvre inspired him, though, made flavors and textures shift and flow in his mind, tease his palate, as he tried to think of a chocolate that he could call *Victoire.*

He liked *La Victoire de Samothrace.* The flowing, exultant winged marble would have represented the essence of his soul, if only he could purify it of all its darkness and make it that beautiful.

After the Louvre, he even went up the Eiffel Tower,

which he hadn't done since a school trip at age ten. He climbed the first two floors on foot, up and up, taking pleasure in the eventual protest of his thighs, and looked down from it at the whole of Paris. His city. He may once have been this city's outcast, but he had made Paris his.

He liked the Eiffel Tower. All those years it had been shining over his city, and he had never until now realized that. He liked the impossible, fantastical strength of it, the way the metal seemed so massive up close. He liked the fact that it had risen above all the complaints and criticism that surrounded its birth and stamped its power not only over the city but the world. He pulled out the little moleskin journal he always carried with him and stood for a long time sketching the curves and angles of the bolts and metal plates, thinking of designs for the surface of his chocolates.

From the railing, he eyed the tiny figures milling around the Champ de Mars wistfully. He didn't know why he was looking for her. She was too thin and too fragile for him, although something about her conversely exuded strength. He didn't even know what color her hair was, and—her features were quite lovely, with the blue eyes and over-full, wide mouth, too full for her thin face; the thick pale dust of freckles entirely charmed him. But . . . there were any number of women with lovely features in his *chocolaterie* at any one time. There was no reason for her to stand out at all, except the way she sat there, too thin, so quiet, hidden in hoods and draping spring sweaters, pulling all the essence of him into her body as if it was the only thing she wanted to do with her life.

The eighth morning, she didn't come.

His heart congealed. Everything lost its flavor. He looked at his elegant, luscious displays and wanted to throw them all out for their worthless, desperate pretense that he was something other than a twelve-year-old sent by his own father to hack meat off bones for a living. The desperate pretense that the truth of life was not there, in that bloody, stinking, cold place while his father at home kept warm with alcohol.

Something moody and bitter rose up in him, the thing that leaked into his chocolates, made them "dark and cruel," as one critic in *Le Figaro* had called them, apparently in approval, because Parisians eager to prove their sadomasochistic relationship to chocolate had rushed to his *salon* the next day.

When she continued not to come, he couldn't stand himself anymore and flung himself on his motorcycle and cut through the streets, dodging traffic with a lethal disregard for life and limb, over to the Île Saint-Louis. Pretending he needed to see Philippe to talk to him about the Chocolatiers' Expo in a couple of weeks.

This type of event forced him and the other top chocolatiers and pâtissiers to cooperate, not their favorite thing to do. Dom was well aware that he cooperated worse than any of them. He couldn't stand his rivals. Being around them made him want to start a fight, and pummel and batter his way to the top of the heap of them, and grin in bloody, bruised victory. *Yes. I can beat anyone.*

He did like Philippe's little fiancée, Magalie, though. Quite a lot. He liked her smallness and those boots of hers and that impervious center to her, as if she couldn't be touched, and he liked the idea of cutting Philippe out, just hard-edged muscling between them. Mostly he liked the rush of violence in the air whenever he thought about it, liked the fact that it was real and dangerous, that Philippe would genuinely try to kill him, and they could fight with fists and bodies and not just with pastries and chocolate.

He didn't because . . . well, it sure as hell wasn't because he liked or respected Philippe. *Bordel.* It made him gun his motor and cut far too close in front of a car just thinking about that as a possible motivation.

He didn't because . . . *putain.* He didn't because he put a wall of embossed rosebuds in his *salle.* He didn't because, no matter how the temptation might whisper at him sometimes, he could choose *not* to be a man who went around destroying other people's happiness. He could choose to be a man who created happiness, even "dark and cruel" happiness, instead. Still, it was perhaps just as well in his mood that it wasn't Magalie he found hanging out with Philippe but Sylvain Marquis's fiancée, Cade Corey. Who looked at a man as if fighting was such a boring and juvenile thing to do that it kind of took all the fun out of it. She was talking with Philippe when Dom walked into the Lyonnais *laboratoire,* still in his motorcycle leathers. Philippe was doing the *gâteaux* and *pièces montées* for Cade and Sylvain's wedding, which had been postponed already once due to some issue in Cade's family— somebody who had been in the hospital, maybe? Dom couldn't care less, but naturally, if there was gossiping to be done, his team was on it. Sometimes their chatter even penetrated his concentration while he worked.

Sylvain Marquis would drown himself in his own chocolate before he would ask Dominique Richard to do his wedding, of course.

"Dominique," Philippe said brusquely, not looking particularly thrilled to see him.

"Philippe." Dom didn't try to shake Philippe's hand, which was covered with powdered sugar. "Cade." He kissed the slim, brown-haired woman on each cheek. Cade had once come into his *laboratoire* to try to buy his soul with a few of her millions, and he might have been tempted if he didn't find Corey Bars as vile as he did. After all, he had sold his soul several times before, and the thing had been remarkably stubborn about surviving the treatment. In the end, the poor little rich girl had settled for Sylvain, and Dom always felt guilty when he saw her, for having forced her to stoop so low.

Dom had flirted with her on principle when she was negotiating for his soul but remained fundamentally indifferent to her. That dark, mean part of him woke up often enough, with the beautiful privileged women who came into his shop, and he took advantage of their eagerness to be used by him. There was something intensely satisfying about being begged for more rough sex by a woman who would have thought him worthless scum ten years ago.

But Cade had never shown the least desire to be used by him, and beyond the satisfaction of sex with them, princesses didn't do much for him. Their lives were too facile, too privileged. Plus, for God's sake, *Corey Chocolate*. He wasn't Sylvain; he had standards. How could Sylvain even hold up that arrogant head of his, marrying the heir to a multibillion-dollar corporation that produced such mass-market pap?

He frowned at Cade Corey, wondering what the hell Sylvain saw in her.

"What?" she asked dryly, and he gave her a look of surprised approval. The first time he had met her, she had wanted something from him, and thus had tried to be conciliating. He liked her better today, when she couldn't care less what he thought of her.

Straight brown hair that was relentlessly silky, blue eyes, a steady I-own-the-world look. Odd, he kept feeling as if there was something different about her he should notice. "Nothing." He shrugged and turned to Philippe. "So are you doing the Chocolatiers' Expo? Cade, do you know who will be there?"

"Corey will have a strong representation." She pointed a finger at herself, which, being Cade, might mean that she thought she, by herself, was the strong representation. "Devon Candy. Caillebaut, Kraft, Firenze . . ."

Dominique exchanged a look of mutual confusion with Philippe. "I meant the *important* people."

Cade made a little growling noise of frustration.

"Me, you, Simon, Sylvain, I think those are the biggest names," Philippe said. "Are you going yourself or sending some of your team?"

"Myself." Simon Casset would probably do one of his exquisite, impossible flights of chocolate and jewel-toned sugar. Philippe favored displays that allowed him to showcase multiple *gâteaux* in some elegant effect. Sylvain . . . "What's Sylvain doing?" he asked Cade, since, being new to the Paris chocolatier scene, she might be naive enough to tell him.

She smiled sweetly at him. "Working. Why aren't you? Is business slow?"

Seriously, if Cade got any more annoying, he might actually end up liking her. Or at least respecting her. She handled herself all right for someone who had originally dropped into the ultra-competitive Parisian chocolate scene acting as if she thought she could buy it up and stuff it in her pocket.

Instead of responding, he studied Philippe's current work-in-progress. All roses and pink and cream. A peek into some other, fairy-tale world. How did the man manage it? Was it that privileged Lyonnais past of his? Philippe was one of the few men as big as he was, but Dominique always felt bigger near him, oversized and clumsy. As if all his own edges were too hard and would break anything he ran into. His hands were far too big for his *métier.* Giant, hard laborer's hands. They belonged to his first *métier,* the one his father had thought he deserved, that of a man who hacked meat off bones.

He compared notes about the upcoming event, but it started getting embarrassingly obvious that he was just restless and had no real purpose in being here, so he strode out, looking for other places to invade and be obnoxious.

He came out of the kitchens into Philippe's Beauty and the Beast palace of a *salon de thé,* with its well-dressed crowd sitting among marble pillars under embossed lions' heads and painted ceilings. And stopped.

There she was. The woman who had not come that morning. She was sitting in *Philippe's salon de thé,* with one of those rosy, airy, fairy-tale concoctions in front of her.

He felt stabbed through the heart. Standing there, oversized for this froth of a place, in his black motorcycle leathers, with his shaggy hair and his stupidly shaved face. He, who shaved at best once every four days, had shaved every single damn morning for the past week. Why? For what stupid reason?

She put a spoon to her lips, enjoying *Philippe* on her tongue. She looked as if she belonged there, probably more than in the rough stone surroundings of his *salon,* despite his stupid embossed rosebuds and velvet curtains. She set the spoon down and gazed at her dessert a moment, her face a little sad, tired.

He shifted, accusingly, and she glanced up. Her gaze flicked over him, his size, his leathers, his hard stare. Her face closed entirely, and she looked back at him just as aggressively, until he half expected her to pull out Mace if he walked too close to her table.

Fuck her, he thought, so bitterly and insanely wounded, anyone would think he had just discovered his virgin bride in the arms of another man on their wedding night. He strode out of the *salon,* and did *not* bump into anything or break it, but probably mostly because people and even things just seemed to shrink out of his way.

It was a pure wonder he didn't have an accident as he headed off into the Paris streets again. People kept shrinking out of his way there, too.

CHAPTER 2

He ran all his errands for the week, stopping by suppliers, bullying his way through traffic with aggressive, suicidal driving. When he got back to his *salon de chocolat*, it was around three in the afternoon.

And she was there.

Sitting at a little table by herself, with a backdrop of rosebuds, her hands curved around a cup of his chocolate. He felt an absurd, intensely painful urge to knock it out of her hands and yell at her for being a faithless tramp, pretending to be his when she had been that very morning closing her luscious mouth over Philippe Lyonnais.

He was losing it. He crushed the urge, the way he crushed all his other destructive urges, like starting a fistfight with Sylvain Marquis at some chocolate show.

His unknown *habituée* glanced up at the sound of his motorcycle leathers or the appearance of such a large mass of blackness in the beautiful room. Her eyebrows drew a little together, in clear recognition that she had seen him that morning.

When she met his eyes, her face closed completely again, as if she was ready to knife him if he got closer.

He turned away, trying to make his expression softer, more encouraging before she saw it again. Damn it, didn't she know he was the one who had made that *tarte au choco-*

lat et au citron vert she was putting in her mouth? Well, not this particular one, because he had been out sulking, but he had invented the recipe and trained his chefs in how to produce exactly what he wanted.

Guillemette came back downstairs with two plates in one hand, meaning they were busy and shorthanded, and Dominique shrugged out of his black leather jacket and ran up the stairs, so that *l'inconnue* could see he belonged there. He even thought of giving Guillemette a friendly order in passing, so *l'inconnue* could see he was *in charge* here.

Damn it, he bet if Sylvain or Philippe walked into their own shops in street clothes, everyone would still know who they were. Customers didn't assume some violent brute off the street had come in and was going to start causing trouble. The women didn't start reaching for their Mace.

Upstairs, in the most beautiful kitchen in Paris, a *laboratoire* filled with light from great windows, and with long marble counters, and with all the glorious, gleaming, luminous space a man could want, he changed into his pastry chef's jacket. Glee shot through him as always at the *bleu, blanc, et rouge* collar, his award for *Meilleur Ouvrier de France,* and it was all he could do not to crush it in his fists like a child overwhelmed by the thrill. But he didn't. He slipped it on like it was nothing, the most natural thing in the world that he should have the right to wear that collar.

Back downstairs, he made sure to start at the farthest table from her, circling the room, pretending to check on his clients' contentment. He was lousy at that shit. He felt servile. If they didn't like it, to hell with them, they could get out. But he pretended, for her, that he did this routinely, the great master chef deigning to talk to the guests just to brighten their lives.

That's how Philippe Lyonnais does it, he reminded himself. He had seen him. Like *noblesse oblige,* a favor from a prince for him to step out of his kitchens and smile at his subjects. And Sylvain didn't even bother, he would bet. He probably thought it was sufficient *noblesse oblige* for him to have graced the earth with his existence in the first place. Bastard. Dominique *wanted* that arrogance, but on him, it always felt aggressive, hard-edged, forced, like some boxer trying to pound his way to respect.

What was the matter with him, anyway? He didn't weasel his way around women. He walked straight up to them, gave them a challenging look, and either they didn't like it, in which case screw them—well, or not, to be exact. Or they loved it, and pretty much that was it for the romance, and they went back to someone's apartment for a few hours.

But . . . for some reason, he didn't want her to look back at him with rejection or reciprocal challenge. He definitely didn't want her to look at him as if she was mentally gauging her ability to kill him to defend herself. He wanted her to look at him like she looked at his chocolate, as if she was absorbing strength and happiness. And was in no hurry to leave it.

It turned his heart all funny to think of being looked at by her that way.

When he reached her table and at last allowed himself to turn so that his back wasn't to her, she was reaching for her purse and had the bill out before her, which pissed him off immediately. All that pathetic spectacle he had made of himself, trying to be Philippe Lyonnais, and she wasn't even going to wait around for him to get to her and finish the performance?

"Mademoiselle," he said to her bent head, and cursed himself immediately for the roughness of his voice. Why

had he never worked on his accent, so he sounded all glossy like Sylvain? Nobody knew the instant *Sylvain* spoke that he was born *en banlieue,* in the rejected hem of Paris, trailing in the dirt. Why couldn't he manage a nice, smooth purr, the way Philippe talked to Magalie? No, instead, rough and *maladroit* and . . . he felt as if he could bruise her just by speaking to her.

She looked up. Her eyes flickered, pupils contracting, and he remembered someone once telling him how much he loomed over people, that he needed to sit or even crouch to put seated people at ease with him. But he had thought, *Good. Let them be uncomfortable.*

It would be rude even for him, wouldn't it, to just pull out the chair opposite her and sit down? He took a step back instead, although it cost him. Stepping back was *not* what he wanted to do.

It worked, though. Her features relaxed slightly. Her eyes stopped contracting in rejection and started to look intrigued. Their blue reminded him of a softening evening, not too bright, not dark, a hint of gray; an oblivious person might not even remember they were blue. She wore a light sweater the shade of garnets with a wide V neckline, its hood draping over her head and hiding the nape of her neck. The fringes of her hair peeked under it, the color of one of his darker, reddish-toned caramels, the passion fruit one, maybe. The wide loose sleeves of the sweater were rolled at the wrists, the chunkiness emphasizing the over-thinness of those wrists.

"Monsieur?" Her accent threw him. Mixed in with the expected Anglo-ness was something else, something that reminded him of the accents of immigrants from French West Africa when he was growing up *en banlieue,* in the teeming, poor, wild projects just outside Paris.

"Cela vous plaît?" He nodded at the crumbs of his work

left in front of her. Not much in the way of crumbs. Had she picked each one up with the tip of her finger and licked it clean? *Do I please you, then? Do you like it?*

Her whole body relaxed, her hands going back to cradle the now-empty cup. The attitude that had first drawn him came back, as if she was soaking up every second of pleasure he could give her. *"Oui."*

He waited, half-hoping for a "thank-you" or "you're wonderful, please can I have some more." But she just looked at him curiously. At least she didn't look as if she wanted to Mace him at the moment.

"Are you one of the chefs here?" she asked suddenly.

So much for his giddy pleasure in the *bleu, blanc, rouge* at his collar. There really wasn't much you could do to get the message across if that failed; it wasn't as if he could embroider his whole jacket with *I am the best, the very best, in the world.* Well, technically, the award was for being the best in France, but in his field, it was the same thing. "I'm Dominique Richard."

The gentleness of his tone reassured him. He had managed to speak to her the way he *wanted* to speak to her, like a caress over her skin.

He was rewarded. Her eyes lit, making him feel giddy again. "Are you really? *Monsieur Richard,* what a pleasure."

She held out a hand instinctively. Definitely American, he thought at the firmness of her clasp. And *putain,* but her hand felt so delicate in his. The very firmness made it clear how fragile it was. But still, her accent—there was something going on with her accent that wasn't the average American tourist. Where did those hard-rolled Rs come from? Some place Creole? Louisiana? Would Cajuns have that immigrant accent?

"Merci," she did say now, gesturing to her empty plate.

Inside he swelled with smugness. Inside, he felt like one

of his own house-made marshmallows, accidentally left too close to a heat source. Puffing up, getting all soft and gooey . . .

"How long are you staying in Paris?" he asked, because he couldn't help it. He had to know.

Her eyes clouded. She tucked her hands together under the folds of her over-large sleeves, like a turtle pulling into its shell. "I don't know."

He cursed the fact that he had let her hand slip away. He hadn't known she was going to hide it. He had this crazy desire to lift it to his mouth and kiss it. *Merde,* she was American. He could probably get away with it. She probably thought that's what French men *did*.

That and kiss with their tongues. His gaze flicked over her mouth, and he had to bite down hard on the inside of his to keep that calm, gentle expression on his face.

"Alors," he said, realizing that he could not do one thing more. He, who had always been instant-sex or nothing . . . he could not even come onto her the tiniest bit more. If he did, she might not come back the next day. She might not be comfortable. "I hope we'll see you tomorrow." He smiled at her easily, casually, as if he was just practicing good client relations, which was hilarious since he had no idea how to do that. And moved over to the counter to speak calmly to Guillemette, although what he came up with for her, he had no idea. His young, crisp, elegant *maîtresse de salle* gazed at him with utter fascination but nodded a time or two as if he made sense. He might have to give her a raise.

He was suddenly conscious of a presence at his elbow, almost brushing him, and his heart seized.

He looked down at *l'inconnue,* hoping he hadn't broken off too obviously in the middle of whatever the hell he had been saying to Guillemette. She was standing almost touching him. Of her own volition. She could have waited until he moved on before she came to the counter. She had *wanted* to be standing almost touching him.

Or else she'd been completely indifferent to whether she did or not, but somehow he didn't think so. A woman who was indifferent about her personal space didn't look at a man as if she was calculating how to knock him out if he got closer, as she had at first done with him.

"I wanted to get a box of chocolates," she told Guillemette on the other side of the counter.

He broke into a huge grin. He couldn't help it. "You already finished the other one?"

Her eyes flicked up to him, arrested. *Bordel,* why couldn't he have sat on himself? He had just revealed he'd been watching her, at least enough to know what she had bought two days before.

I'm not stalking you, I promise. Seeing you at Philippe's was a coincidence. Plus, he couldn't stalk in his own place, *merde.* He was just ... so damn big. He had the hands of a butcher. How would she be able to sit there again, worrying some brute might be spying on her? Up there with his hands plastered so hungrily against the glass. Thank God he had shaved.

"Yes," she said. "I loved them."

Bordel, there went that gooey, swollen marshmallow feeling again. What was *wrong* with him?

Guillemette, meanwhile, slipped on a white cotton glove and pulled out one of his flat metal boxes.

L'inconnue looked up at him. "Which ones would you pick?" she asked softly.

Arousal washed over him. It shook him how helpless he felt before its flood, like a man who didn't know how to swim. Women had come on to him before with that question; usually it meant he was going to have sex within the next few hours. Maybe that was all his reaction was:

Pavlov's dog. But he knew how to swim in those waters. He knew completely how to control them.

And women with faces dusted all over in freckles did not come on to him that way. It was the glossy women, imperviously confident, or the pretty delicate ones with a pierced nose and belly button who liked to play bad, or women who were cheating on someone and had to act quickly.

He held out a blind hand to Guillemette, who placed a white glove in it. He slipped that on, moving behind the counter. It cost him a little, to move away from her when she had come so close on purpose, but the counter between them also allowed him to relax just a little. He couldn't accidentally hurt her, since there was a barrier between them. And he could maybe smile at her just a little more deeply without her feeling pursued.

He did let a smile soften his mouth, hold her eyes for just an extra second, let her see the warmth in his. "Tell me . . . what flavors do you like?"

He could barely recognize himself. Him, with his all-out, aggressive, take-it-or-leave-it approach to women, he was so reined in, so subtle, so gentle. *Slow, slow, slow,* he told himself. *Slow. She's a cream or a pastry or a chocolate to be tempered just right. Think about her that way. Sloooow.*

Let her absorb you. Just the way she sat in the salle *day after day and absorbed everything you made, as if it was the only thing in life she wanted to do.*

He was losing his mind. He didn't even know who he was, to be feeling like this, to be acting like this. With a woman he didn't even know, just because she had come into his *salon* and sat so still in it, consuming him, two times a day for seven days.

"Probably anything of yours," she said frankly, ruefully, and another wave of arousal swept through him. *Putain,* he thought, like a man just catching a hint of a tsunami on the horizon with no time to get away. *This is going to be bad.*

"Just . . . whatever you think," she said quietly. "You pick for me. I would like that. I would be honored."

Honored? He couldn't breathe properly. He felt like a schoolboy when the sexy math teacher bent over his homework. Or the way he imagined that would have felt, based on books; he had left school before puberty. He was suddenly so nervous he was grateful for the white glove to hide his damp palm. All of his flavors were wild, all his chocolate was dark, challenging. That was what he was known for. That smoky chocolate, there, for example— that might be too much. But then again, she might love it. Maybe he should stick with his least wild flavors, like this straightforward dark single origin chocolate—but it was so very dark, so bitter at first bite, with its long, lingering, slowly gentling aftertaste. What if it was too bitter for her, what if she couldn't wait for that gentling?

For the first time in his life, he wished he had just one chocolate that was a neutral, trustworthy 50 percent cacao with a touch of Tahitian vanilla.

"Which ones did you like best from the other box?" he asked hopefully.

A smile flashed over her face, rueful and happy. "All of them."

Another warning wave crashed through him. Yes, he thought, as that tsunami got closer. This was going to be bad.

He looked down helplessly, starting to get frustrated with himself. These were his chocolates. How could he be nervous about them? How could he not dare offer them to her? They were the best thing in his life he had to offer.

If he couldn't offer this, then he might as well forget it. He had nothing else worth anything.

"What is that one?" She pointed to a square printed

with an elusive pattern in an even deeper garnet than her sweater.

She couldn't point at one of his least challenging ones, could she? "It's a balsamic vinegar caramel center with a blend of Caribbean dark chocolate."

Her gaze flashed up to his, round and fascinated. "Balsamic *vinegar*?"

If he blushed, he was going to have to go hang himself. What was the matter with him? This was his *chocolate.* "If you would like something a little more traditional . . ." He didn't really have anything traditional, but maybe the lemon-thyme was comparatively subtle? She had liked that éclair the other day. Besides, she might be used to some of these flavor combinations if she knew chocolate; other chocolatiers copied him all over the world these days, and even if they didn't do it as well as he did, some of the flavor combinations that had been outrageous when he first came up with them were growing widespread. Imitation might be the best form of flattery, but it sure as hell was an annoying one. At this rate, he might have to start working with milk chocolate and vanilla just to continue to be the rebel. He just so did not see himself as a milk chocolate and vanilla kind of guy.

"No, I want to try it," she said definitely. "If you came up with it, it has to be good."

Warmth infused him, scarier and more powerful even than the arousal. Still, his fingers hesitated before he closed them around the garnet-marked square. What if he disappointed that conviction of hers? That was the problem when you took such risks with your flavors; some of the risks were bound to offend someone. Of course, he *liked* offending people. Why was he suddenly wishing he made things that were safe?

He forced his gloved fingers to close around the chocolate, slipping it into the corner of the box. The whole vast expanse of the flat square of metal gleamed back at him, still to fill. It was insane how terrifying that expanse looked.

Dominique, ça suffit, he told himself sharply. *Act like who you are: someone who believes in himself when no one else does.* "Perhaps this one?" He closed his fingers around a chocolate square printed with a fragile petal-shape of white. *"Jasmin."* He felt awkward, offering her the Jasmin, a lumberjack presenting a princess with a fistful of flowers.

But she would like that one, he thought. It would bloom on her mouth, like a hint of some magical night in Provence.

Unless she thought it was too perfumey . . .

"Jasmine," she said wonderingly. "Oh, yes."

He looked up at her, his mouth softening helplessly. "And this one." Confidence started to unfurl feathers in the ashes like a phoenix. Why she had burned his up in the first place, that was still the question. Her presence had been so very quiet, from the first. Not at all likely to leave a strong man in ashes, surely? "It has this tiny, secret semi-liquid tangy lime-caramel center that melts over your tongue just after you bite through the bitter dark chocolate."

Her eyes kept brightening, flicking from his face to his hands and back. "That sounds so fascinating." She said it as if her tongue curled around the idea, hungry for fascinating things.

Warmth and arousal battled in him, blended in what was for him a heretofore unheard of fusion. Probably a normal person's fusion, like chocolate and vanilla, but *he* didn't know it.

"You should at least try this one." He picked up a square with a golden pattern that evoked just a hint of a sea of waving grain. *"Ganache à l'avoine."*

Her eyes flickered, and he realized she didn't know the word. But while his English was minimal, given his lack of schooling, he certainly knew how to describe his chocolate in it; his tourist market was enormous. "Oats."

She laughed out loud with delight. "A ganache with *oats*? *Yes,* I want to try it."

He had to form himself back up out of a puddle behind the counter after that laugh. He hoped he was subtle about it, and she didn't realize he had melted to the floor.

He grinned at her. She could have been his mirror, the way she sparkled back at that grin, lighting up. All those days, she'd sat so deeply quiet and still in his *salon,* and now he was waking her up.

Triumph surged in him. "This one." He pointed. "It's so dark. You can't rush it. You can't bite into it expecting something sweet. You have to let it melt on your tongue, wait for the aftertaste, the way it just soothes and soothes and soothes."

Her lips softened apart. Her gaze trailed slowly up his body, searched his face, snagged on his lips. Came back to his eyes, as if she wanted to search out the meaning of him. That would be hard. His eyes were close to black, not at all like her clear twilight blue, which made it very easy to see her pupils dilating.

Yes. He wanted to pump his fist in victory.

Slow, Dom. Slow, slow, slow. But he felt himself sparkling, as he went through his chocolates, as she lit brighter at every single one, was eager for every single one. He offered her one of his more controversial ones to try on the spot. She blushed and tried to demur, and he overrode her, happily, growing cocky. She took it from his fingers, and he couldn't decide whether to be grateful for the glove, which helped veil his giant butcher's hands, or regret it, for it meant he couldn't feel that fleeting brush of her skin.

Her eyes widened at the flavors in her mouth and then closed with an intense concentration of pleasure. "It's like an adventure in your mouth. The whole world here in your body while outside, you're safe and warm." Her hand, indicating the *salle* at the words "safe and warm," seemed to linger a moment in his direction, but that had to be an accident. His *salon* was an elegant haven, but no one had ever associated safe and warm with his own physical self.

An adventure in her mouth, though—now *that* he could provide. "Here, have another." He pushed the square into her hand. "No, try this one."

Her flush blurred her pale freckles, but she smiled and took it. Her enthusiasm, or maybe even more the blush, tempted him to abandon this medium-size box and pull out his largest, fill it with everything of his and three times over. But he caught himself. He wanted her to run out. He wanted her to have to come back here to get her next fix.

The expanse that had seemed so vast at first grew too small. He played as long as he could with that last empty square of metal, teasing her to choose which of the remaining flavors would fill it. But he did eventually have to put something in there.

He slipped it precisely in and looked up into her face, trying to gauge the moment. Could he push it? Could he ask her out? But if she balked, if that made her uncomfortable, he wouldn't see her again.

It was a lot easier to ask a woman out if you didn't care whether you saw her again, he realized. All his strong come-ons, his hard confidence with women, had it all this time just been pure cowardice? When he had something to lose, he didn't know what to do?

Why did he think he had something to lose? He didn't even know her name.

She looked entirely intrigued, engaged, eyes bright, a blush on her cheeks as his eyes held hers a little too long.

But he hadn't really flirted with her yet, not in a way that could be positively identified as flirting. She could, all this time, have pretended to herself they were only chocolatier and client, talking about his profession . . . in a passionate way, because it inspired passion.

"You must come back tomorrow," he finally said, testing, "to tell me if you liked them."

She smiled as if he had made her very happy. So *maybe* that was exactly the right thing to say. Or *maybe* he could have pushed it, maybe she would have said yes. Damn it, how had this grown so hard? "I will," she promised.

He grinned, entirely satisfied. One sure step forward was better than a long lunge that might end in a void.

Which was the first time since he was eighteen years old that he had ever thought such a thing. He was all about the lunge.

Guillemette slipped the box into one of his specially designed sacks with the adamant DR on its side and stepped behind the cash register. He frowned as *l'inconnue* reached for her wallet. He didn't want her to pay for his chocolates. He wanted them to be his gift to her. But if he offered them to her, would that be too much? Would she feel uncomfortable coming back the next day?

Putain. This was going to drive him insane.

He turned brusquely away from the sight of her paying, deeply uneasy with it, as if his whole joy in that past half hour of chocolate selection had just been messily squashed.

She glanced up with a smile as she took the sack and hesitated at his frown. A little of that strong coolness of hers came back, that look from the very beginning, as if she would be happy to hang on his smiles but wasn't going to allow his anger anywhere near her. "Thank you very much, Monsieur," she said.

And he was still feeling the *monsieur* like a wound in his soul when she walked out.

CHAPTER 3

J aime walked down the Boulevard du Temple, away from
the roiling life around République, back into the more
sophisticated Marais, the sack from Dominique Richard
hanging from her fingers. She felt happier than she had in
three months, and the happiness seemed to fill her like he-
lium did a balloon, opening up the cramped limp person
she had become until she could finally dance in the wind
again.

As a test, she tried to think about older moments of
pure happiness, times when she had seen how her work
with cacao farms had changed people's lives so completely.
And she hit a huge ugly wall, just as she always did these
days. Hit it and flinched back, unable to reach those memories.

So. Dominique Richard. Her body tickled all over at
the memory of him looking at her, feeding her chocolates.

How different her impression had been the first time
she saw him, standing in Philippe Lyonnais's *salon de thé,*
aggressive, hard, arrogant, dangerous. Maybe he had been
angry about something. He probably hadn't realized he
was giving her that hard stare. Maybe the strong lines of
his face, the black shaggy hair, the glittering, somehow
rough eyes, gave him a false air of aggression. Once he
started talking about his chocolates, he turned into a pas-

sionate boy. No, that wasn't quite it, not a boy. Watching him choose his chocolates for her was like being stroked all over, gently, by those big, hard hands of his.

God, she could stand to be stroked. Even if it was just for a short fling, to soak up that warmth and pleasure as long as she could.

She flushed all over, wistfully. A fling how, exactly? She could hardly buy him, not *Dominique Richard* of all people, and she didn't really know what besides money she had to offer him right now. She felt emptied out. And she hated the way her bones were sticking out and making her look so fragile. She wanted to look invincible.

At the best of times, she was small and kind of silly look-ing, with all her freckles. Not someone men with no fi-nancial interest swooned over. Most men she met knew she had money, but her few experiments hanging out with her friends anonymously in bars had made it clear that the men who didn't know who she was were going to pick out her friends and ignore her. Once in a while the shy, awkward men settled on her while their cockier friends went for her girlfriends, because the ones who lacked self-confidence and didn't know who she was thought she seemed a surer bet. More likely to take what she could get, maybe.

It had taken the boyfriend disaster and those bar exper-iments to make her fully grasp how much her ready sup-ply of dates was predicated on her last name. Before that, she had thought at least some of them must . . . just like her. Not for any particular reason. Just because she was her.

That naïveté had faded. Still, she had believed in herself, in the value of her passionate ability to change the lives of the downtrodden. And now she had lost that, too. The only non-monetary value she knew she had.

So how could she possibly draw a big, sexy, intense man

who could produce chocolates like miracles out of his own hands?

But there was nothing wrong, of course, with indulging a crush by sitting in his *chocolaterie,* thinking about him and letting him sell her chocolates.

It was not as if she had one single other thing in life right now that she would rather do.

"You should be running Corey Chocolate, that's what you should be doing," her grandfather told her roughly. James Corey, or Grandpa Jack to Jaime, still officially lived in the town named after his family, in the U.S. But no one would know it, judging from how much time he was spending in Paris, now that both his granddaughters were there. "Your father is such a pain to work with. Always trying to be in charge."

Jaime raised an eyebrow. "You want me to take over Corey Chocolate so you can take me over?"

"Just to show you the ropes!" The old man's blue eyes glinted. They were sitting on the terrace of the apartment he and her father had recently bought. It offered a magnificent view of the green sweep of the Jardin du Luxembourg in one direction, where the Palais du Luxembourg rose proudly from the gardens and tiny little specks of color floated on the great *bassin,* sailboats being chased by children. In the other direction, the Eiffel Tower rose past a stretch of Paris rooftops. "Since you've spent your entire life refusing to learn them."

"Pardon me for wasting my life doing something unimportant," Jaime said, dangerously mild.

"Oh, your work had its uses." The old man waved his hand, completely oblivious to the danger. "Good publicity, for one. Made it easy to lead the pack for that fair trade chocolate craze. I've got to hand it to Cade, I thought she was just on another one of her gourmet snob kicks when she backed you on the fair trade thing, but she was right about that one. You helped us corner the market."

A muscle in Jaime's jaw tightened. In her mind, a twelve-year-old boy carried loads she couldn't even lift. She had tried to heft it. The photo of her failing, falling to her knees under the effort, had created an international furor. It had almost gotten the photographer a Pulitzer prize. "Publicity and market share weren't why I did it."

Grandpa Jack winced. "I know, Jamie, but you don't have to keep reminding me. I'm trying to imagine you as future CEO material of a major multinational corporation."

"Don't hurt your brain. I'll never be CEO material. Talk to Cade." First-born Cade had been the heir assumptive, and Jaime had taken pains to make her own refusal of the role clear. Her participation in anti-capitalist protests and wild parties in college had made her stance a public scandal years ago.

Her grandfather grunted. "Have you tried talking to Cade lately? She's gotten almost as impossible as you've always been. It's getting lonely over there in the States. You can't leave me and your dad together by ourselves, I might have to start spanking him again."

Jaime grinned involuntarily. "Did you ever really spank him?" It was hard to imagine her father as a little boy, in someone else's control. He controlled half the world.

"No." Grandpa Jack looked disgruntled. "I told your grandma we were wasting a golden opportunity, but she always insisted on giving him extra chores instead. And look where that got us."

"He works all the time?"

"*And* he's bossy to his own father."

"I don't think I can stop Dad from being bossy, Grandpa." She grinned at the older Corey.

The truth flashed out of him in a sudden desperate rage,

lightning from what had seemed an innocent white cloud: "At least you would be *safe.*"

Jaime drew back into herself, hair rising all up and down her arms in spite of herself. "What happened didn't make me *helpless,* Grandpa."

Just incapable of doing any damn thing.

Maybe if she took over the reins as Corey heir apparent, she would at least be capable of *something.* Even if it was only running half the world.

CHAPTER 4

"**B**onjour." The low, rough, gentled voice stroked over her, and Jaime looked up at Dominique Richard helplessly. This crush was overwhelming her, too sudden and intense. Her defenses were all down: physical weakness; her sense of purpose hiding in a fetal ball; and now her heart was going to cop out, leaving her a pushover for a gorgeous bad-boy.

Thank God for her heart. The only part of her that still knew how to seize life.

She smiled up at him, just to thank him for existing and letting her sit there all squooshy about him. Men like him were wonderful. They *made* themselves larger than life, superstars, someone you could sit in a corner and fuzzily swoon over.

Well-mannered toward his guests, he could have no idea of the effect his courtesy had on her. Superstars didn't. It might cross their minds that women came to them easily, but they had no idea how hard the woman was fighting to keep her head on straight. They never understood how much power they had without even trying.

Not that Jaime was trying to keep her head on straight. She was using all of what she had once thought a considerable willpower for other things. Besides, why resist?

Thank God she was able to enjoy the fun and infinite security of having a crush on a man out of her reach.

His near-black eyes brightened at her smile. He definitely liked female attention, no matter whom it came
from. She gave him a little more of it, the way she used to
throw her panties onstage with all the others lying at a
rock star's feet. *You're amazing. Here's my tribute.*

He came closer to her table, and this time she relaxed
into the sense of being loomed over. There was no harm
in him. He meant no threat to her.

"Did you like the chocolates?" he asked with a smile
that made a woman feel at the center of his world.

She blushed. After her workout at the gym the evening
before, she had lain in her bed, nibbling on his chocolates
instead of falling asleep, lured deeper and deeper into fantasies about him with every bite. Some of those fantasies
sparkled back through her mind as she looked up at him,
and the blush was uncontrollable. "Of course. I like everything you make."

His smile widened into a grin. Oh, he liked to be
praised, didn't he? He looked like a boy who had just won
the marbles off everyone else in the schoolyard when he
grinned like that. It melted her middle.

He pulled out the chair opposite her, and she started.
How much time did one of France's most famous chocolatiers-pâtissiers have to spend with her? Talk about courtesy to his clients. And what did you do with a crush when
he actually sat down and talked to you?

"Which was your favorite?" he asked hungrily.

It amused her to realize that he just wanted his vanity
stroked. Now that, she could do, especially if it kept him
near her longer. "All of them."

He radiated pleasure. It reached right into her eroge-
nous zones and radiated there, too. *"Allez,"* he coaxed,
lapping up her praise and begging for more. "There

must have been one or two you liked a little more, a little less."

She shook her head. "I liked *all* of them." Flavor after astonishing flavor, always a surprise, always delicious, combinations of exotic flowers and herbs and vinegars with a darkness that came inside and shook her mouth and through it her whole body. She had *loved* his chocolates. Tonight she was going to go right back out on another trip around the world, escorted by their dark and delicious creator, curled up in her bed. Imagining him pulling her in against that hard body and feeding them to her . . .

"You ate them all?" Was that a visible swell to his chest?

Yep, vanity. She gave him another starstruck smile, enjoying how easy it was to feed his ego and make him happy, and nodded.

He was pretty much openly gloating at this point. She half expected him to get up and do one of those soccer victory dances. "Do you like caramels, too? Would you like to try some?"

"I liked yours." She had never had any other caramels besides the chewy mass-market ones a Corey subsidiary produced, and she hadn't especially liked those. But three of his had curved like a gift around the plate under her hot chocolate the other day, a very nice little client-relations gesture. Warm and buttery and just delicately chewy, like condensed sunshine.

He sprang up as if he couldn't sit still any longer—the man was probably always in motion—and went to the tall columned displays of his current caramel flavors, grabbing several. The fast, hard, graceful enthusiasm of his movements made her whole soul weep a little with thwarted longing. Like being at a party with one of her favorite movie idols, watching him flirt and play and dance in real life.

She looked at his big hand as he offered the caramels to her and had to lick the inside of her lips. The little things gleamed bright and warm, light shining off the plastic that wrapped their golden colors, held in that hard, large palm. She took one, delicately, and her fingertips brushed his skin.

Oh, boy.

This was better even than that time she had run into a favorite sexy movie star and convinced him to autograph her arm in permanent ink, but it might be more than her heart could take. It was beating like mad already.

The caramel yielded to her teeth, soft, smooth, creamy, while the flavor of it slapped her palate awake. "What is it?" It reminded her of her travels in the tropics, both the good and the bad.

"Passion fruit mango." He watched her eagerly, maybe even a little anxiously, which charmed her. Anyone would think if she hadn't liked it, it would have crushed him. Dominique Richard. Who, according to her sister, was so outrageously arrogant he made Sylvain Marquis and Philippe Lyonnais look mild-mannered and humble. How dearly he must love to have his ego stroked.

"It's delicious." She bit into the other half. Such an intense flavor, such a luscious texture. Tonight she was going to lie awake fantasizing that he was there stretched out beside her, feeding these to her, too.

Her skin prickled all over, in protest at this torture, in longing. What she wouldn't give to have those big, rough hands stroke her in real life.

Uh-oh. With the movie stars and the rock stars, she had never drifted past fantasy into any kind of real life longing.

"What about this one?" He unwrapped it. Big fingers on that tiny, delicate twist of plastic, opening the sun for her . . .

Dulcet texture and stinging flavor. She looked up at him helplessly. Maybe if she gave him her rented apartment number, he would be interested in a one-night stand, despite her ordinary looks. She could be his groupie. It might break her heart, but she thought she had proved she could survive being broken.

"You're going to kill me, *Monsieur.*" She laughed. "An overdose of deliciousness."

Displeasure flashed across his eyes. "You can call me Dominique," he said brusquely. "I'm not very formal."

His eyebrows lifted a touch as he looked at her. Waiting either for her to say his name or to give him hers. But it would be so safe and warm to keep him on his stage. "I wouldn't presume."

He frowned. The light in his face faded radically.

He hesitated a long moment, and then finally nodded and moved away from her. Back to work. Clouds crowded over her moment in the sun, and it was her own fault. He spoke to the elegant young woman who seemed to run the room, glanced back at Jaime, hesitated again, then ran lightly up that gorgeous spiral of stairs, disappearing into the heavens from which he had descended.

Which was funny, given that he looked much more like a devil than an angel. Maybe, post-fall, Lucifer had discovered he could bribe his way back into heaven with sufficiently good chocolate. It would work with *her* if she were God. She watched him go, part of her relieved, part of her wistful. As she cradled the cup in her hands near her face, the heat rising off his chocolate seemed to warm her whole body.

When she was leaving, the elegant young woman gave her a small, very elegantly ribboned bag, inside which a dozen caramels gleamed like captured suns. "From Monsieur Richard. He wanted you to have them."

Jaime reached for her wallet again, confused.

"Non, non. Il vous les offre." It's a gift. He offers them to you.

How incredibly sweet. He must just love his open admirers. She slipped it into her worn, woven purse, wishing it was the kind of memento she could keep forever instead of one that had to be eaten within days or lose its quality.

She heard the music as she stepped out of the shop. Her heart already lifted, it was easy to turn toward the sound, to head toward the Place de la République and its crowd of dancing people.

Dominique always liked that first moment when he stepped into the street, carrying the scent of cacao with him so strongly that people turned to look at him, trying to catch his flavor. It was so vividly better than stepping into the street smelling of blood and death. Better, even, than stepping out smelling of the cacophony of scents he would pick up cooking, anything from onions to pumpkin, when he had been apprenticed to a chef; or that butter and flour scent when he had been shifted over to pastries.

He heard the music from the Place de la République and smiled. He kind of liked forging his way through protests on his way home from work. And he loved the way people would come into his *salon* to relax over sumptuous desserts after an hour or so of energetic protesting. Paris. Nobody did life better.

It was a pro-immigration or anti-discrimination protest—he could tell before he even got close enough to see the signs, from the diversity of the crowd, every ethnicity from the nearly pure black of Senegalese to the bronze of Moroccans to the white skin and bright blond hair from Poland. With a liberal dose of *nos-ancêtres-les-Gaulois* French who sympathized with the cause. A punk rock group was playing on a stage under the proud statue of Marianne, symbol of the French Republic; he could only make out half the words, but the group was known for its anti-discrimination themes.

All the streets were blocked to car traffic, and the white vans of riot police formed stern lines up the edges of those streets, reminding the protesters what would happen if things got out of hand. But the police themselves lounged tranquilly in the vans as the crowd danced with bobbing signs for the television cameras but continued to play nice.

He spotted his *inconnue* dancing happily near the fringe as he came closer and felt a little jolt to his heart. She had a big grin on her face, as if she didn't want to think of anything in the world but dancing.

He stopped unnoticed a few meters away from her at the edge of the crowd and was just thinking about joining her when she stopped grinning and moved out of the crowd.

Two men followed her, closing in even as he moved forward to meet her. He had just time to glimpse the stark, ferocious expression on her face, out of all proportion to the situation, when he reached them. The two men were grinning, moving far too close to her and looming over her; he caught the words "my dick."

He grabbed her arm and yanked her from between the two of them so that she fell against his chest. "Fuck off," he told the two men, showing the edge of his teeth.

He had an instant to realize he had scared the hell out of her when she jerked wildly, and then all the tension drained out of her and she looked up.

She relaxed to—an incredible degree. He couldn't possibly be that reassuring.

The two men bristled, and instantly the berserker urge swept him, the violent pleasure at the idea of taking them on and anyone else in the mob they pulled with them. What did he care if he ended up bloodied and beaten? He had survived it before. He grabbed her shoulder, ready to fling her out and straight toward the protection of the riot police.

But the older *con* flicked a glance over Dom's hard body

and carnivorous expression. *"Connard. Je t'emmerde."* The asshole turned sullenly back into the crowd, the younger one growling but following suit. If it took two of them to go after one small woman, one by himself was never going to face off against Dominique.

Dom watched them a second, to make sure they didn't return with reinforcements, then took his *inconnue* out of the crowd, still with a hand on her shoulder, guiding her far enough down one of the boulevards to be out of the mob. *"Pardon,"* he said to her, when they were far enough away from the noise to hear each other. *"Ça va?"*

She had recovered from that instant of relief and now looked—and felt, her shoulder in his hand—tense and brooding.

"I'm fine," she said roughly. "Perfectly fine." She hesitated and then looked up at him. That brooding anger got confused, distracted; fascinatingly, she blushed.

That—had to be promising. All the hardness in him melted like chocolate too close to a flame, and he smiled down at her, helplessly enthralled.

"That was very nice of you, though," she said. "Thank you."

Nice. He could have let her save herself, walking toward the riot police or into the nearest bar; it was not as if the men could have done anything but harass her with a few crude words in this spot. He could have walked up, smiled at her, and put his arm around her shoulders, ignoring the men altogether, which would have made them instantly turn their attention elsewhere, with no chance of violence. Instead, he had just nearly started a fight, in circumstances that could have turned a peaceful protest into a tear-gassed mob scene. If that was her idea of nice, they might actually suit each other.

"My pleasure," he said, which was unfortunately all too true. Violence must be like nicotine; you never quite got over the addiction. He still felt the powerful desire to go back into the crowd, haul both those men out of it, and drive his fists into their faces. "I hope I didn't scare you."

She shook her head minutely. "Startled me, for a second." Which was a lie if he ever heard one; for a split second, her reaction had been pure terror. But that terror had been so instantly, so oddly, so completely allayed. An odd, faraway look came over her. "You smelled like chocolate," she murmured. He remembered that instant when she had relaxed against his chest, before she had even looked up and seen his face.

Desire surged and fisted around him. He wanted nothing in life but to strip them both naked, to wrap her in his scent. It made his breath ragged with the effort not to say it, not to lean into her, aggressive and guttural, and say, *Come smell me all over.*

His scalp prickled with the struggle not to be as crude and direct as the two strangers he had just driven away. He cleared his throat and forced himself a couple of steps back out of her personal space, before he violated every centimeter of it. "It's better in the middle than at the edges," he said, trying to focus on practical advice because he didn't want her getting in trouble on her own some day while he was up in his *laboratoire* and had no idea. "The troublemakers always hang out on the edges."

She made a little face. "I hate being in the middle of a crowd, though. I used to enjoy it, but these days, it feels as if I can't get out."

Hunh. It must be odd to be so small. He could shove his way through most masses of people. Crowds didn't trap him. They just made him want to hit people. "I don't like being in the middle, either." He was adamantly against hitting people who didn't deserve it. "You could just avoid protests. Tear gas is no fun."

She grimaced. "I know."

"You *do*?" She *was* American, right? He had gotten the vague idea that Americans were too passive for protests, but maybe that was just one of those media stereotypes.

She shrugged oddly. After a second, she held up three fingers.

"That's exactly how many times *I've* gotten tear-gassed," he said, considerably startled.

"Most of mine were as a student." She sounded so stiffly defensive, she must be talking to someone else in her head. *He* wasn't going to start judging anyone for getting into trouble.

Most? "All of mine were as a teenager," he admitted, feeling a tad out-gunned. Like a reformed addict, ever since he was eighteen he had avoided situations that might lead him back to his addiction, if that was the best way to describe his rapport with violence.

"Two G-8 summits," she said, for some reason embarrassed. "I was a spoiled brat."

"*Banlieue* issues. I was mostly just a troublemaker. But not like them," he added hastily. Not one who harassed women half his size. "What was the one *not* as a student?" curiosity compelled him to ask, even though she clearly didn't want to volunteer the information.

Her eyebrows crinkled, her expression shifting to something very sober. "That one—I was in Africa," she said with what had to be deliberate vagueness. If she had actually traveled in Africa, she was surely capable of distinguishing countries within the continent. "And—very naive to join in a protest. There were—there were actually military sharpshooters on the rooftops, shooting people in the crowd in the head. Peaceful protesters in the crowd."

Putain. She must be incredibly strong, was the first thing he thought. In fact, he wanted to close his hands around her shoulders and hold her still for him while he took a good long look into the depths and strength of her. The fleeting thought crossed his mind that his heart might have protected itself for so long and then thrown itself so ridiculously after her because it had incredible survival instincts.

But no, then, surely he wouldn't feel so helplessly kamikaze.

"Don't do that," he said involuntarily.

She looked questioning.

Don't put yourself in positions where people might shoot you in the head, he wanted to say, lamely. "Don't join in protests in strange countries where you don't know how the government might react." Starting with G8 summits.

"I don't anymore. Mostly."

He narrowed his eyes. "You're that familiar with the way French riot police might handle a crowd or what's likely to make that crowd degenerate into a riot?"

She looked disgruntled. "I was just there for the dancing."

Now he did close his hand around her shoulders. He couldn't help it. Somebody had to get a grip on her. "Don't join in protests in strange countries where you don't know how the government might react. Even for the dancing." He started to release her, hesitated. "And don't go to nightclubs by yourself, either. Go find the dance groups on the quays, if you're looking for dancing."

Although he didn't entirely like the thought of her being there on her own—hit on by all comers—either.

Merde. This time he did manage to force himself to release her. Before he could start getting jealous of someone whose name he didn't even know. Wouldn't *that* be a chip off the old block. *Les chiens ne font pas des chats.* "I'll see you tomorrow?"

She hesitated, flushed a little, but held his eyes as she nodded.

CHAPTER 5

Jaime concentrated on not feeling guilty about Dominique Richard's chocolates when she sat down across the table from Sylvain Marquis that evening. Her future brother-in-law, named by some as the best chocolatier in the world, would be outraged to learn she was frequenting Dominique Richard's *salon*.

So would the other man at the table, Philippe Lyonnais, come to think of it. And her sister Cade. Probably the only person who wouldn't mind was Philippe's fiancée Magalie, who might consider it good for the men to have their arrogance tweaked.

They were sitting in Hugo Faure and Luc Leroi's three-star restaurant in the Hôtel de Leucé, full of crystal and gold opulence and the kind of powerful people who could afford three-hundred-euro-per-person dinners. Of course, everyone at their table felt quite at home, or in Magalie's case, at least pretended. Jaime had a feeling Magalie was good at pretending to feel at home. Massive bouquets of roses decorated the place today, creating the impression that people were dining in a forest whose canopy was red velvet roses.

Sylvain Marquis sat at the head of the table, with her sister Cade on his right hand and Jaime on his left. "Indulge me," he had told Jaime. "This way, I get to be surrounded by beautiful women"—he winked—"and keep as far away from Philippe as possible. Also, it will annoy him no end to find me at the head of the table when he gets here." But what it also accomplished, gorgeous, gracious poet that he was, was to place Jaime, the only one without a partner, squarely in the middle of the gathering and not at its outer edge.

Philippe Lyonnais, considered one of the world's best pâtissiers, had clearly been dragged to this dinner by Magalie. Jaime supposed that if you were competitive enough to become one of the best chocolatiers-pâtissiers in the world, you were too competitive to form easy friendships with your rivals.

She had a flashing vision of adding Dominique Richard to the mix and grinned involuntarily. Sylvain was a nice guy, who already had to bear being engaged to a Corey of Corey Chocolate, a *mésalliance* if ever there was one.

He seemed to be dealing with it surprisingly well, though, as if in her annoyingly perfect sister he had caught a prize. Sylvain was the ultimate proof that Cade could land anything she set her mind to. Countries, even. Major world businesses as subsidiaries. Jaime had heard that landing Sylvain had involved breaking and entering. She had to admire that in her sister, that confidence, that ability to go after a dream. She had had it herself once, not so very long ago at all, but it was hard to sift through the ashes and remember what that confidence had felt like when it was alive and thriving.

Cade was the more attractive of the two sisters, with an even-featured elegance and no freckles, but she wasn't drop-dead gorgeous or anything, and Sylvain really was, in an intense, passionate, poet's way. *He* seemed to think Cade was drop-dead gorgeous, though. It made a girl feel sad and lonely just to watch that glow in his eyes when he looked at her sister.

Right now, Sylvain wasn't looking at her. He was busy singing the praises of all the most fattening dishes on the menu, trying to get Jaime to order them. And when Sylvain went out of his way to convince a woman something was delicious, it was pretty hard to ignore.

She thought about ordering the salad for her first course just to be provoking, since that was how she reacted to pressure. But she was pretty full of Dominique Richard's chocolate, which seemed to just snuggle up cozy and warm in her tummy. So she did something even more provoking. She refused to order a first course at all and opted for the lightest main dish.

Cade frowned anxiously, causing Sylvain to redouble his efforts with Jaime.

"I'm full," Jaime said. "I've been wandering around the city trying pastries all day." That and going to the gym near her new temporary apartment were her main occupations.

"Whose?" Sylvain and Philippe asked in the same indignant breath.

Oops. "I just like to walk around. Visit the Louvre. Explore the different quarters. There are tempting boulangeries everywhere."

"Oh—boulangeries," Sylvain said, partially mollified. He didn't do bread. Jaime bit back a grin. Yep, if she *could* have her fantasy date here right now, Sylvain and he would be at each other's throats all evening.

"Are you sure you're all right on your own?" Cade asked, setting Jaime's back teeth. Did she look so helpless? She might be the younger sister, but she was the one who had spent the past few years in all the wildest, most challenging corners of the cacao world, reforming working conditions and changing people's lives. Okay, right at the end there, she had been helpless and had the scars to prove it, but it wasn't as if anyone else could have survived better.

And she didn't like having that moment of helplessness rubbed in her face. "I'm fine." She had spent the first few weeks of physical therapy living in the spare bedroom in Sylvain's apartment, the one Cade now shared with him, but even though Sylvain's place was fairly large for Paris, it was still too small for Jaime to share with an anxious sister.

She had rented her own little place by the week, up toward the northern corner of the Marais, near Dominique Richard's *salon*. She would have been welcome to use the luxurious place her father had bought in the Sixth, when Cade had declared her intention of remaining in Paris. But Jaime had spent her summers all through college doing internships with professors in the far reaches of the world, and she had spent the three years after she graduated entirely on her own in those far reaches, continents away from her family. She liked that. Being far away from the Coreys and anything they could want of her. Maybe not quite as far as usual right this second, but . . . she needed her own place, a place she could curl up in, without any chance that someone else would turn the key in the lock and pop in unexpectedly.

This apartment put her no more than a twenty-minute walk from Cade, but Cade got all hovering and anxious nevertheless. It drove Jaime nuts.

"It's a little wilder up near République, isn't it?" Cade asked. "You're careful, aren't you?"

Jaime gave her sister an ironic look, which was better than strangling her. For one thing, what Cade meant by "wilder" probably was just that the area north and east of République was considerably more working class and ethnically diverse than the Sixth, where Cade was. For another, Jaime was in the Marais, one of the most elite quarters in the city, even if she was only a couple of blocks from République. And finally, wilder than *what*? Madagascar? Côte d'Ivoire? Papua New Guinea? Cameroon, perhaps? Cade had no real clue what Jaime had been doing, did she?

Cade flushed a little under Jaime's look and set her jaw stubbornly. "I know it's a romantic city, but it's a city, nevertheless. Just make sure you pay attention. Don't go wandering down empty streets in the middle of the night. Make sure no one's within grabbing reach when you enter your code on the street late at night." She shot an odd, sudden glance at Sylvain at that last and bit her lip. Sylvain, inexplicably, grinned.

Jaime ground her teeth and focused on Philippe, sitting across from her, beside Magalie, who was so fashionable and sure of herself she made Jaime feel very freckled. She also wore such high heels that she always looked taller than Jaime, which was unfair, because Jaime was pretty sure she herself would be a couple inches taller if they ever got to meet on even footing. "So," Jaime said brightly to Philippe, "I hear you are doing the, what do you call them, the *pièces montées,* for Cade's wedding next month. I'm sure they'll be stunning."

Philippe nodded his tawny head absently, clearly not finding any doubt in that and not remembering he should pretend to be modest. "We've got the expo next week first, though." He nodded at Sylvain.

Sylvain rolled his eyes. "If Richard doesn't ruin it. I'm going to have the table right beside his again, I know it. We need a chocolatier whose last name starts with P."

Philippe shrugged. "He won't do anything that would damage his work. Just ignore him when he tries to start a fight."

Jaime's eyebrows went up. When he tried to start a fight? She remembered the moment when he'd looked ready to take on a whole mob. But—that was circumstantial, right? With her he had been so *nice.*

"I wouldn't put it past him to do something to destroy

someone *else's* work," Sylvain said broodingly. "Trip someone carrying a chocolate sculpture, for example."

Philippe considered that, square chin on one hand. "He's managed to restrain himself from doing it in the past," he pointed out, not as if he felt it was any guarantee of future results.

"I know. But you can feel the restraint."

"Look, don't ask *me* to defend Dominique Richard." For some reason, Philippe glanced at Magalie and away, his mouth hardening. "He's an arrogant bastard. But you know, so are you, Sylvain."

"I am *not* a bastard," Sylvain protested. "And I'm not arrogant, I'm just realistic. Richard is a bastard."

"C'est vrai," Magalie suddenly intervened, her mouth curving in amusement. "Sylvain's a sweetheart compared to Dom. That is, Sylvain, you just assume everyone will fall at your feet when you walk by, the same, ah, realistic way Philippe does." She cast her fiancé a dark look. "But Dom—he knows he might have to bludgeon some people into bowing. He's ready to do it."

Bludgeon. The word evoked an unfortunate visceral reaction in Jaime. But in her head, that hard face softened into boyishly grinning pleasure. Magalie didn't mean bludgeon literally, she reminded herself.

"Since when do you call him Dom?" Philippe asked Magalie sharply. "Are you getting to know him so well?"

"He's just being Dominique." Magalie waved a dismissive hand. "Don't let him get to you. That's all he's trying to do."

Philippe curled one hand around Magalie's under the table, his face hard. Magalie leaned to whisper something in his ear. His mouth softened enough for one corner of it to curl up as he glanced down at her.

Had Dominique Richard hit on Magalie? Jaime toyed with her fork. It figured. Magalie was intensely vivid and cute. There was just something about having the movie star flirt with someone she *knew* that made her . . . wistful.

Still, what did she expect? Even though she wasn't really attractive in the way Magalie and her sister were, she didn't normally base all her worth on her looks. She had changed *lives.* Saved *children.* Found a break in the world and fixed it. She had been someone even a man like Dominique Richard could love, if he could get past the freckles. But right now . . . well, what did she have to offer him?

Hey look, you know, I'm not gorgeous or anything, but I used to know how to fix the world, and now . . . I'm scared of it.

She sighed and shoved the wistfulness away. If he hit on Magalie, he did; it wasn't her business.

And if his rivals thought he was a bastard, what did it matter? They probably thought that about each other and all their other rivals, too.

She was quite sure plenty of her teenage movie star idols had been bastards when you got to know them. And like a teen idol, Dominique would probably be appalled that she might think something could develop between them. So she would just enjoy the crush for what it was.

Bastard or not.

CHAPTER 6

"**I** can't keep shaving every day," Dom cursed the next morning, looking into the mirror above the sink outside the *toilettes* in the corner of the *laboratoire*. "It's making my skin break out in a rash." He ran his hand over the path of tiny red bumps around his jaw. He supposed a man with a rash looked less threatening than a man with a four-day growth of black scruff, but it couldn't be sexy, could it?

How long was this normal style of getting a woman interested in you supposed to take, anyway? He had built hopes yesterday, but then she had refused to use his first name and refused to give him her own, and he had known he had to pull back again or lose her. Then, later after the *manif*, he hadn't dared, not so soon after letting her glimpse his true colors. He might have dipped himself in chocolate, but the fact was that no one who bit through his chocolate exterior would find a soft, sweet ganache inside. Even after years of therapy, he was ready to let fly with his fists at the first provocation. She hadn't seemed to mind, but then she had just proven she had no sense about danger. *He* had minded for her.

Merde, but this stuff was complicated. He kept trying to pretend she was chocolate because at least he understood that you could never rush chocolate, but since she persistently resembled a woman instead, it was hard for him to treat her like something he could stir with a spoon.

Unfortunately.

He sure would love to stir her with his "spoon," he thought inappropriately, caught his own wicked grin in the mirror, and sighed. He was never going to learn to be a gentleman, was he? He wondered if she would let him make love to her for hours, though, absorbing him the way she did when she sat in his *salon,* the way she took his chocolates home and ate them all up in a night. She could eat *him* all up in a night.

He was going to drive himself crazy thinking these things.

"I'm not meant to shave this much," he said, coming back into the kitchens, rubbing the back of his hand on his jaw.

"That's you, thin-skinned," Célie said dryly, stretching her short body far out over the ganache she had just poured, in order to smooth it flat between two metal frames. She had started training under him when she was eighteen, escaped herself out of a bad situation. He had only been twenty-four back then, setting out on his own after six years training in other kitchens, none of which specialized in chocolate, an act of pure, stubborn insanity.

"Such a sensitive man," his caramellier Amand mocked, recovering a pot from one of the long sinks along the wall.

"Famous for it, even," Célie said.

Great, his shaving issues were going to be the joke of the day.

"Do you make sure to let the shaving cream sit for a couple of minutes before you shave?" Amand asked helpfully. "That makes all the difference."

Dom gave him an indignant look. His young caramellier had fine light brown hair and had to stop shaving for three days before you could even tell. What the hell did he know?

"I have this really great cream I use on my legs afterward," Célie volunteered. "Do you want me to bring you some to try?"

He was probably the only maître chef in Paris who had employees who mouthed off to him this way. They followed his training to the minutest detail when it came to the production he was famous for, but they made up for it by being smart asses. As a rebel himself, he was lousy at imposing his will. His employees actually used *tu* with him. He could guarantee Sylvain's and Philippe's teams didn't do that.

"Just trying to be helpful," Célie smirked, and smoothed the next frame of ganache.

Putain. He hesitated beside Célie en route to the "hot" room, the *cuisine,* where the caramels, and baking, and cream-heating were done. "Does it smell very feminine, your cream?" he asked awkwardly, sotto voce.

Célie grinned. "Just like gardenias. That's not a problem, is it?"

Bordel de cul. He went to talk about the day's work with his pastry team, all of whom had some advice on shaving. He wondered wistfully if he could fire Amand for passing it on so fast, but unfortunately, he liked the guy. Amand had been loyal to him from day one, had a hilarious sense of humor, and could work like a demon during the Christmas season. For that, Dom just had to put up with being the butt of his own staff's jokes.

Guillemette came up the stairs and lifted her eyebrows at him. Definitely he needed to give that girl a raise. She, at least, had been subtle.

His heart pounding, he ran down the stairs.

When he saw what was waiting for him at the bottom, he nearly ran right back up and fired Guillemette on the spot. Turned out, her eyebrow raising was way the hell too subtle.

★ ★ ★

Jaime looked up right away at the sound of feet on the metal stairs. She followed all movements involuntarily these days, but never with that leap of hope in her heart.

It reminded her of her freshman crush on a senior in high school. Finding excuses to linger with her friends places he might pass, giggling, imagining at night their great love story, not even jealous of his beautiful girlfriend because it was a *crush* and it was normal he wouldn't be interested in a freshman. Other than her movie star crushes, it had been the funnest, safest interest in a man she had ever had.

Dominique came down the stairs with the graceful speed of an athletic man who knew this territory so well he could have raced the twisting stairs blindfolded, not looking where his feet went, glancing . . . right toward her table.

He smiled immediately when he saw her, and her heart started pounding. How could any man be so hot? That shaggy rebel black hair that needed a cut, the hard size of him, the way he moved. The intent almost-black eyes, the square smooth jaw, those big hands that made her body shiver with longing, as if they could lift her up like some baby chick, cupped warm in them and utterly secure. That rough, gentle voice of his, talking about flavors, until she wished she could become one of his.

She would give about anything, at that moment, to look like the tall, elegant, beautiful brunette waiting at the cash register. If she did, she would have had a chance at nabbing him for a little while.

Dominique noticed the brunette when he was nearly at the bottom of the stairs. His step faltered, and he had to grab onto the railing for balance.

Jaime's heart sank to her toes. Shit. She had already ordered. She was going to have to watch this. She reached blindly for her purse, with its book-loaded iPad, which she had never before turned on in his *salon*.

The lovely brunette turned away from the counter at his approach, gazing at Dominique Richard as if she expected all of his attention.

She got it, too. Dominique glanced once at Jaime, then focused on the other woman. The gentleness vanished from his face, leaving it hard-edged, dangerous. The kind of face that got better women than she to walk right up and tuck themselves behind him on his motorcycle. He had to have a motorcycle to go with those leathers she had seen the other day. Probably a loud one.

Jaime turned on her iPad. She felt sick, as if she was watching a train run over someone she loved and doing nothing to stop it.

"Dominique," the brunette said in a beautiful sexy voice. How did Frenchwomen *manage* that little husk and catch? As if they were constantly on the edge of an orgasm. This woman's voice layered silk in it, too, suggesting she and Dominique had a history among sheets of just such silk.

Jaime stared blindly at the list of book titles on her tablet.

"*Bon . . . jour,*" she heard Dominique say.

She flicked a glance despite herself. The woman's smile promised . . . God. Jaime wished she was French. How could the other woman promise fifty million orgasms with just a smile?

This was a lot worse than spotting that senior crush making out with his girlfriend. It was more along the lines of the time she had discovered her real boyfriend in college making out with the girl who attracted him for her body and not for her money.

Maybe she needed to get out of here before she took one more blow than she could stand.

CHAPTER 7

Dom was in a flat panic. The sight of the woman by the cash register had alarmed him, but then *l'inconnue* pulled out her iPad and everything went to hell. She had never once done anything else in his *salon* but focus on him. On all the best he had to offer to the world.

Offer for one hundred euros a kilo, of course. He didn't owe the world shit.

He scowled at Guillemette. If he had known what was waiting for him, he could have stayed upstairs and made the brunette come to him, dealt with her there where his little freckled *habituée* couldn't see.

Every line of the brunette's body made it clear she was throwing out an invitation for sex, and certainly it was flattering and even a little bit arousing that she had liked it so much the last time. But he couldn't even remember her name, and . . . he was going to lose his *habituée* over this. If she had started to drift toward the bait he was dangling for her on a hook, this appearance of a sleek shark was going to drive her right out of his waters entirely.

Out of the corner of his eye, he saw *l'inconnue* rest her head on her hand and tap the screen of her iPad. *She wasn't wearing a hood today.* If he could get closer, he could see at last what her hair was like. Was it all that same reddish-caramel color?

"Dominique," the brunette breathed, clearly believing that the tone was enough to wrap around him and pull him straight toward her.

And it might have been. He was pretty good at quick, wild sex that involved no cuddles afterward. He had a special talent for it, even.

At her table, *l'inconnue* pulled a scarf out of her purse and looped it loosely over her head, her Audrey Hepburn look. Which was kind of romantic and sweet, because a face less like Audrey Hepburn's would be hard to imagine. Maybe a little in the cheekbones.

Merde, no, it wasn't sweet. She had come *out,* she had come here today ready to be just a little more naked to him, and now she was hiding herself again, and he hadn't even gotten a good look at her hair.

"How are you?" Dom asked the brunette crisply, trying to make himself seem unavailable without making *anyone watching* think he was a rude, crude, and socially unacceptable human being who had sex with women whose names he couldn't remember later and then treated them badly. Everything else might be true, but he did *not* treat them badly. This woman had pursued *him,* had gotten exactly the little fantasy she was looking for, and months later, must have started fantasizing again.

The woman gave him a small, intimate smile. "Thinking of you."

Putain. She was as aggressive in her glossy way as he was, and since she didn't give a damn about him and therefore had resilient feelings, brushing her off wasn't going to be that easy to do.

Certainly not without giving the definite impression to *people who happened to be watching* that he used women and was heartless to them afterward.

Which he *was,* but in his defense, they were heartless to him, too. Hearts weren't involved. He used them because their only reason for coming on to him in the first place was that they wanted him to use them.

He could feel himself floundering in panic, and then his guts caught up with him and kicked his brain into action. He wasn't going down without a fight.

"Come." He took the brunette's arm and led her out onto the sidewalk, out of sight of the windows. Then he turned to look at her. Had he ever even *known* her name? Or had she told him to call her *bébé* or something?

He had a talent for that, too. Women who wanted to be anonymous. Who didn't want to leave anything behind with him, not even their names.

Like his *inconnue,* who sat there, holding on to her name like a treasure, not letting him have even that one scrap of her.

"I'm sorry," he told the brunette roughly. *"Non."* He had to do this quickly. The longer he was out here, the worse his absence was going to look.

The brunette stared at him, her smile disappearing.

"I don't—I've met someone." His heart pounded to admit that out loud. *I've met someone.* Another woman whose name he didn't know. But he had touched her shoulders yesterday and she hadn't jerked them away or anything. She hadn't screamed to the riot police for help.

Putain, but he had it bad. Some part of him pointed out that he was being inordinately stupid, turning down easy, hot sex with a stranger in favor of a painstaking, tentative, slender chance of even going to dinner with another stranger. But this beautiful brunette had never sat in his *salon* as if his very existence made up her happiness, as if she could spend hours soaking him in and still want more of him. She would be happy for hours of sex, sure, but it wasn't . . . it just really wasn't the same thing.

Maybe he had been living on the sexual equivalent of

desserts for too long. His whole being craved proteins, a long, slow, complete meal. And the dessert on top of it.

Frustration and injured pride flashed across the woman's face. She lifted her chin. "Just what are you saying *non* to, Dominique? Did you think something was on offer?" She looked him up and down, her lip curling.

His shoulders relaxed. Thank God for women who could give as good as they got. "I suppose I was just fantasizing that it was as good for you as it was for me. You can't blame a man for dreaming."

A tiny soothing of her pride. She shrugged, to soothe it more. "Oh, it was great, but these things are better not repeated, you know. They lose all their appeal."

"Yes, of course," he said. He knew that very well. And was rather pleased with himself for having managed not to be the one rude enough to point it out. He glanced back at the gleaming windows of his shop, in the most ridiculously counterproductive urge to show off to a certain someone how very well-mannered he was being.

"I just came by to pick up some of your chocolates for some houseguests," the brunette said dismissively. "And thought I would say hello while I was in."

"Bien sûr." *Merde.* That meant he had to let her back in.

Inside the shop, a cup of chocolate and a double dark chocolate réligieuse sat in front of *l'inconnue.* Untouched. She was standing, laying bills down on the table.

Oh, God. "Guillemette," he said sharply. "Could you assist madame?"

"Madame" gave a brusque turn to her head when he left her side, but he prayed Guillemette's elegant control of the room would cover even that situation.

L'inconnue looked up when he approached her table. Even with her standing, he loomed over her. Her eyes were wry, cool, her face unblushing. That was bad, the lack of a blush. How to handle this so that it didn't look like exactly what it was, a man trying to juggle two women?

"Mademoiselle, bonjour," he said quietly, forcing off all his hardness, trying to shove it away into some closet he could slam and lock. It was more difficult this time. He felt hard. Something vital was being threatened, and he only knew how to fight for what he wanted, slugging with all his strength. But his freckled stranger wasn't a boxer. He couldn't get what he wanted by slugging.

"Bonjour," she said distantly.

"You're not hungry?" he asked with a little smile at the food left on her table, exactly as if his heart wasn't pounding frantically at the sight. *She hadn't even taken a taste.*

"I forgot I have an appointment."

That was a lie. The pounding of his heart was making him sick. He was so much bigger than she was. Could he just wrap her up and take her away and explain . . . what, exactly? Maybe he could explain with his hands and his mouth on her body. The thought surged through him. God, yes, tracing freckles. What a lovely, delicious morning that would be. There wasn't any other way to communicate . . . whatever it was he wanted to communicate.

"Did you like your caramels?" he asked with another smile, willing her to respond to it the way she had the afternoon before.

Her eyebrows flexed, troubled, and smoothed again. "I did," she said, but didn't smile.

He kicked his smile up another notch, coaxing hard. "Which one did you like the best?"

"All of them," she said, resigned. She looked away from him, slipping her wallet into her purse.

"Would you like to see how they're made?" he asked on a sudden inspiration, stretching out a hand. Could that prove an irresistible temptation? "Could you call your appointment, put it off?"

She stilled and looked back up at him, her eyebrows knit. She glanced past him, toward the counter, where Guillemette boxed chocolates for the brunette. He didn't dare glance back at what the brunette's expression might be, but *l'inconnue*'s face grew more troubled.

"Surely you don't have time for that," she said slowly.

"It will be a pleasure," he said firmly.

Again her gaze flicked to the brunette and back to him, incredulous. "You don't even know my name. Do you?" she asked warily.

"No." He raised his eyebrows expectantly.

Once again, she didn't respond with the correct politeness and tell him.

Really. And here he was trying so hard to prove to her *his* manners. "I've told you mine," he prompted encouragingly. "Dominique."

But that, unexpectedly, made her laugh. "Everybody in Paris knows *your* name, Dominique Richard," she told him with . . . with what he could only describe as affectionate humor. As if she was going to ruffle his hair indulgently next.

Hmm. He was not her little boy. And yet, the idea of her hand in his hair, even patting it like a little boy's, made his whole body curl with longing.

"Come upstairs," he coaxed. It must, indeed, have been irresistible bait, because she moved with him to the bottom of the stairs. "You'll love this."

"Ciao, Dominique," the brunette said silkily as she took her sack of chocolates and made a little gesture to her ear, *I'll call you later.*

La salope, Dom thought with respect. That was probably why he had been attracted to her in the first place. He liked a woman who fought back and fought dirty.

He looked down at his *inconnue,* her eyes once again cool, distant, incredulous. Well, it wouldn't be the first time he had to surmount an impossible handicap from his past. He smiled down at her. "Come up." *Come see me at my best.*

He just barely remembered, last minute, to fall into step behind her rather than lead the way. Someone, some exasperated girl when he was a teenager, had complained about his lack of gallantry, and that had been one of the things she had pointed out—that he was supposed to follow behind the woman up the stairs. He had refused to care. The very last thing he was able to do back then was put himself in a position that suggested he was anyone's servant, man or woman.

But as he followed behind *her* up *his* stairs, he thought it wasn't so bad. He didn't feel like her servant, he felt like a Peeping Tom. He could see her butt as she climbed and planned to put some more meat on it by stuffing her with delicacies while she was upstairs. And if she slipped on those narrow spirals, he could catch her.

A light came on in his brain. Maybe *that* was the reason he was supposed to follow a woman up the stairs. Did that mean he was supposed to go before her on the descent, too?

That wouldn't be nearly as much fun, because he wouldn't be able to see her butt, but he kind of liked the idea that if she tripped, she would ram straight into his broad shoulders and cling to them. And he wouldn't let her fall.

He grinned a little. Maybe if he was lucky, she would trip because she was so busy watching *his* butt. He'd been told he had a good one, although the context felt uncomfortably sordid and dirty as he followed Mademoiselle Nameless up the stairs.

"She's *not* going to call me later," he mentioned into her ear, brought to the level of his mouth by the two steps between them. "She doesn't even have my number."

Her step faltered and he actually got to reach out a hand and put that gentlemanliness into practice, catching her . . . maybe just a little lower on her back than was quite well-mannered, maybe just a little too much of her butt, but he didn't want her to *fall*.

She tripped again at the touch, but she didn't knock his hand away. *This is it, Dom. Either she's desperately afraid of heights, or she might be ready for you to ask her out. She might not disappear if you do.*

He ducked around as soon as they reached the top of the stairs, to see her expression when they first came into his *laboratoire*.

When her face lit up like a sunrise, he wanted to kiss her right then.

Damn, this whole going slow stuff was hard.

Jaime had never seen anything like Dominique Richard's kitchens. While it had some things in common with Sylvain's, Sylvain concentrated purely on the production of *chocolat,* no pastries, no caramels other than those incorporated into the chocolate itself. And Sylvain's was on the ground floor, with windows high up, in a more expensive part of Paris and therefore a more cramped space.

Dominique's . . . really was like ascending into heaven. The spring light of Paris came in from all the great casement windows, two of which were open on this gently cool day, to let in air. He was a couple of streets back from République itself, not on a major traffic artery, and the street noise was just a gentle reminder that the world was alive.

Gray marble gleamed in long, polished counters full of equipment. People moved around in white, along with one girl in her early twenties in black. Five small *enrobeuses,* nothing at all like the great factory machines that she knew, were placed in one area of the main room, one coating chocolate right then as a woman fed little squares of ganache into it while another touched up squares as they left the flow.

Metal forms of all shapes and descriptions hung from nails on the walls, reaching halfway to the high ceilings. A young man was artfully placing pastries on plates, adding little decorative touches before he left the room to take them down to the tables below. The girl in black passed from an opening on the far right end of the room to an opening on the far left, carrying a big bowl. Someone started to roll out dough on one of the marble counters.

The girl in black reappeared in the opening to the left at the same moment as a tall, brown-haired man appeared in the opening to the right. The two of them looked at Dominique and Jaime and then exchanged fascinated, charmed glances before they disappeared back into their separate rooms, with . . . twitching lips?

"Come!" Dominique said happily, pulling her in. He reminded her of children on the cacao farms, how they would talk to any adult who would listen, desperately wanting to show off how well they could do something of value. Like carry loads twice their own weight on their shoulders, or, later, after she had made her first rounds and reforms of the farms and was coming back to ensure her plans were being carried out, how well they were learning their letters and how to draw and what their doll's name was.

"This is *beautiful,*" Jaime said wonderingly. She had never imagined a *laboratoire de chocolat* so beautiful. Light, open, full of happiness. His *salon* was exceptionally beautiful, but this was even brighter, more active. It felt like the kind of place *her* cacao should end up, the cacao harvested in the hushed heat under the banana leaves, broken free from red or yellow wrinkled pods by willing hands, starting out as white fruit sweeter than a mango. Dominique insisted on fair trade chocolate from his processor, which got some of its supplies from farms under the Corey umbrella. She knew every step of his supply chain, might even have spread the beans out to dry in the sun with her own hand. She knew the fruity alcoholic smell these beans had once had as they fermented, the stinging sweetness of the memory blending with the rich, dark, warm intensity of the chocolate it had become.

An enormous block of chocolate rose above them on a counter that must be designed for such weight. Chisels in different sizes lay beside it, but the block itself was untouched. "What's this?"

"I've got to do something for the Chocolatiers' Expo next week, but I'm still thinking." His hand flexed into her back, and he studied the great block as if his gaze could pierce through it. "Sometimes you have to see what comes out of the chocolate."

She smiled, wondering suddenly if she could talk him into letting teenagers from the cacao farming cooperatives have an internship in his *laboratoire*. She could create a four-week scholarship, rotating through different farms, giving one teenager at a time that month in Paris. Make them part of the beautiful final end product their work went into creating.

The image of an excited adolescent was blotted out, knocked from her mind by darkness as if by a blow to the head. She took a deep breath of that comforting scent of chocolate and concentrated on the feel of Dominique's hand against her back.

He kept his hand there, her body yielding to his lead as if she was waltzing, as he guided her down the length of the room, stopping spontaneously at anything he thought would please her. "Try this." He offered her an éclair fresh from a tray.

His eyes brightened at her expression when she bit into

it, the dark, dense flavor of the soft, cold cream, the spark in it of something fresh, something tantalizingly different she could not identify.

"Pâtes de fruits." He stopped in front of a tray of gleaming sugared jewels of color. "Have you ever tried my *pâtes de fruits*?" He started to hand one to her, realized her mouth and hands were still full of his éclair, and hesitated, then ate it himself.

Her eyes snagged on his mouth, jealously, wondering what flavors were melting in it. Not chocolate. Something brighter, clearer, tart maybe, making his tongue sting just a little—

Something sparked in his eyes, lambent, hot. She looked away before she could blush—oh, damn, too late. What *had* been going on with that beautiful brunette downstairs? What had he been thinking to send her away in order to show Jaime his kitchens? Had he gone blind? *Could* he possibly know Jaime's name and need financial backing? He had opened this extravagant new space quite recently, and the economy was probably affecting people's indulgence in exorbitant chocolates; maybe he had over-extended.

He turned them into a doorway and shifted her in front of him. The heat from his body sank into her back and butt, curled through her body, the way the heat from the cream steaming in front of her wafted over her face, bringing with it the scent of some witch's secret garden. "This is the *cuisine,* where we do all the hot work, the baking, the caramels. Amand's working on a caramel right now, see?" She looked across the workspace to the tall, brown-haired man stirring a large pot, releasing scents of butter and sugar into the air. The pot had not yet started to boil, but he concentrated on it intently, biting down hard on his lower lip. The corners of his lips twitched.

"Do you know anything about how chocolate is made?" Dominique asked eagerly. His presence only inches behind her was melting every muscle in her spine and thighs until it was all she could do not to sway back against him.

She still hadn't decided what to say to that question when he started explaining it to her. "See, we have verbena infusing right here." He guided her to a pot full of cream in which floated a branch of long, narrow green leaves.

The lemony, fresh scent of the verbena wafted over her face, brightening the tranquil scent of the cream. His big hand on the small of her back was like some hot stone in tribal massage, its heat dissolving her.

"Once it has infused, we'll add the chocolate for the ganache."

His hand curled over her hip and whirled her around, to guide her into another room. "And this is a cooler room, where we set our ganaches and keep our new batches of chocolates to refill the displays."

The young woman in the black chef's jacket stretched her body far out over two long metal frames, scraping chocolate ganache smooth between them. She focused diligently on that smoothing, and every couple of seconds her lips trembled and she had to press them tightly together. She shot one glance up at Dominique and Jaime, her eyes alive with laughter, and bent her head quickly over the marble table again.

Past the marble table at which she worked were wheeled wire shelves, scattered with metal flats, half full of lovely finished chocolates. "*Tiens,* try this one, it's one of my favorites." Dominique proffered a chocolate, his thumb almost brushing Jaime's lower lip.

She caught her breath and looked up into his eyes.

What in the world was going on here? Did he like sycophants so much he would turn down a beautiful woman in order to melt a perfectly ordinary specimen into a puddle at his feet? Or *did* he know who she was? Or . . .

She closed her mouth around the chocolate, because,

whatever his reasons, hers were . . . that it allowed her lips to brush the hard tips of his thumb and index finger. Their warmth and texture shivered from the sensitive skin of her lips all through her, as his chocolate hit all the taste sensors in her mouth, from a touch of *fleur de sel* to bitter to sweet, and started melting on her tongue.

She didn't care what his reasons were. She didn't care if he could be attracted by money, and she didn't care if he just liked groupie sex. No matter what his motivations, she would still be the person who ended up receiving the most. All his sun and warmth and intensity . . .

"Dom," someone said, and it took a moment for the word to penetrate, both for him and for her. She blinked, confused, as those dramatic black eyebrows slashed down and he finally turned toward the speaker.

"Excuse-moi," said the speaker, a short, broad-shouldered man who sounded genuinely regretful. "I'm not sure I understand what you want me to do here. Could you—?"

Dominique gave him a dark look, but excused himself to Jaime and moved away into the cooking room. Jaime looked after them with raised brows. His team called him *Dom?* Used *tu?* Sylvain's team called him *Chef,* or *Monsieur,* and kept a punctilious *vous* at all times.

She tore her gaze away from Dominique's broad back and wandered around the *laboratoire.* The enrobing machine's flow of chocolate had a hypnotic pull. Such a delicate, intimate cascade compared to the great flows of chocolate in the giant enrobers back home in Corey. Much darker, too. Little chocolate centers disappeared under it, fed by an older woman in white who set them quickly and rapidly on the wire mesh, coming out the other side glistening with their chocolate *robes.* A tireless acrobat, the younger woman wielded the tiny tip of her knife like a fairy godmother's wand, bending to fascinating right angles to touch those *robes* up to be perfect for the ball.

Jaime wanted to be those ganache centers. Disappearing in melted chocolate, hidden from the world inside that warm darkness. She glanced involuntarily toward Dominique, half-turned toward her as if he was trying to keep her in sight, and bit her lip.

She realized the two women at the *enrobeuse* were sneaking bright, curious glances at her, smiling a little, and flushed, shifting away.

All the walls around the stairway were pure glass. Could she see that beautiful *salle* from here? Maybe the white rosebud wall? She slipped around to the point where the glass, framing the open spiral stairs, made a tiny one-person space against the farthest wall from those rosebuds.

Yes, just here you could see parts of the *salle*. That was the table where she usually sat, right there. A waiter was clearing off her uneaten pastries.

A movement back in the kitchens drew her eyes. Dominique Richard had returned to find her. On the other side of the stairwell and through two walls of glass, their eyes met. He stood very still. Very big.

Something in his stance made her glance around for her escape routes, like prey. But there were none. If she left this slim, final corner of glass, she would be moving toward him, and he would be able to track her movements every step of the way.

A hungry predator, he didn't wait for her to come to him. He prowled after her, closing her into that final corner of glass.

Predator? Where did she get these ideas? She wasn't the yummy brunette. He was too big a predator to track someone her size as his prey. It would be like a panther tracking a cricket. Something a panther would only do if it was starving, and he could not possibly be starving.

He stopped in front of her, blocking her into that little corner between glass and wall, his shoulders brushing either side of it. The void of the stairwell fell away behind her, just the other side of a sheet of glass.

His body heated the whole space. She shivered in it, stroked all over before he even touched her. He was so close she could see even the faint pink breaking out along his smooth jaw, and that sent another wave of heat through her. Was his skin so soft then? Or did he just shave too fast, impatient to burst on with his life?

"Do you ever stand up here and peek at the *salle,* if there's someone famous?" she asked.

He glanced toward her usual table and back at her, an odd, wary expression on his face. "There's often someone famous. And we're usually very busy."

"And you're famous yourself." Too famous to linger here, spying on clients, of course.

He grinned, quite pleased he hadn't had to point his fame out. "Are you?"

It sounded like a genuine question. Maybe he didn't know who she was, after all. "No," she said honestly. Not for her accomplishments, anyway.

He leaned in a little closer. No, that was her wishful thinking. She was definitely the world's most pathetic groupie. She wanted him to pick her up and press her back against that glass wall. She didn't want to remember how exposed the glass left them to the world. She tilted her head, her lips soft and openly begging. What stroked *his* skin all over? "Your kitchens are so beautiful. I've never seen anything like them."

For once, a compliment seemed to glance off him. She wasn't sure he even heard it. He closed one of those big hands around her wrist and rubbed his thumb over the bone there. "You don't eat enough," he said softly.

A shaft of anger shot through her. She wanted to yank her wrist away to spite . . . to spite her own face, since she was the only one who would suffer for it. All she did was eat and go to the gym and wander around this city, which was another kind of exercise. She was devoting her whole existence to getting strong again. Damn it, she was doing the best she could.

His gaze drifted over her set jaw. A frown flickered across his face. Then he rubbed his thumb over her wrist again, and she dissolved. She couldn't think past the feel of his thumb on that ultra-sensitive skin. "Do you ever go out with strange men?" he asked, low. "And let them feed you mortal food?"

Her gaze shot back to his face. Heat bloomed all through her, taking over her sex and her nipples and the color of her face, that hated scarlet blush of hers flaming, a red flag to guarantee he noticed all her weaknesses. "It's hard to stoop so low. After yours."

Again the compliment seemed to glance off that absorbed focus of his. Okay, if *that* didn't please him, what about her could? Hero-worship was pretty much the only arrow she had left in her quiver.

His gaze roamed all over her face, seeing every bit of that blush. Thank God she had pulled on a scarf, so he couldn't see the way it swept over her throat and breasts, too. "I've got to go," he murmured. "I promised to do this stupid cooking show session."

Oh. She would have pulled back in acceptance of the rejection, but she couldn't pull back. She was in a corner between glass, stone, and him.

"Are you doing anything tonight?" he asked very softly.

The blush swept back through her so hard she felt as if she would burn up from the inside out. Burning oh-so-particularly in all the parts of her body that she wanted to have pressed against him.

She was—she was probably supposed to go have dinner with her sister, so Cade could worry about what she ate, but she could cancel. She wobbled her head uncertainly.

"Can I come pick you up?"

She nodded unsteadily and every muscle of his body surged in response. And a very quiet rabbit looked up and realized she was cornered by a tiger.

And shivered in helpless delight at the fact that he wanted to eat her.

"Where are you staying?"

Staying. Not *Where do you live?* So impermanence was one of the base assumptions here.

"I'll, ah—" She dug into her purse for pen and paper. She turned toward the glass as a writing surface, his breath on the nape of her neck as she tried to make the pen work at that angle. Excitement kept licking over her skin. And yet at the same time, he smelled so deliciously of chocolate she could curl up in him like a comforter. She felt a deep, intense sense of coming home after too many years away. He leaned over her as if he couldn't help it, watching her write hungrily.

His hand closed carefully around the paper when she gave it to him. Not crushing it at all. He took a long, long breath, staring down at her. Then he turned his body like a heavy, reluctant gate that had not had its hinges oiled in some time. If she hadn't handed him her address as a password, would he have blocked her in that corner with his body forever, until she yielded?

Damn. Maybe she should have written more slowly. Dropped her pen a few times. Gotten their bodies tangled as they both reached for it.

Any second, and she would just lean into him, layer her weight onto him, let him do with it what he would.

Fighting resistance, as if trying to get her body into motion through thick melted chocolate, she forced herself to take a half step. It was either that or look so desperate he would retract the invitation.

"Seven thirty, then?" He checked as her body brushed

his. She could have gotten past without brushing him, but . . . why miss an opportunity? He might never even show tonight, and then she would regret it.

Would he stand her up? She glanced over her shoulder at him. He was staring at her with an intent, dazed look as if he was trying to see her through a fever. Maybe he was coming down with something that was making him act insane. "I would like that," she said, and he grinned, fast and hard.

That grin warmed every part of her body, even the stubborn achy one that usually refused to be warmed. It kept her warm, a golden, hopeful glow inside, as she forced herself to leave that source of heat, that scent of chocolate, and go out into Paris in the springtime.

As soon as she was out the door, the *laboratoire* erupted.

"Whoot! Whoot!" yelled Célie, clasping both hands and shaking them over her head in victory.

"Chef, you did it!"

Someone catcalled. Amand gave a long wolf-whistle.

"Oh, shut the hell up," Dom said, rubbing the piece of paper between his fingers over and over as if it was silk. He couldn't entirely suppress a grin, even though he was flushing.

Célie propped one *fesse* on a marble counter. "So what's her name?"

"Oh, *putain de bordel de merde.*" Dom looked down at the piece of paper. A number, a street. No name. "I still don't know."

CHAPTER 8

It turned out it was a good thing Jaime had to wait nine whole hours for Dominique to come get her, because she had to go shopping. And she had no idea how to go shopping. She hadn't done it in years, dressing herself entirely from market stalls, or else old clothes out of her closet whenever she visited home. Most of what she was wearing now had been picked out by Cade, while Jaime was still in the hospital. Jaime had added the hats and scarves herself, and expanded her selection of long-sleeved things that hid her arms, but that was about it.

What did you *wear* for a date with a man like Dominique Richard?

Her first instinct was to call Cade, but she absolutely could not stand to have Cade teaching her the ropes of something so basic, as if she was the goof-off, *helpless* baby sister. Magalie Chaudron had a killer fashion sense, but Jaime didn't know her well enough to call her. Anyway, she would have had to get her number from Cade.

So she was on her own.

Exactly as she was used to, so it would have to do.

She felt more helpless before this task than before any number of things, although a feeling of helplessness seemed to be her predominant trait right now, didn't it? At least this was a much more pleasant way to be helpless than some. Walking the streets of Paris with no limit on the money she could spend to get ready for a hot date, unable to make up her mind. It sounded like most women's dream. She reminded herself of that, tried to let it be a dream for herself, too—just pleasure. This was all about pleasure. No guilt, no regret, just pleasure.

The shop windows were full of things that did not look as if they would flatter her nearly as well as they did the mannequins. What kind of thing was she supposed to wear? What would *he* wear?

It didn't matter what he would wear, she reminded herself fiercely. For God's sake, she had been a major socializer in college. The woman set the tone. The man could wear jeans, what did it matter?

She wanted to wear a dress, but it was cool in the evening, and what if he drove his motorcycle? And she was still working on the muscle tone of her too-thin legs. Finally, after *seven hours* of shopping and because she was desperate, she forced herself to settle on patterned thin leggings and a long tunic top of midnight blue, loose enough to soften her body, with a heavy metal belt to draw attention to the Parisian-worthy thinness of her waist. Loose, super-soft knit sleeves narrowed to close-fit wide cuffs that stretched partway up the back of her hands, ending not so much in a ruffle as in the faintest hint of a ripple.

On her short hair, she tried a pageboy hat and glared at it, because she didn't look at all like the pictures of movie stars in magazines. Besides, having it on just seemed to emphasize the bareness of her neck, and she *hated* having her nape exposed.

Maybe Dominique would make it feel less exposed. The thought of him being right beside her seemed to still all the cold chills down her spine, stroke the hair on the nape of her neck back down with one warm hand.

She finally left the hat off and very carefully coiffed her

short, expertly feathered hair, using a little sapphire but-
terfly barrette to make sure the left side stayed in place the
way she wanted it.

Looking at herself in the mirror, she felt . . . unpro-
tected, and she reached for a scarf, clenched her fist and
drew her hand away, reached for it again, pressed her hand
to her thigh . . .

And the buzzer sounded.

Dom didn't worry about what to wear because it never
occurred to him. Even at award dinners and on cooking
shows, clean jeans and an untucked pressed shirt were the
height to which he aspired in terms of fashion. He would
have felt a complete fool showing up in a suit, but since he
had always seen his unknown in simple clothes, it never
crossed his mind.

His main goal for the evening in terms of *her* fashion
was to get her damn hood off her head.

So when she came downstairs with her hair naked, he
was knocked off his feet from the start. He was waiting for
her, tense and eager, trying not to stand too intimidatingly
close to the door, and when he saw that reddish-caramel
hair feathered around her face, he nearly muscled her right
back through it, backward straight up the steps, and into
her apartment. After which, a wall would probably do
fine. All he wanted was a closed door between him and
her and the rest of the world.

No, a bed, he told himself severely. *Don't even* think *about
anything else.*

So his mind did focus, obediently, on beds, but that
might not have been the most helpful direction for it to
head right at the moment.

"You look beautiful," he said involuntarily, and then
cringed because he sounded like he had at sixteen, back

when he had still thought he could get someone to love him despite everything.

Her eyes shot to his, skeptical even while she flushed a little. He caught his hand just short of her hair, realizing he had been about to stroke the fine feathery cut. It was too short for her face, really. Maybe that's why she hid it. Maybe it was a recent cut she was less than satisfied with. Maybe he could convince her to grow it out a little more, until it curved under her jaw.

He had to stop losing his mind. It took time to grow hair, and she had made it clear she was a visitor here.

Would it be a good time to ask for her name again? But if she said no, he might have a hard time not getting pissed off, so instead he took her hand firmly in his and headed them down the sidewalk.

Her lips parted, and she looked up at him with eyes big enough to drown in. No, skydive in, the cloudless twilight sky of them, float and float and float until you forgot to open your parachute and slammed into the ground.

He hadn't held a woman's hand since—well, ever. It hadn't worked out at sixteen. He *liked* it, that slim cool feel of her fingers entrapped in his. God, he hoped his hand didn't seem like some monster enclosing hers.

"Is there anywhere you would like to go?" he asked. *Merde,* maybe he should have put on a suit after all. His name could get them in anywhere, even without reservations, and it would have been a great chance to impress her. But he didn't really want to be in some elegant, hushed place with everyone watching them tonight.

"Not fancy," she said. She had not made one single effort to free her hand from his. "Just some place small, and warm, and . . . fun."

"Fun?" His eyebrows went up. Did she want him to take her someplace wild? If he got in a fight and got arrested, it would ruin the false impression he was trying to cultivate.

She had to lift both hands to illustrate what she meant, but he just let her carry his hand with her, not about to let go. She pushed the free hand toward the one he held, apparently trying to gesture closeness. "Warm," she said again. And then she did something that undid him to the last faint whisper of his soul: she gave his hand a squeeze with fingertips that could just barely reach around his, apparently using *him* to indicate what she wanted to say. He meant warmth. He meant this word she couldn't find.

He turned and kissed her. Wrapped her up in his arms, scooted her back into a green doorway with his body between hers and the brush of passersby, and kissed that full mouth of hers.

He met closed lips, because she hadn't been prepared for him at all. But he slanted his mouth over hers, too hungry to give up, and anyway, he had forced a hell of a lot of doors to open in his life. No force here, no force, just your mouth . . . please . . .

Her muscles loosened to him, her weight sinking onto his arms, her lips parting. Her fingers came up to close around his shoulders through the leather, and he wished it was already off his shoulders, trampled on the ground, who cared, just so he could feel her hands.

Her mouth, letting him in. After all those days eating everything he made, did she like the taste now of *him*? *Please take me, too.*

He couldn't say *please,* he couldn't, but . . . he said it with his mouth. Coaxing hers. Taking hers. God, she didn't need much coaxing.

It went through him like fireworks, the way she opened for him, and his arms tightened and lifted her higher on his body, and—

"*Excellente technique, jeune homme,*" a middle-aged woman

said acerbically, walking past, and he brought his head slowly up and gave her straight back an annoyed but grateful look. You could always count on a fellow Parisian to let you know when you were making a complete fool of yourself.

"*Pardon,*" he whispered to *the woman whose name he still didn't know,* turning his head back to rest his forehead just gently against hers. "*Pardon.* I couldn't help—" He stopped himself just in time, because he despised men who said they couldn't help things.

All her weight lay still yielded to him, her face flushed, her lips parted, her eyes clinging, her body his to hold. Oh, God. He looked back toward her apartment building, only a few doors away.

He had promised her dinner, hadn't he? *Not* fast-food sex.

And just because she *looked* as if he could lower his mouth back to hers and nibble her lips and turn her body entirely limp and take her straight upstairs didn't mean he . . . he shouldn't . . . he—

"We had better keep walking." He straightened so roughly she stumbled, and he cursed himself. He never could wash those six years of brute hacking out of him, could he? He closed his hand around hers again, more tentatively.

She didn't say anything at all, but she curled her fingers around the edge of his palm—all she could reach from the inside of his hold.

She wasn't wearing a jacket, he realized when he shrugged off his own at the bistro. He grinned with heady anticipation. It was going to get cooler by the time they left the restaurant, and he would be able to give her *his* leather jacket, wrapping her up in his warmth for all the walk back to her apartment.

"Do you like it?" He smiled down at her, enjoying

deeply the fact that he could now use *tu* with her, as they waited at the bottom of the steps for the waiter to arrange a space for two in the crowded little place, its room set just a few steps down from the street. He had brought her to one of his favorite bistros, on the edge between the Marais and the République area. The kind of place where you could get a good steak, fresh cut *frites,* and lather it with *sauce Roquefort,* all of which he was planning on talking her into ordering. *Were* the bones on her wrists just starting to soften a little, after ten days of his *salon?*

Her smile warmed him all through. *"C'est parfait,"* she said shyly. She had grown very shy since that kiss.

That shyness put him in power, and he felt corrupted by that power already, inclined to lure her into his clutches and keep her there forever. Surely it wasn't a very smart thing for her to do, to let him have the power here.

Any woman who let a man have power over her was a complete fool, but when he was the man in question . . .

Well. She wasn't here for very long, he reminded himself. He could surely manage to be a decent person for as long as she was in the city.

"What are you doing in Paris?" he asked, holding her hands across the table because he didn't want to lose the privilege in case she recovered some shred of sense, and sliding his fingers under the close knit of the cuff of her sleeves to stroke against the inside of her wrists. He wasn't really trying to manipulate her, he just couldn't stop himself. He loved the feel of her skin, he loved that access, he loved the way her eyes grew dazed and dreamy.

But his question made her pull her focus back in, her eyes clearing and growing distant. "I have family here."

It hit him like a slap that there was some lie there. Here he was, her melted marshmallow, and she could keep herself together enough to lie to him. He had thought he had the power? "But you're not staying with them?"

Like, whose apartment did he need to direct them back to, in order to have her all to himself?

She shook her head. "I like to have my own space."

Great. That unshared, private space of hers was not very far from this restaurant at all.

"What family do you have here?"

"My—sister," she said reluctantly, watching him, for what he didn't know. "My father and grandfather, sometimes. My family has always liked Paris. My mother used to get us all to come here sometimes when we were little. It's where she and my father had their honeymoon."

He smiled. He didn't have many privileges of birth, but he did at least have that one: he was born in a city that made women's hearts mushy and romantic just by whispering its name.

Well, he hadn't been born quite *in* it. Even with that privilege, he was on the outskirts, the muddy hem of the elegant gown. But he had claimed Paris fully now. "Is that why you speak French?"

"Mmm. Partly. My mother died when I was ten, and my father didn't want to come back here after that. But I guess my sister and I always had a—tie to Paris, because of her. We both studied French in school, and my sister just recently moved here. But most of my practice is from development work in French-speaking countries. That's what I"—she seemed to hesitate a long time over her verb tenses—"I've been doing."

Bon Dieu. An infinitely better person than he was, then. "How long have you been doing that?"

"Since college."

College. So she had about ten years more education than he did, too.

"But I did summer internships even during college, so I guess you could say longer."

He massaged the back of his neck and didn't say any-

thing. It was as he suspected. He didn't have much to offer her but great chocolate and great sex. Why she kept sitting in his *salon* acting as if she could absorb something
more from him was a mystery.

Well, no, it wasn't a mystery. It was a testament to his
own ability to construct illusions. She had never suggested
she wanted anything else.

The best he could do was delay her realizing her mistake as long as he could. Or was that how his father had
gotten his mother? By hiding his real self just long
enough? "Odd," he said without meaning to. "I lost my
mother when I was ten, too."

Her fingers squeezed over the hand that still held hers.
He instantly dropped his hand from his neck to recoup
her other hand. If there was squeezing going on, both his
hands wanted some. "It's tough," she said quietly. "I'm
sorry. Was it an accident or did she get sick?"

He shouldn't have brought this up. "A boyfriend," he
said dryly. Dryness was about the best tone he could manage about this event, and that had taken a lot of practice.

Her eyes widened, shocked. "A boyfriend *killed* her?"

He flinched. "No." Well, God, now that she suggested
it, he realized he couldn't know. They said women repeated cycles, so she might very well have run off with
someone who treated her the same way his father had.
"She ran off with him. Would you like a red wine, do you
think? This Médoc is supposed to be good."

Was his mother all right? He had bitterly hated her for
so long, and now suddenly he felt a desperate urge to track
her down and make sure she was hale and happy. Something she had never made sure of about *him*.

His Still Nameless Date was staring at him with her lips
parted, her eyes uncomprehending. See, and her parents
had loved her, too. The knowledge squeezed his heart with

anguish. He didn't deserve her. He shouldn't be sitting here, luring her into his clutches.

"Whatever you want," she said absently of the wine, blinking, trying without success to stop staring.

He flicked a hand at Axel, the waiter, and ordered her a glass. She raised her eyebrows when she realized hers was the only one being poured. "I said whatever you want."

Here it came. "I don't drink."

She blinked a couple of times, and then burst out laughing.

Well, that hadn't hurt as much as he'd thought. He raised one eyebrow, waiting, while her laugh twisted and tumbled in his middle, doing all kinds of unethical things to him.

"You really don't? But—you're French!" she burbled. "Oh, I love it. You must love saying that to people."

He hadn't, actually, ever loved saying it before. People looked at him as if he had grown two heads, and he sure as hell wasn't going to explain the reason. But—he found himself smiling, his thumbs gently stroking the back of her hands.

"Is chocolate your only vice?" she suggested cheerfully.

"Well—not my only," he had to admit.

She looked down at their joined hands, and her mouth curved in a way that made that tsunami of warmth and arousal beat through him. She could have been looking right through the table, straight at his currently most pressing vice, which was surging at the imagined attention.

Her lashes lifted suddenly, and from under them, she gave him a long look. His hands squeezed slowly tighter.

"So, did your father raise you on his own or did he remarry?" she asked randomly. Probably grabbing at topics to make the sexual tension halfway bearable.

"Mmm." This was what he got for taking a woman out

to dinner. Conversation, for God's sake. He did much, much better just going straight to sex, before, during, and after which no woman ever looked at him with the slightest hint of pity. "He didn't remarry. This is really good." He pointed to the healthiest first course on the menu, trying to make up for all that sugar he was pouring into her body. "The chef sautés the chèvre very quickly over high heat, and then lays it over a bed of mâche, with balsamic caramelized figs—"

He stopped, because her eyes had flicked from his finger on the menu back to his face, and they were narrowed, a little annoyed.

What had he said? Damn it, the whole sex-and-that's-it policy had been working so well for him. What had inspired him to change it?

Her hands shifted in his as if she might be wanting to free them, and he couldn't help it that his fingers tightened a little. It was instinct. He looked down at her hands caught in his as the twitch stilled and she changed her mind, then up to the freckles over her cheekbones, her wide mouth, her blue gaze back on their hands, the blush that had never entirely faded from her cheeks that evening. That warmth washed through him, beating his helpless body. Oh, that. That had inspired him to change his policy.

"You want me to be quiet so you can concentrate on the menu?" he hazarded.

She shook her head, gazing at their hands. "No. No, whatever you said sounds good."

It wasn't until the first course arrived that he realized one of the worst aspects of this dinner idea, that he had to let go of her hands, too. He angled his legs under the small table so that they kept brushing against hers instead. And she looked up at him with those skydiving eyes of hers and that sunset blush and let him do it. And she ate all of her

salad and only a third of the steak, but then she kept soaking up that Roquefort sauce with fries and nibbling one
more from time to time while he ate *his* steak, until her
whole rich concoction of pure cream and Roquefort was
gone, so he felt he had accomplished something. Plus, he
had the brilliant idea to talk about the best places to visit
in Paris instead of family history, so his own enjoyment of
the conversation improved radically. Her eyes sparkled as
she talked about what she had seen, asked him about what
he liked. He was a little embarrassed to realize she had visited more of the cultural monuments of his city than he had.

He draped his jacket around her shoulders as they left
the restaurant, entirely smug about his forethought in
wearing one and her lack of forethought in not. They
didn't say a word as they walked through the streets. He
knew he should keep up conversation, not let her start
having second thoughts, but his heart was beating so hard,
he didn't dare open his mouth. He knew his words would
come out choppy; she would hear his struggle to breathe.

What was the matter with him? How could he be nervous about *sex*?

At the door to her building, she turned and looked up
at him, her hands burying in the pockets of his jacket, her
eyes very wide.

He leaned into her, bracing his arms on either side of
her head.

"Tell me your name." He tried to keep his voice coaxing, but he was pretty sure he didn't succeed. Damn it, he
was *not* going to be her wild one-time nameless fuck, her
little visit to a porn shop. His whole being rose up in re-
bellion against that role he had embraced for so long.

Bordel de cul, she wasn't going to tell him. She looked
away, her face growing thoughtful and distant. Braced over
her, his body surged with ways he could wring it out of her,
and she shot a glance up at him, a wistful, hungry smile.

"*J'aime,*" she said, with that choppy English J of hers, and his whole body jerked.

And then went still, more still than in that last second before they got to the Rs when the *Meilleur Ouvrier de France* award was announced and even his peers finally agreed that, yes, he was one of the best of the best choco- latiers in the world. He forgot all about her name. "What do you love?" he whispered. His—chocolate? His body? Being with him?

Her eyes widened, and she stared at him as if trapped, which she was: he had his arms braced on either side of her and his body looming over her, and there was no way he was going to let her go. Her face turned so crimson he could tell even in the silver-gold night lights of the city. "That's my name." Her voice came out a strangled whis- per.

He blinked a moment, while his insides scrambled and congealed and tried to be reasonable and didn't know what to do. "Your name is *Jaime?*" He couldn't say the hard J; his English training consisted of the swear words he had picked up from films and all the marketing vocabulary for his chocolates, practical things like *oats* and *black heart of the ganache with its virile notes of olive oil.* He silked it out, her name, and her head tilted back as if he had just petted her with it.

He sank one too-big hand into that short hair, curling halfway around her skull, and then drew it down over her neck, over her shoulder, down her arm, heavily, petting her for real.

She sighed and sank back against the door.

His body kicked into overdrive. *That was a yes.*

He pressed his hand low over her belly between the sheltering panels of his jacket and rubbed it up over her ribs, a slow drag, until it was just below her breasts, and her eyes were closed, and her lips were parted. "Jaime," he whispered, her name sounding so much like something else that fear and desire knocked through him, some strange wild harmony.

She shivered and turned her head a little to the side, the line of her chin and throat all exposed to him. So he took the offer, brushed his lips very gently from the corner of her mouth, over the line of her jaw, down her throat.

"Jaime," he whispered, and his heart tried to stop in pure terror at the word, but his body kept it going. "What's your code?"

Her hands sank into his hair. He had to force himself enough away from her that she could turn in the tight shelter of his body, her shoulder rubbing against his chest, and tap it in.

Don't be stupid, some voice from his teenage past wanted to tell her. *Don't let me see your code. Don't let me in.* He quelled it ruthlessly.

When the door released, he pushed it open instantly and herded her inside, letting the door close behind them, shutting out the street, shutting them into darkness. In that darkness, he lifted her up, riding her on his thigh so he could free a hand, running it up to cup the breast he had just resisted on the public street. His mouth closed over hers, and this time her lips were already parted for him.

A door—to something of value—that was *open* for him. That welcomed him in.

She liked to eat things in slow bites, he reminded himself. She liked to sit there for hours. She liked to take her time. So he gave himself to her in slow bites, a flicker of his tongue, a taste of hers, a nibble of her lips, an elusive slide of his. It was so hard his body shook with it. His forearms corded against the door on either side of her head with the effort to keep himself off her. Her arms clutching his back were all that were holding her up on his thigh.

He loved that. He loved the way she clung to him.

He had to force his mouth away from hers again, panting. "Tell me where to go." He must sound like a savage. A man who had no control.

She showed him the stairs, and he picked her up so that her legs were wrapped around his hips and carried her up them.

He had to stop a few times because his breath was too short, and not from the stairs or the weight. He had to stop and kiss her, grabbing onto the banister so he kept some purchase in the world of her kisses and didn't send them tumbling down the stairs.

She liked this. She liked it. She liked the taste of him.

He had to take the key from her at her door because she seemed so lost in kisses, she could let him kiss her against her door forever. But if there was one door in his life he was going to get open, it was that one, by God.

He got them in, then threw the deadbolt on the whole damn world outside.

Bed, he reminded himself as he looked around, managing a blurred vision of a small space, of hardwood floors and red curtains. *No walls, no floors. Bed.* Or maybe a couch, because one was right there and—*Bed!*

The suitcase on the floor of her bedroom made his heart flinch, curling from a blow. The lid was propped up against the wall, and it was fully packed, with a few clothes folded loosely on top of a dresser. She hadn't even put her clothes in the drawers in the room. She was living out of her suitcase, ready to go.

He ignored his heart. No one in his life had ever dealt with it with much patience, including himself, and he wasn't about to start now.

He turned on the nearest lamp, and she stiffened against him and pulled away.

"I don't—turn it off," she entreated.

He paused with his hand on the switch. "Really?" he

asked, disappointed. She stood there in that midnight blue tunic that didn't even show the mark of his hands where he had slid them on her body, but her face was so flushed, her mouth so full and bruised looking, her eyes so dark and hungry. He wouldn't be able to see whether the rest of her body blushed in the dark, or where her freckles went, or what happened to them under his hands.

Her mouth grew stubborn. She started to fold her arms around herself.

He turned the lamp off.

In the light from the street, he could still see her, but more as a lighter form in shadow. He couldn't make out those pale freckles or shades of blush. *Next time,* he promised as he reached for her, alarming himself with his continual attempts to make this long-term.

She knelt suddenly on the high bed, bringing her face level with his, and when his mouth closed on hers this time, her hands slid under his shirt and found the T-shirt underneath. Damn it, he had worn too many clothes. But she pushed that barrier away, too, slid the knit up his skin.

He pushed his jacket off her, which drove her hands away from him, then grabbed them back and brought them to the buttons on his shirt.

"I can't believe you—" She broke off, kissing him, just like he had dreamed she would, long and slow as if she could savor him forever.

"Can't believe what?" he asked against her mouth, attacking his own buttons from the bottom since she was taking so long from the top. But his own hands got lost, too, slipping away from his forgotten buttons, running over her body through the knit tunic. He got her belt off, dropped away that annoying metal that kept getting in the way of his hands.

"It doesn't matter," she whispered, sliding her hands all

over his chest through his double layers of shirt. "I don't care."

He couldn't bite his own tongue to shut himself up, because it kept getting tangled with hers, and so he heard himself protesting, in a breath against her mouth as he took her down onto the bed, "Yes, it does. It does matter. I care."

His heart went wild to see her lying there for him. He drew her low, slouchy boots off, running his hands down her legs through the thin leggings, over slim, stubborn muscles, too thin but not weak. His hand curled slowly around that thin calf, harder than he should. He stared down at it, not looking at her. "Tell me the truth," he said suddenly, harshly, in the dark. "Are you sick? Have you had cancer? Are you all right?"

A moment's silence while he waited in paralyzed fear for the response, not at all sure what he would do with it. But, "No." She sounded angry. "I'm *perfectly fine*."

He did an involuntary tally of the calories she must be consuming in his shop. Unless she didn't eat one single other thing, it didn't add up. "*Do* you eat normal food?"

"No." Definite anger in her voice. He was ruining the mood, idiot that he was. "I only eat the best food in the world. But yes, that includes lots of healthy servings of fruits and vegetables." She didn't actually say *Back off*, but her tone rang with it.

"*Pardon.*" He slid back up her body, propping himself on his elbows above her on the bed. "I just—" His thumb stroked her cheekbone. Her skin felt so soft, the bone under it so strong and so delicate at the same time. "I just—" What had he been going to say?

He lowered his head and kissed her again, and this time he didn't have any trouble taking a long, long, long slow time. He rolled over onto his back, pulling her on top of him so he could feel her weight, still kissing her. He dragged her hands back to his buttons. "Take it off," he whispered against her mouth. "Please. I want to feel your hands."

He knew better than to take her clothes off yet. She might be able to spend an hour savoring him, but he was pretty sure that as soon as he got her naked, he would devour her.

She pushed herself up on his chest, her palms pressing into his muscles, and looked at him. *Why* wouldn't she let him turn on the light? He was positive she must be blushing. But she sat all the way up, knees slipping to either side of his hips to straddle him and his very unmistakable arousal.

She had to be blushing. She had to be. And when his hips surged up against hers uncontrollably like a beast that kept slipping off leash, she had to be. She drew her lower lip in under her teeth, and longing squeezed him in one hard fist. He grabbed her fingers, pressing the tips of them against his buttons. *At last,* she gave them her attention.

He kept thinking he couldn't get more aroused, and she kept proving him wrong. Feeling her hands slip the panels of his shirt away and smooth over his T-shirt, feeling her ride his arousal as she did it, pressing down on him without flinching, feeling her hands push his T-shirt up, sliding over his skin . . . desire shook him like a worthless cur. No.

No, that wasn't right.

Desire shook him like some sparkly, beautiful star from which she wanted to wring all light.

He sat up to let her pull the shirt over his head, and that brought them face to face, with her astride him still. *"Ma minette,"* he whispered, running his hands down her arms and catching her wrists, stretching her hands away from him before he lost it. "Can I have more than one try?"

She pressed her face into the join of his neck and shoulder and nodded.

CHAPTER 9

Yet another reason to insist on no light, the blush she could feel covering her entire body. Her skin transparently showing the heat he generated inside her.

He made her so hot. And so warm, both. She had no idea what had inspired him to give himself to her, but like some dry, desperate sponge, she was going to soak up every last bit of him that she could. He could wring her every way he wanted, afterward, to get himself back, she would still have him, have some of him to keep.

She just hoped he got something out of it, too.

She turned her head from his throat, pressing kisses over those big shoulders. Why did a chocolatier-pâtissier have such shoulders? His work was physical, but this was brute strength, here, the shoulders of someone who did heavy construction or who devoted serious effort at the gym to maintaining them. She squeezed her hands into the biceps that matched them, letting her fingernails test their resilience. He had taken a shower between his work and meeting her, washing away the chocolate scent that made her feel she was coming home. Here, in the night, his scent was his own essence, the cacao in it elusive, as if she could chase it all over his body and still find only him. The scent of totally new territory.

So why did it feel like the place she wanted to belong?

"Jaime." Her silked-out name shivered over her.

"What?" she whispered, trailing her lips over his chest. It rose and fell. He pulled her hips in harder against his. "Nothing." One of his hands dragged over her back, through the knit. "I just like saying your name." His hands scooped under her bottom, flexing into the muscles there. "Say mine."

She pressed her face into his chest and let him feel her grin. "Monsieur?"

His fingers flexed punishingly into her bottom. "That's not funny."

Really? Well, maybe she did have a peculiar sense of humor.

He pulled her head back from his chest enough to look at her in the darkness. "Well, maybe a little funny," he allowed. "Some other time."

This wasn't a one-night deal? Some other time they might play erotic games? Maybe "some other time" was just a figure of speech. She wrapped her arms suddenly as much around him as she could, squeezing herself hard to him, as if she could imprint all that heat of him inside her body forever.

She must have been stronger than she realized, for she felt the breath leave him, puffing against her head. He pushed her tunic up until his hands were rough against her bare back, and that made her shiver all over. They were so rough. They were so big. They were so . . . tender. Her whole body wanted to cry out like parched earth for rain at that strength and that tenderness, as if he healed everything about her. "Say my name," he said again.

"Dominique Richard."

He shook her hips in punishment, a tiny movement that rocked her tormentingly against him. "Just me."

She loosed her stranglehold on him enough to slide one hand down his arm while with the other she still held on tight. Those muscles in his arms. The way they flexed to her touch. "Dominique."

He rolled them down, onto his back, then twisted them onto their sides, pulling her leggings off her, those rough big palms scraping over her naked butt and all the way down her legs. She twisted restlessly, cool air flowing against her sex. He had caught her panties with the clinging material of the leggings. She wasn't sure at first he realized it, covered as she still was by the long tunic.

Then his hands slid slowly, excruciatingly slowly, back up her bare legs and . . . he realized it.

"*Chérie,*" he whispered into her mouth, kissing her again and again as his hand rubbed her open. "Do you want me so much then?"

Of course, he couldn't *see* that she was all one big blush, but it wasn't as if her wet and hungry sex was being any more subtle about it. She twisted against him, burying her face in his body, nodding helplessly as her arms wrapped around him, slid over him.

"Do you, Jaime? Do you really?" He slipped the tip of one of those big, blunt fingers just a half-inch into her. She panted against him, the top of her head pressed hard into his chest so that she could hide her face from him and see his hand between her thighs at the same time. Her fingers dug into him frantically. "Just a little bit?" he whispered to the back of her head, slipping his finger a tiny bit farther into her. "Just a little at a time?"

She twisted her head back and forth against his chest, wildly denying it. No, not a little bit. All, all, all.

But he ignored her, letting his finger sink only one half-inch more.

"I like this," he breathed to the back of her head. "Oh, I like it, the feel of you yielding to me. You like it, too, don't you, *chérie,* you like taking me inside you. Tell me you do."

Her fingers dug and dragged against the muscles of his

back. "I do." She felt close to weeping with desire, but her lower body was doing that already for her. "You have to know I do."

"I want you to tell me." His finger slid just a little deeper, his other hand curved around her thigh, not forcing her but encouraging her to be still for him. The walls of her sex yielded to him and then squeezed back tight against him, her lips curled hungrily over him. "I like you to tell me."

Oh, yes, praise. He liked praise. She let her head fall back so he could see all of her, her desperation. "I love it," she whispered. "I love it. I want you inside of me. I won't get enough of you. I want you. Don't—don't torment me."

"*Torment* you?" He scraped a hand over her hair, cradled her skull. "*Minette,* I thought you would like it slow. I wouldn't torment you."

She managed something like a smile, her body shaking with need. "Some—some other time, perhaps." She gave him his own words back. "Right now, I just . . . really want you."

"Jaime." He drew her hard against his body, turning her so that her back was to his chest and his arms were wrapped around her in a hard embrace. She loved that embrace, but her body twisted, bereft at the withdrawal of his finger.

"You can have me," he whispered to the top of her head. "Jaime. Let me just make sure of one little thing first."

"What?" Her body writhed against him, loving the friction created between their skin but trying for so much more.

His hand pressed hard against her sex, holding her pelvis back against his, still veiled in jeans. "Just one little thing, Jaime."

He slipped his thumb over the tiniest center of absolute power on her body. She jerked and sagged back against him, flowering helplessly as he stroked the nub of her sex.

"There it is." His rough, gentled voice was like sex itself, more powerful even than the stroke of his hands. "*Cette petite chose.* Do you like that, sweetheart? Do you like it harder? Do you like it . . . just right here? There you go, *minette,* there, I've got you, give it to me, give me . . . you're so beautiful . . . yes, oh, yes . . ."

She came so fast for him it would have been embarrassing if she had any thought left. Her body flew straight into him as if he were the sun. She shook in his hard hold uncontrollably as she rose. He held her so completely as the world dissolved around her. Her body arching, shaking, against the hard muscles of his arms.

"*Yes.*" There was no mistaking the triumph in his voice, the hand actually closing into a fist of victory against her sex. He rocked his knuckles against her, gently, riding the orgasm out, letting her enjoy the lingering waves of it. Until at last she was still, rubbing her face against him weakly, and he rolled away from her long enough to push off his jeans and dig in one of the pockets and come back. Of course he had come to pick her up supplied with condoms. That had been what they were both after, right?

He knelt on the bed between her legs and drew her tunic over her head. When he threw the dress on the floor, he had to take a minute, his hands fisted hard on his thighs. She didn't think she had ever seen a man so violently aroused.

He breathed hard, his knuckles pressing into the muscles of his thighs. "Will you—will you take it off for me, Jaime?"

He was staring at her bra. Still shaky with the aftershocks, entirely malleable, she pushed herself up on her elbows enough to reach behind her and undo the clasp. When she relaxed back onto the bed and slowly pulled the straps off her shoulders and lifted the bra away, she felt as if she was making some kind of sacred vow. The virgin sacrifice. The offering.

"Oh, God." His voice harsh, he came down over her, wrapping her thighs around him, and managed a fleeting grin. "See, this is why I had to make sure. But you did promise me—" He pushed slowly, just his blunt tip, inside of her. "You did—do you like that, Jaime? Would you like some more?"

She hit his bicep. "Don't *do* that! Don't do that bit by bit thing!"

Even with sweat beading his temples, the muscles of his entire body corded with his efforts at self-restraint, that grin broke out. "You mean you would rather I did—this?" He surged hard inside her, all at once, filling her entirely with him.

"*Yes!*" She grabbed for his butt, trying to pull him even deeper, angling her body to take all of him. The feel of him inside her was—wonderful. It felt as if he was entirely making her new again. A hard, intense use of her body that was so utterly for her pleasure.

"*Putain,* Jaime." He stopped grinning. His face now was severe, wild. "You did—you did promise me I could have more than one try. I think I'm going to need it." He drew out and drove into her again, if possible even deeper.

He caught himself there, to her intense frustration. "I thought I said *not* slow!"

"No." He gave his head a slow shake, like a boxer trying to surface from combat. "I'm . . . at the end of my control here. You tell me—you tell me if I hurt you."

She stared up at that hard, bad-boy face, the dark shaggy hair clinging to the sweat on his temples, his eyes pitch-black in the darkness, and laughed incredulously. "*You*—hurt me? You're crazy. Just—*please*. Please just—all of you. As much as you can give."

"God." He sounded destroyed. "Well—you'll be happy, *chérie*. It's not going to be slow."

CHAPTER 10

Jaime dreamed dappled sunlight. It fell through the thick shade of banana leaves, through the second tier of cacao leaves, and it speckled the brown leaves that crunched softly under her feet. Her hand stroked over the ribbed, dimpled outside of a cacao pod, curled over its football tip. Delicate blossoms peeked at her from the trunk. A man smiled at her and offered her a pod, splitting it open for her with one deft hack of his machete, holding the pod he was splitting in one hand. The fruit tasted like nothing else: white and pulpy, it had its own flavor, not a peach, not a mango, not a kiwi—cacao fruit, nothing like the chocolate it would eventually become.

"This is amazing," she told him. She was proud of him, proud of herself. It was so recent and yet so elusive, like something lost in a bad dream, that pride in herself. He had been determined to make a success of his own farm without resorting to the slavery he himself had known, kidnapped as he had been at age eleven. She had brought Corey funding in. She had helped set up a program on his farm, which kept children completely in school until fourteen, and then allowed them to work up to three paid hours a day in conjunction with schooling, until age sixteen. Many parents were convinced that schooling itself was impractical, training children for opportunities they could never have, so this combination had been the most palatable to the area. No slavery here, no beatings, no insane loads for kids to carry. The program had spread to other farms; everyone around him had wanted in on it. And she had brought them in on it. Changed a whole region. She could change the whole damn world, if she kept at it.

The man grinned at her, pleased. She kept walking, sinking deeper and deeper into the plantation, until, in a dream's transition, she was along the banks of the Amazon River, an ocean away, the cacao growing in its natural state, the forest dark and thick around her. She smiled, because she was safe here, and happy. And then the riverbank caved in under her and hard hands yanked her from the water, and . . .

She woke up with a gasp, pain shooting all through her.

No. No. Damn it, this dream had started out so promisingly. When was she going to manage to escape its ending?

She rubbed her face and peeked around. In case she had screamed in her sleep and . . . maybe attracted someone to her rescue.

He was gone. It was barely dawn, but he was gone.

She sighed. She hadn't really expected him to be there. It would have been nice, but . . . she wasn't given to delusions, and she hadn't indulged in any here.

She tucked her hands behind her head, images of the night pushing that final second of her dream far away. She smiled in a kiss-bruised, sleepy way, thinking about him. They had made love for *hours*. Or he had made love to her for hours. He had worn her out. She remembered growing more and more malleable, saturated with him, and still willing for more, just as long as his hands and his mouth kept sliding over her.

It was the first time in months that she had woken up conscious of aches in her body that didn't make her mad, or determined, or cast a darkness over her just from their existence. Instead, they felt—good. Well-earned. Alive.

What an extraordinary night. She never, ever would have pegged herself for the panty-throwing girl the rock star *actually picked up*. Maybe the fates had wanted to give her one dream come true, after everything.

It made her smile, all through her determinedly healthy breakfast and her shower. When she was dressed, she opened the floor-to-ceiling casement windows to the spring morning and turned on her computer for the first time since her last try a week ago.

She was going to do it. Going to be strong again. She could feel it, as if she had drained all Dominique Richard's strength from him and filled herself with it.

Dear Jaime, read the message from Antoine Soumbounou, head of one of the largest farming cooperatives under the Corey umbrella. *Thank you for the e-mail from your secretary, letting us know you are well.* Cade was the one who had put an assistant on all those well-wishing e-mails. Jaime hadn't been able to face it. *When do you think you will come back to Abidjan? I am hoping we will still one day soon be able to do this Round Table on Sustainable Cocoa Economy you have talked about. Between the fight for power and the sanctions, things are bad here. Farmers are having trouble surviving, and you know what that means . . .*

It meant that labor practices got nastier and more desperate. Exploitation and trafficking grew.

We are all so happy you are better. When will we see you again?

First she pressed her forehead into the table, hugging her belly. Then she wrapped her hands over the back of her head and the nape of her neck, spreading the fingers wide to cover as much as she could.

Then, just when it was about to take hold of her, the sickness, the sweating, huddled dread, she leaped up so fast that the chair fell behind her and she bruised her knee against the table. Slinging her purse over her shoulder, she headed out of the apartment.

Out there, on the streets, away from what she couldn't bear to do and knew she couldn't abandon, she felt better already. Paris welcomed her, with its green doors, and red-eaved cafés, and elegant people brushing by her, and its utter distance from the rest of her life.

She glanced up the street, in the direction that would lead to Dominique Richard's *salon,* with a little smile.

But she knew better than to go that way. It was one thing to be a groupie and another a clinging leech. She just wished she had stocked up on more of his chocolate before sexing herself out of the right to linger there.

Cuddling to herself the memory of the evening and night with him until the warmth and pleasure of it filled her and everything else faded away, leaving a big happy smile, she turned southward toward the Seine.

"Whoa!" Cade stopped on her heels in the Tuileries, where she and Jaime had promised to meet up. "What happened to you?" She stared at her sister. "You look— you look—" Her eyes rested on Jaime's throat and narrowed. "Have you met someone?"

"Can I have a little bit of a private life?" Jaime said stiffly, pulling her scarf around her throat. Dominique did have a prickly jaw.

"No," Cade said. "No one needs as extreme a sense of privacy as you. You get on my nerves. Who is he?" Her face brightened up like sunrise. "Is it a *Parisian?*"

Jaime stared at her sister for a moment. "Why does that make you so happy?"

Cade turned the sunrise off on purpose, with that boardroom control of hers. "Oh, I don't know." Cade shrugged indifferently. "Just, you know—" She looked around at the kids pushing the little colorful sailboats on the pond. "It could be kind of *nice* if you decided to live in Paris, too. The opposite end of Paris, of course." She frowned deeply at Jaime.

"Who's going to run Corey?" Jaime asked dryly.

"Dad. He's fifty-three and not ready to release power anytime soon, no matter what he says. I'm not ready to pull my fingers completely out of the pie, either, but I think long-term, when Dad wants to quit, we might hire a CEO. It's fifteen or more years down the road. Good Lord, you didn't think any of us were assuming *you* would want to do it?"

Well, she wouldn't. But still. Jaime folded her arms. She didn't know why it was so annoying, when you spent most of your life trying to convince people of your unsuitability for a certain role, that they *accepted* that unsuitability, but right now, pretty much every suggestion that she couldn't do whatever she determined to do rubbed raw nerves. "Grandpa Jack wants me to do it."

"Would you?" Cade asked, astonished. "I thought you liked doing the farm-level work. It's"—she hesitated over the praise but said softly—"it's amazing what you've done. You know that, right, Jaime?"

Right now Jaime didn't want to do much beyond sit in Dominique Richard's *salon* eating chocolates and *mille-feuilles*.

He would get sick of her eventually. You couldn't just glue yourself to a man's life like some kind of leech, sucking everything that was beautiful about him into you. She had spent all her life trying not to be a parasite.

Right now, she was afraid to go back there, anyway. Last night . . . his hands on her everywhere, her complete openness . . . she felt herself blushing right in front of her sister.

"I absolutely do not want to run Corey, no," she said.

Although if she wasn't doing anything else, maybe she should make her father and grandfather happy? It would be a first.

Last night . . . that *was* one-night-stand sex, wasn't it? Get it all out of your system, saturate yourself, never see the person again. Sex with a groupie.

She could go back to his *salon* and see if he still smiled at her today. She longed to go back. But what if he looked at her the way he had looked at that brunette? What if his lifted eyebrows said, *Haven't we finished this already?* After she had been so . . . naked to him.

Mostly guys didn't slip out while you were asleep if they wanted to see more of you. She had accepted, going into it, that it was a toss-your-panties-on-the-stage-and-have-the-rock-star-pick-them-up kind of fluke. She shouldn't try to force it into anything else now.

"Are you okay?" Cade asked, as they took a seat at one of the outdoor cafés. The food at the Tuileries cafés wasn't particularly good, but it was certainly a nice place to relax with one's sister on a spring day in Paris. Jaime had spent the morning next door in the Louvre gazing at *La Victoire de Samothrace*. That great statue of Victory, headless, armless, her wings outspread, looked as if, marble or not, she could leap into the sky and rise above everything.

Sometimes it was a huge help to her, *La Victoire de Samothrace*. And sometimes it made her feel like a total loser, unable to rise to the standards of that soaring marble.

"I wish everyone would quit asking me that," Jaime said, annoyed. "I'm perfectly fine."

"You look fine, for once. I'd be interested in meeting this Parisian who makes you look so fine."

"Will you stop?" She requested an apricot juice from the waiter and scanned the crêpe menu. The crêpes here were terrible, but the ambience was everything. They ordered, and she snuck a glance at her sister as she handed back the menu. "So who else did you research when you were trying to buy Sylvain?"

"I did not buy him," Cade snapped touchily. Apparently the accusation kept coming up.

"I didn't say you did, I said you tried to. The whole world knows you actually stole him." The blogs had made for some hilarious reading while Jaime was stuck in a hospital bed, avoiding her own e-mails. Once the swelling went down around her eyes enough that she could read. "Who else did you look at?"

This was Cade. She might have thrown her hat after a windmill, but she had most certainly researched the top twenty windmills before she did.

"Well . . . I visited Philippe, but chocolate really isn't his primary concentration. Still, his name has the cachet I wanted for the line, so he could have worked." Cade brooded darkly. "If a single one of these chocolatiers-pâtissiers in Paris had the sense to appreciate their own economic benefit instead of acting like an offer from a major American corporation was a coarse insult."

Jaime grinned. "Who else? Dominique Richard?"

"Oh, him." Cade rolled her eyes. "I believe he would have been quite happy to sell me some sex in his office, but not his chocolate, oh, no."

The knife went right into her gut, out of the blue, like the other time, the other time her guts had been bludgeoned. Jaime sat there with her legs stretched to the side of the café table, looking as relaxed and happy as Paris in the springtime and feeling like she needed to curl in the dust and gravel and vomit. "A flirt, hmm?" she managed through numb lips.

"If you like that kind of thing." Cade shrugged. "He's very aggressive and not very romantic."

Jaime's eyes crinkled a little, doubtful. Were her standards and her sister's that different? What did Sylvain do for romance, scatter rose petals everywhere she walked? And what did she call "aggressive"? A smile? An excruciating thought occurred to her: Dominique might have been more instantly interested in Cade and therefore come on to her much more strongly. Cade was pretty. Very elegant and classy, with a charismatic, own-the-world confidence.

Jaime stared into the gravel and dust of the Tuileries at her feet, trying intensely to visualize *La Victoire de Samothrace* soaring armless but wings spread above that staircase in the Louvre, trying to see that and absolutely nothing else.

"I mean, he came out of an abattoir, which is impressive, but sometimes you can really tell."

"He came out of an *abattoir*?" That dusty ground jerked out from under her feet. "A slaughterhouse? Like—where the carcasses pass by and the people who work there have to hack the meat off bones with great big machetes?" There had been a whole series of Pulitzer Prize–winning articles about work in such plants in the United States that had come out when she was in college; she remembered studying them in one of her classes on local economic development. She had wanted to visit one as part of a project for the class, but none would allow visitors, and when she tried to sneak in by getting herself hired, she hadn't even been able to pass herself off as a potential employee. Too small, too educated, too accustomed to privilege so that it must leak out of her every pore; she had not looked rough, or tough, or needy enough. "And it's *cold,* isn't it? And . . . and . . . brutal."

"I think so. I've never seen how one operates in France, but how different can it be?"

"I don't understand," Jaime said slowly. "He's one of the best chocolatiers-pâtissiers in France."

"It's an incredible story. His father put him to work in a

slaughterhouse when he was twelve, he worked there until he was eighteen, then he managed to get himself apprenticed in the kitchen of a good chef in Paris, and from there to pastry apprentice at one of the top places in Paris, and from there to his own chocolate *laboratoire,* which was almost instantly named one of the best and started supplying all the great hotels around here. All that in the space of a few years. At first you could only get his chocolates by eating at the hotels, and it would be their names on the chocolate, and only people in the know were aware who had really made it. That was one of the reasons I thought he, at least, might be amenable to helping us develop a line. But no, he's clearly risen above *that.*" Cade got an annoyed look again. "Then he won *Meilleur Ouvrier de France* last year—you know, those insanely impossible trials they do here to be named *best in France.* They're so difficult that almost no one can succeed. He used that to help launch this *salon* he now has. Everyone raves about it, although personally, I find some of his flavors really wild and difficult."

Jaime sat frozen. She had known from the first she couldn't possibly deserve him, the spoiled rich girl who couldn't manage to get back on her horse after the one bad throw she had ever taken, and now . . .

La Victoire de Samothrace shattered in her vision, its beautiful, ancient, invincible marble battered into dust and pieces. She could have cried, but she wouldn't. One beautiful night was enough to go on for a very long time.

She really, really wanted to cry.

"Are you all right?" Cade asked again suddenly. "Your arm's not hurting?"

God damn it, but she hated it when people asked about her weaknesses. "No." She tilted her head back and stared at the peeling bark of the plane-tree above her. "I'm perfectly fine."

CHAPTER 11

He had ridden her so hard, like he hadn't meant to at all, and it had felt so damn good. She just wrapped herself around him and begged for more. The sound of her *Yes, yes, yes, please!* as he came in a last hard drive into her, her teeth biting into the muscles of his forearm as the nearest thing in her reach, still echoed in his mind as he kept trying to taste his newest ganache and kept resurfacing with no idea of what he had just tasted. It all tasted of her.

He had made love to her for hours. He would come back from disposing of a condom in the bathroom, thinking to fall asleep exhausted beside her. He would snuggle up against her, his arm around her, kissing the nearest skin, just because . . . he wanted to cuddle. And he would find himself, slowly, letting his mouth and hands drift farther, until he was making love to her again. He couldn't get over the way she pulled him to her, the way even as she grew more tired than he was, her hands stroked sleepily over him and she yielded to him, *absorbing* him. He had had many women who couldn't get enough of sex, but this was as if she couldn't get enough of *him*.

Putain, maybe he was completely deluding himself.

When he'd left her in the dark hours of the morning to go to work, he'd kissed all the fingers curled up on the pillow. "Jaime," he whispered very softly against those curled fingers, the word shivering through him. He peered hopefully at her face in the dimness, but she didn't waken, and he finally had to drag himself away.

The great block of chocolate greeted him in the dark *laboratoire*. He gazed at it as the lights came on, gleaming gently off the marble, making the windows turn black to the pre-dawn world. He knew suddenly, in incredulous, hopeful fear, what was trying to come out of that chocolate. Changing clothes, he vaulted up onto the counter and got to work.

At first, he believed in the sculpture the chocolate wanted him to make. But when she didn't come that morning, his heart sank down until it wasn't even in his body anymore; it was something lost in the mud. She didn't come over and over. At 10:01, at 10:02, at 10:03. At 11:14, at 11:15, at 11:16. At 2:03, at 2:04, at 3:19, at 3:20. She didn't come ever. Minute after minute after minute of ever.

Bordel de Dieu, not her, too. Surely she hadn't . . . gotten what she wanted. *All* she wanted. Already. *She liked to linger.*

"Inspiring, was she? So what's her name?" asked disrespectful Célie, nudging her own boss and one of Paris's top chocolatiers hard in the ribs with her elbow when he came down from his sculpture to help with the daily work and because the sculpture was starting to terrify him again.

He hesitated, then smiled *shyly,* oh, for God's sake. "Jaime." He couldn't say her name the way Jaime herself did, the blunt start. When he said it, every time, it was soft and silky and it hung in the air like an elusive promise, never completed. *I love*—what? Your hair, your smile, your freckles, the way you look at me, the way you feel in my hands.

The only thing it couldn't ever be was *I love you,* because that would have started differently, *Je t'aime,* no other meaning possible.

"It is *not!*" Célie said incredulously. "She made that up! Jaime?"

He hesitated, that squooshy feeling inside of him freezing a little. Could she have?

"If that's her real name, that is so incredibly sw-e-e-e-et!" Célie caroled ecstatically, dancing off with her pot of ganache toward the cooling room. "Which is hilarious because it's you! You being sweet! I love it! Are you seeing her again?"

"Célie, can you get to work maybe and butt out of my private life? *Putain.*" He growled his way over to save Amand's caramel. 3:27. He was about to rip that clock off the wall and throw it into the street below. She still hadn't come.

He went to the gym as soon as he left his *laboratoire.* He killed himself with weights first and then went for rounds of *boxe* in which he annihilated his opponents, punishing them mercilessly for the fact that as soon as he left there he was going to go beg at her apartment door, not at all sure if she would let him in.

He was coming back into the weight room, when he saw her. The scariest thing was that his heart didn't stop when he saw her. It started again. He had been doing all that brutal weight workout, all that *boxe,* without the benefit of his *heart.*

She lay on a bench, flushed and sweating, her face wrought with the strain of the weights she was pressing. She was wearing a sleeveless knit blue shirt but separate arm sleeves, so that only her shoulders were bare, which was odd, because she looked very hot. She had closed her eyes briefly in the effort, and she didn't see him right away.

He crouched beside her. So close to the straining shoulder muscles and the slender curve of her biceps working with all her might. Close enough he could trace the sheen of sweat on her skin with his fingertips and then lick the taste of it off them. God, why the intermediary? Close enough he could bend forward and place his mouth right on that taut muscle in her shoulder . . .

"Jaime," he murmured. How he loved saying her name. It made something tremble inside him, every time.

Her eyes flared open, her arms wavering, and he reached up and guided the bar into the supporters, taking the weight off her. It wasn't much. He could handle it one-handed, even from that angle. Odd. He would have thought someone with such a stern expression on her face as she pressed, someone who seemed so determined, would be able to lift a bit more. A recent interest of hers, strength?

She came up onto one elbow on the bench, panting, her face very much flushed. From the effort? From him? From memories of last night?

He smiled at her, wanting to lick her all over.

Maybe he could get her to leave the light on this time, let him check out what happened to those freckles in the wake of his hands. Would she blush all over?

She smiled back at him, just a tiny, shy smile, and the urge to pick her up and haul her out of there swept through his body, trying to goad his already-engorged muscles into action. He was such a brute. He wondered what she thought of the sight of him, sleeveless, his biceps so engorged from his own workout, the sweat making his hair cling to his temples. "I didn't know you came to this gym."

"Just for two or three weeks now," she said. He loved the sound of her voice, hoarse, fast, interrupted by her pants, as she tried to get her breathing back to normal. He wanted to do something to her that made it impossible for her to get her breathing back to normal. "I usually come in the morning."

But not this morning, he thought with a slow grin. This

morning, when he had left her in the early hours to get to work, she had perhaps slept very, very late, lingering in his scent in the sheets.

His gaze drifted over her body to her mouth. It was all he could do to only look. If they hadn't been surrounded by clanging metal and grunting bodies, he would already have had his mouth all over her.

"You didn't come today," he murmured, and her color flamed back. "I missed you."

Her mouth trembled. She stared at him as if he was the world's worst liar attempting for the first time ever to tell the truth.

He found he knew what to do here. He had had her body all night long, and it had taught him something. She needed to be reassured.

He closed his hand around hers, rubbing it open so that his thumb could lodge securely against her palm, and kissed it. For one thing, his body leaped in silky, hot rejoicing to have some contact with her again. And if there was ever a moment to take advantage of all those stereotypes about Frenchmen, this was it. "Are you almost done?" he asked softly.

Against the clingy knit of her exercise top, her nipples peaked. Again he had to fight the surge of his body. *Public place, Dom. Not even you can jump on top of her here.*

"I've—I've actually just started," she said reluctantly.

He stroked his thumb from her palm up over her wrist. "How long is your workout?"

"About an hour." Her eyes kept snagging on parts of his body, his biceps, his shoulders, his mouth, his jaw. He drew the back of his free hand down his jaw involuntarily. *Merde,* it was already prickly. If he had to start shaving twice a day, he was going to break out in hives. He checked her throat, trying to tell between freckles and a blush whether he had marked her the night before.

His thumb climbed higher, teasing in little figure eights over the sensitive inside of her arm. "Can I come back for you? Can I take you out to dinner?"

Dinner? his body howled. *Not again, damn it! That will take hours!* Hours before he could nibble his way over all those little, straining muscles of hers. *Putain,* but his body needed to learn some self-discipline. After a workout like this, the last thing she needed to do was skip a meal.

She stared at him, the blue of her eyes slumberous as she pulled her lower lip in to nibble it with her teeth. "It will only be six o'clock," she mentioned softly. No restaurant in Paris served before 7:30. A whole hour and a half to fill.

"It's a beautiful city to walk around in," he heard himself say.

Oh, you bastard! his body wailed. *You masochistic bastard.*

But some other part of him poised for her answer, eager, afraid. "Would you like to walk with me?"

She blinked rapidly, and really, that crimson blush *had* to be for him by now; surely she had recovered from the weights. "Yes."

You know, you're a lot better at sex than romantic walks, his body pointed out bitterly. *You might have remembered that.*

Shut up, he told his thoroughly undisciplined and over-indulged dick.

Well, what are you going to say to her? Got any scintillating conversation? Don't you dare bring up your childhood again!

It's a romantic walk! Can't we just hold hands and be quiet?

His *putain de bite* sulked. *Personally, I think it would be much more romantic to—*

Just shut up already!

CHAPTER 12

Maybe he liked the full romantic experience, Jaime thought, looking up at the big man who walked beside her, his hand hard around hers. Maybe he needed all of it, great sex, but also somebody's whole heart, ripped out of her body by these walks along the Seine. Maybe if Cade had been interested in buying sex in his office, he would have walked her down the Seine in the same way, with that same softness around his mouth.

Maybe he would have held her hand like that, like someone would have had to chop his arm off to get her away from him.

Maybe it was just instinct: to lap up all the praise from the latest worshipper fallen at his feet.

She looked down at his big scarred hand, holding hers so firmly. She looked back up at him.

He smiled down at her before he looked away. If it had been remotely possible on his hard-boned, bad-boy face, she would have thought that smile shy.

He didn't talk, but a man who had Paris in the springtime didn't need to talk. Better not. Better just to concentrate on the cool breeze off the river, stirring his shaggy black hair, the bridges that stretched away through centuries, that fresh young green on the trees along the quays.

Evening was falling later and later. The sun was only start-ing to set now, easy blurred shades of pink and gold and gray through low strips of clouds. The sky above them was blue, clear, but blurring toward gray. Half the world looked in love, couples strolling hand in hand along the Seine. At the edge of that sunset, in the west, far away along the river that shimmered with pink and gold, the Eiffel Tower rose, gentled by the low haze.

"You're the visitor. Is there anywhere you would like to go?" he asked softly.

She had been here three months now, and in any case, she had visited Paris before, but never walking hand in hand with him. "Just like this. Just like this is fine."

His hand flexed on hers.

He took her as far as the Louvre and the Pont des Arts, and they stood there on the wooden pedestrian bridge, hand in hand, watching the sun set. A group played jazz a little way down the bridge; two lovers huddled into each other against the chain railing, bumpy with lovers' locks in all colors; a group of students broke out beers and wine, laughing and talking. All around them the life and love of Paris were in full bloom, but their little moment of it seemed utterly sheltered, just the two of them.

As the pink faded from the sky, the Eiffel Tower burst into sparkles, demanding all the attention, promising a beautiful evening. They watched it without speaking, but Dominique's hand left hers to circle around her shoulders and pull her in hard against his body. After a minute, he shifted her to stand in front of him, her back tucked against his chest, the panels of his jacket to either side of her, his arms wrapping around her. He still didn't speak, just held her there on the wooden bridge, watching the effusive Tower. She could feel his arousal, but he didn't say any-thing about it or even nudge her with his hips. Just watched the lights with his arms wrapped around her.

When the sparkle faded, *la Tour's* glowing nighttime robes remained, more burnished and more elegant than any star's red carpet gown. Dominique's breath left him in a long sigh. For a moment more, he didn't move. Then, "You must be starving after that workout. Let me feed you."

His phrasing did odd things to her middle. *Let me. Let me feed you.*

She wanted to question his motives for being with her, but she couldn't, because they barely knew each other. She could take it or leave it.

And these days, she was a taker.

He drew them through the courtyard of the Louvre, past the glowing Pyramide and fountains and the handful of young men trying out wild antics on inline skates in its light. Then he headed into streets north and east of it, until he stopped by a place from which warm light spilled onto the pavement. There was a couple in front of them and the place looked packed, but Dominique had hardly stepped inside when someone coming downstairs from the kitchen spotted him.

"*Mais mon cher Dominique, quel plaisir!* I suppose you did not think to reserve? You never do. *Non, mais, pour vous, Dominique, pour vous . . .*"

Jaime tried not to worry over that "you never do" while they were seated in a space that hadn't existed two minutes before and didn't look entirely as if it could exist now, it was so small and she and Dominique were so close together. There were any number of circumstances in which a man could come to a restaurant without reservations—with friends, with family, by himself even. It didn't always have to be with a beautiful woman.

Dominique smiled at her across the tiny table, looking pleased with himself. "Warm enough?" he said. "Is this what you like?"

And she forgot a little about the "you never do." He might have eaten here before, but he had picked it out tonight because of *her* tastes. What he knew of them.

"You've probably heard of the chef," he said, and when he told her, she had. In fact, she had eaten at Daniel Faure's more famous restaurant only a few days before with Cade, Sylvain, Philippe, and Magalie. "I got my start under him. He's one of the best men in the world." He said it firmly, brooking no dispute. "But I don't know if it's as widely known that he has three restaurants. He calls the most famous one his place for the *aristos,* then there's his *bourgeois* one, and this one"—he grinned—"is for the proletariat. *Poulet roti, steak, frites . . .* but his style."

I love you. The need to tell him swelled through her like some giant balloon, bigger and bigger, pressing everything else out of her, until she was afraid if she opened her mouth, that was the only thing she would be able to say.

On the bridge, between his body and the stretch of Paris's gleaming nightfall, she had wanted to turn and rub her face all over his chest, bury herself in him. Wasn't that a terrible thing to do to a strong man? Have nothing to offer him, but wrap the burden of *I love you* around him after two dates, like a clinging vine. Not hard to guess that she had been born to be a parasite, she thought bitterly. To use the earth and other people to her own ends.

She looked down at the table, trying to breathe slowly, trying to control herself. Words on the paper placemat blurred before her:

Je suis comme je suis . . .
J'aime celui qui m'aime
Est-ce ma faute à moi
Si ce n'est pas le même . . .

Je suis faite pour plaire . . .

I am how I am . . . I love the one who loves me, is it my fault if that one is not always the same? I'm made to please. What more do you want from me? Jacques Prévert. The chef apparently liked poetry on his placemats.

"Are you all right?" Dominique asked.

"I'm fine," she said. *Perfectly fine.* If she could get through that wall, if she could become again the woman who saved the world, could she keep him? Could a privileged princess, who had played at saving the world but was now curled into a fetal ball at the first hard shock of that world, ever deserve a man who had been given over to a slaughterhouse when he was twelve and still become—that grin, those hands over her body, those rosebuds and rough stone and wildness of flavors and delight. "Stupid poem." She pushed the placemat away from her.

"I've always rather liked that one," Dominique said slowly, as if he might be rethinking his tastes.

Of course. It might have been written for him: *I am who I am and it's not my fault you like me. What more could you want from me?* She smiled, with an effort. "You come here enough to know all the poems on the placemats?"

He opened his mouth, hesitated, and closed it, catching back whatever he had been about to say. "We can trade." He slid his across to her.

Cet amour
Si violent
Si fragile
Si tendre . . .

She looked up at him. *This love so violent, so fragile, so tender . . .* He was gazing back at her, his eyes intense, very dark.

"*Vous avez choisi?*" a cheerful young woman asked above them. *Have you chosen?*

Dominique rubbed the nape of his neck and looked away. Anyone would have thought the waitress had just asked him a terribly rude question.

"No," Jaime said. She hadn't even looked at the menu. "No, I still need time to consider."

His mouth twisted. He shook himself and smiled. "You're not going to take anything blindly. Smart woman. Let me see if I can talk you into something."

This time it was easier to go slow. One night, he was just someone's erotic fantasy, her need to let off a pressure cooker of sexual steam. But two nights—there was no pressure left. He had made love to her all night long just the night before. Now, if she lifted her head to him when he kissed her, if her eyes closed, if her muscles grew soft and yielding in his arms, it was because . . . she liked having him there. He wondered if she might even have let him in if he didn't have great sex to offer in return, if all he had wanted to do was climb upstairs and curl up in her bed around her and fall asleep.

That wasn't something he wanted to put to the test tonight. His spoiled dick would freaking kill him.

He liked this, oh, he liked this, the slow. He had never done it, touched someone as if she was precious, and as if . . . by some strange chance . . . his big, rough touch might even be precious to her. Not just a quick, hard way to get off. He liked it, that she let him back into her apartment building with that blush all over her body. He liked kissing her for it. He liked stroking her so gently, everywhere, kissing her on the stairs leisurely and thorough, as if he had all the time in the world with her. As if it wouldn't end.

He wanted to throw that suitcase out the window when he almost tripped over it. Probably throwing her things through windows would ruin his disguise as a nice guy.

Maybe he could unpack all her clothes while she was sleeping in the morning, drag the suitcase away with him, and leave it out on the street to help the first homeless person who came by. An act of charity, almost.

You selfish bastard. That's her escape, when you revert to form.

He kissed her again, managing just barely not to give the suitcase at least one hard kick.

He didn't like it that she wouldn't let him have the light on again. His hand fisted around the lamp base, and he had to force himself to turn it back off, like a petulant boy.

But the sight of her lying on her side beside him on the bed, the city lights gentle over her, was still beautiful.

"It's like moonlight," she said softly, once, her hand tracing slowly from his shoulder down over his ribs to his hips in a way that squeezed him with anguished, frantic longing and fear, as if *he* could be precious.

"Moonlight?" Him? he thought, with a jolt of confused, wary pleasure. It sounded beautiful, but . . . intangible. Transient.

"The city light."

Dominique, you're pathetic. You thought you could be moonlight? "I've never been anywhere outside of Paris. I've never seen moonlight without all the city lights to compete with it, or spent a night without some kind of light."

Her eyes widened with wonder. "I've been in places where there were no lights, no man-made lights, for so far, if you stood on tiptoe, the stars would get caught in your hair. And when there was a moon, it just filled the whole world up." Her fingers flexed into his shoulders. "Oh, you should come see sometime! You would love i—"

And just when his heart was leaping like a praised puppy, she broke off, her face closing, her body stiffening.

One thing was for sure, the accidental inclusion of him in her future plans turned her off like a light. He had to work hard, ignoring with his usual impatience his own hurt heart, to relax her again. To turn her muscles all malleable to him. To hear her breath catch. To make her body twist, rubbing her skin against the sheets and against him.

"Jaime." He said her name over and over again. *J'aime. I love this, I love this, I love the way you let my hands shape your head as if you trust me with it. I love pressing a kiss right there on the curve of your hipbone. I love—* "I wish you would let me see you. I like the colors of you."

A flicker of hesitation, and then she said dryly, "You mean, you like to see me blush. No."

"I do," he admitted unabashedly. "I want to see where it goes. Do you blush down to here?" His mouth brushed over one breast, just above the aureole of her nipple. "What color are these, anyway?" He breathed over the little raspberry, watched it tighten still further. "Are they pink, like your blush? Or brown, like your freckles? Are there freckles here?" He curved his hands around her breasts. His hands looked so big, so brutish against her small breasts, with the nipples peeking out like some last desperate cry for help before being hauled under by the mauling monster.

But she liked it. He looked up at her face and slowly, gently brought one of those rough thumbs to rub a circle over her nipple. Oh, she liked it very much. Her eyes closing, and her breath coming fast, and her hands sliding over his biceps, gripping, not finding much purchase. His biceps were too big for her small hands. But he would hold still for them. Whatever purchase she found, he would let her hold him.

He lowered his head to nestle his face against her breasts, and she shivered all over. He twisted his chin enough to rub it against the back of one hand, still cupping her breasts. He had shaved between the gym and meeting her again, which meant *twice* that day, and five hours later it was already faintly prickly. Now that was just unfair. How the hell did other men get smooth jaws? He wished he had started practicing this gentlemanly stuff years ago, before he met her, so he would have a clue how to carry it off.

He lifted his head. Her eyes were closed, her hands flexing helplessly into what she could manage of his biceps. She seemed to like prickly. He ran a little test with his jaw over the upper slope of her breast.

She made a little sound, and her hands slid up over his shoulders, soft hands, so soft. Oh, God, he thought he could detect against the smoothness of his shoulders just the faintest hint of a little callus or blister from her newly acquired sport of weightlifting, and it made him return to her mouth and kiss her for such a long time.

He wanted to wrap his arms around her and squeeze her the way a man dying of thirst might squeeze every last drop of water from a sponge. But he didn't. He didn't.

He just kissed her. Taking his time. Licking up her response. Diving for more.

He liked this. Oh, how he liked this. He pulled her wrists above her head and rolled over onto her, trapping her, watching her eyes widen, her breath catch, then rolled again and let her trap him. He lifted her because he could, because he could manipulate her body so easily, and he *loved* that.

He tangled and rolled and took charge and yielded, kaleidoscope glimpses of the different ways they might make love if they had a lifetime to try every mood.

He liked this so much, too much. "Can I keep you?" he whispered against her skin. But he was down at the small of her back at that point, and he didn't think she heard.

She certainly didn't say yes.

He trailed his jaw and his lips back up the line of her spine, thinking of ways he could get her to say yes. And he licked the nape of her neck until she was all one shivering moan, completely his. For this moment, completely his.

"Can I?" he whispered again into her ear, although he didn't know if she had heard the first question, so when she shivered and nodded, all she was really saying yes to was his touch. Still—on her head be it, right? You should never agree to something unless you had read every line of the contract. His mind flashed ideas of ways to keep her: a golden cage, a treasure in a box and him with the key, the pure brute force of his arms. None of them worked. He kissed over her shoulders, down the length of her arms. None of them worked in real life.

Addiction.

Maybe he could just get her so addicted to him she wouldn't be able to tear herself away.

He laughed a little, a harsh puff of air against her skin, mocking himself for the pipe dream. But . . . like the time he had asked for a job from one of the top chefs in Paris, after being just freed from arrest and with only an abattoir as his past experience, or the four years' merciless training and then the brutal trials for *Meilleur Ouvrier de France* . . . it was worth a shot.

He shouldn't, of course. He shouldn't try to make her completely his, because he was a bad bet. But when a man had his teeth sinking oh-so-gently into a woman's naked butt while she made a little moaning sound was probably not the best time to ask him to think of anything except his own wild wants.

So he laid her out in that city light she thought was like moonlight and went to work on being addicting.

Chapter 13

When Jaime woke, there was a note on the pillow beside hers: *Come by*.

No signature. She picked it up and rubbed it between her fingers. She looked around for a moment, then dug into the bottom of her suitcase, coming out with a small round box that had been given to her by the grandmother of a child in Côte d'Ivoire. She folded the note and placed it carefully in the tiny box, then slipped it back down into the bottom of her suitcase.

She didn't try to turn on her computer at all that morning. She was terrified she would find more e-mails asking her to leave.

When Dom came in to his *laboratoire* later than usual, Célie and Amand were already there, in the *cuisine,* the hot room where things were cooked. Célie was talking to Amand: ". . . I think it's adorable. He's fallen so hard. Would you ever have believed it? Mr. Take It and Leave It. And I got a look at her. She's not a movie star or anything. She looks just—normal."

Dom barely forewent growling. Like an . . . adorable teddy bear. It was enough to make a man break something, but . . . he sighed. He did kind of like it. Being adorable.

"I just hope she doesn't crush him. Didn't Guillaume say she sounded like a tourist?"

"Well," Amand said reticently. "You can't say he doesn't deserve to have his heart crushed."

Thanks, Amand. People always thought that about him. Even when he was six years old, the people who loved him thought he deserved what he got. He shoved a mold that clattered against the tile backdrop.

"Or to be loved and left," Amand said, not catching the hint.

Oh, you fucking bastard, Amand. You're welcome for hiring you when you were a clueless teenager who didn't dare go back home.

Dom filled the doorway, so that Amand looked up from slicing off great pats of Isigny butter and Célie from weighing chocolate. "Please," Dom said, "don't let me interrupt."

Célie stuck her chin out at him. "Then I won't. *I* think it would be extremely salutary for you, if somebody loved you and didn't leave you. It's a lot harder work."

Dom stared at his chocolatier for a long moment and then turned abruptly and went to the far opposite end of the main room, carving bits of long Grecian skirt from his sculpture. Just until the shakiness inside him calmed down.

When Jaime got there a few hours later, Dominique was growling into his phone. He gave her one delighted look, a kind of surreal syncopation with his immediate return to growling, and offered her the nearest fresh pastry to eat.

While she bit into flakiness and a chocolate cream so dark and intense she wasn't sure how he got it to fluff, she circled around the great block of chocolate, intrigued. The bottom seemed to be turning into rough-hewn folds.

A person maybe, the folds of a long dress? Was that what he saw coming out of the chocolate?

He shoved his phone into his pocket. "If he really can't get us enough of our vanilla because of the cyclone, we're just going to have to find another supplier. But first, I'm going to see him in person and make sure he's not letting someone else talk him into giving them what he's got."

"Vanilla?" Jaime raised an eyebrow, licking cream off her lips. His dark eyes immediately went to her mouth, and he smiled, just a little smile, as if he was kissing her there. "You?"

"It goes in as a base flavor in all kinds of things. And I'm not about to start using some inferior product from Papua New Guinea."

"The vanilla there is quite good!" Jaime said rather indignantly. She saw a lot of friendly faces when he said "Papua New Guinea."

He dismissed those friendly faces with a wave of his hand, as not at all relevant in the quest for the best vanilla, and reached for his motorcycle jacket. Then he gave Jaime a slow grin. "You want to come?" From the expression on his face, he had known some women before her who liked riding on his motorcycle with their legs wrapped around him. "I'll drive carefully."

She sighed, because there wasn't a lot she could do about the fact that she wasn't the first woman he had met, and that he had learned a lot from the other ones. "Yes. I want to come."

He even had an extra helmet for her, with a hibiscus on the front, female size. A jasmine scent lingered in it. "If I get lice from one of your women," she muttered.

"What?" he asked blankly.

She just glared at him, refusing to expand.

He looked from her to the helmet. "That's Célie's. She

comes in on a moped." He slipped his leather jacket around her and zipped it up. "Lice." He was grinning. *"Salope,"* he whispered to her respectfully.

Jaime had ridden on a moped behind a proud teenager in Papua New Guinea only six months or so ago. And she had driven herself around on mopeds quite a bit. It seemed so much more appropriate than arriving in a phalanx of expensive cars to pretend you cared about the little people who couldn't afford bicycles. But she hadn't ridden on an actual motorcycle behind someone since she was seventeen years old and still throwing her panties on the stage at concerts.

And her eighteen-year-old driver back then hadn't been as big, hadn't been as hard, hadn't been as much to wrap her arms around. Compared to the other bikes that passed them, Dominique drove with extreme care: slowly, no weaving in and out of traffic. She tightened her arms around him, trying to help offset the wind that must be cutting through his clothes, since he had given his jacket—which was also his protection against any fall—to her.

As they left the heart of the city, they entered a different world of bigger, uglier buildings, big supermarkets, warehouses, square-cornered practicality, the cheaper world where the large things of this city were exiled. He pulled in near the door of a small warehouse with several vans parked in front of it.

"Do you drive that carefully when I'm not on the bike?" Jaime asked, taking off her helmet and automatically running her hand over the left side of her head, making sure her hair was still in place.

Dominique grinned and didn't answer.

"Would you?" she asked because she couldn't help herself.

He stilled, his helmet just off his head. Probably taken

aback by the nerve of a woman he had slept with two times trying to take over his driving. He lowered the helmet enough to gaze at her for a long moment. "Drive more carefully? Did you just ask me to drive more carefully?"

"Yes," she said sternly.

He stared down at her with those almost-black eyes of his and didn't say anything at all. Not yes, not no, not "that's none of your business." He looked oddly shaken. When he turned toward the warehouse, with his helmet tucked under his far arm, his mouth curved a little.

That smile disappeared under a sudden flare of outrage. "*Putain!* I knew someone was stealing the supply."

Sylvain Marquis was just leaving the building, and he nearly ran straight into them. He started to raise one of those haughty eyebrows of his at Dom, and then spotted his companion.

"*Jamie?*"

Dom jerked and closed his hand too fast, too hard around Jaime's nearest shoulder, as if Sylvain had reached out and tried to grab her away. The woman who had just told him to *drive carefully*. As if he *mattered*. "You know *Sylvain?*"

What had *he* done to get her name? Maybe that explained what she was doing with Dominique. Maybe she was some kind of chocolatier groupie, concentrating all her attention on each of them, one at a time, until . . .

"*Jamie, qu'est-ce que tu fous avec lui?*" Sylvain demanded. *What the hell are you doing with him?* Sylvain liked to pretend he had risen above the *banlieue*, that he belonged among the aristos and bourgeois over there in his Sixth Arrondissement, so the sight of Jaime with Dominique had definitely hit him hard for him to swear. Or maybe it was the influence of their environment, out here on the margins of Paris, a degree closer to where they'd both grown up, bringing out the worst in him.

"Your *banlieue* is showing, Marquis." Dom's teeth showed, slashing, sharp, as he shifted his body a step in front of Jaime. "Careful, or I'll let you see mine."

Sylvain gave him a scathing look. "You still haven't learned how to solve problems with anything other than your fists?"

Dom sneered at him. The supercilious bastard who thought he had managed so much better. "If you think I'm going to fight you for her with a delicate game of chocolate, think again."

Jaime grabbed *Sylvain's* arm. Not Dominique's. Dom flinched as if he'd been whipped.

"You. Come here," she told Sylvain. With *tu*. She was on *tu* terms with that bastard.

She dragged Sylvain off, out of earshot, while Dom spun on his heel and snarled, not sure if he should lunge after them and beat the crap out of Sylvain right then or if that was one of the destructive urges that would ruin his whole life if he revealed it in front of Jaime.

He knew far too well how easy it could be to ruin things by letting your fists fly. He had seen it from the point of view of the things ruined.

Jaime was keeping her voice low, but her whole body language was a yell. As she whispered, her fist clenched, and she poked Sylvain in the chest with it. Dom snarled harder, hoping she would haul off and hit him for real, and then Dom could leap, let off any leash of civility.

Sylvain was trying to keep his voice down, too, but words escaped: "Dominique *Richard*?" And ". . . womanizer . . . *un vrai salaud* . . ."

Thank you, Sylvain. I'll kill you.

Jaime poked Sylvain harder. It was close to a punch this

time. Her face was flaming with temper; he was surprised that short hair of hers didn't stand up around her head like a fire. If he could get control of his own wounded, panicked rage, it would be kind of fascinating to watch. He hadn't known she had a temper. He had suspected, from those little glimpses of cool steel from time to time, but hadn't known for sure, that she could stand up to a man.

He *loved* women who could stand up to men.

And . . . and . . . he settled back on his heels a little, less ready to lunge. He even folded his arms, to show how calm he was. She was standing up for *him*. She was fighting Sylvain Marquis over *him*. The anger in him unflexed, stretched, started to show a little hint of a hard-edged grin. So how do you like that, Sylvain "Dieudonné"?

But why hadn't she grabbed *Dominique*'s arm to stop a fight? Hadn't she believed she could stop him?

He stiffened as Sylvain closed his hand over Jaime's fist, holding it back from his chest. Jaime could poke the man as much as she wanted, but that didn't give *him* the right to touch *her*. *What* made him think he could close his hand around her fist so familiarly?

Sylvain said something more, got a response he didn't like, turned and strode away a few steps, turned back to Jaime and flung out his hands. She just glared and spoke quickly.

Sylvain folded his arms, stared at the ground, and shook his head a few times.

Jaime put her hands on her hips and said something more.

"Fine," he saw Sylvain's lips shape. "Fine."

Just how long was he supposed to allow them for this lovers' quarrel? Dom strode back up to them and got an immediate glare from Jaime. Apparently longer.

Sylvain turned his head and gazed at him, with a set jaw. Sylvain was tall enough to meet him eye to eye, but he was leaner. He got to look like a gorgeous passionate poet, while Dom was the rough butcher boy. "You really are a bastard, Richard."

"Fuck you, Marquis."

Sylvain narrowed his eyes and looked back at Jaime. "After all the chocolates I made for you. Please don't tell me you actually prefer his."

Sylvain . . . making chocolates for Jaime . . . Dom's fists strained against his will. If only he could teleport Jaime somewhere else, so she wouldn't see this, and then *kill that bastard.*

"Is this all just about chocolate egos?" Jaime demanded furiously.

Sylvain barely bothered to indicate Dom with his aristocratic jaw. "With him—probably. But I meant what I said, Jamie."

Dom growled.

"Don't even think about it, Richard," Sylvain said, his tone so sharp and severe it startled its way through Dom's anger. "There's no way I'm indulging you in a fight right in front of her. *No way.*"

Dom's eyebrows drew together as he stared back at his most despised rival. What was the meaning there?

Sylvain shook his head, looked once more at Jaime, then turned on his heel and walked away—to his van, which was currently being loaded with big boxes of the vanilla beans Dom had come for.

Dom refused to give him the honor of glaring after him and turned away. And to be even clearer, he laid his arm proprietarily and extremely gently—*no anger, don't let her feel any of the anger*—across Jaime's shoulders, still in his jacket, and led her toward the farther corner of the building.

At the corner, he dropped her shoulders and leaned

back against the building, pressing his butt into it, trying to glue himself and any violent urges to the concrete. He folded his arms across his chest for extra measure.

"Is your name Ja-mie or Jaime?" He was so mad he almost managed to say that hard J in her name, the way that bastard-Sylvain, with six more years of school and therefore of English classes, could.

"Jamie is a nickname." Jaime spoke not so much as if she was mad at him but as if she was just globally hostile, anger spreading out from her like a radius of self-protection.

A nickname. Sylvain not only knew her name but her *nickname*. "How do you know Sylvain?" he growled.

Jaime shot him a glare. "That's none of your damned business."

It was probably fortunate that he found it vastly reassuring when she talked to him that way, as if she wouldn't put up with shit from him. It calmed part of him down, even while part of him still strained to do murder. "Have you slept with him?"

She gaped at him. Then her eyes flamed with rage. "What do you guys do, practice internecine sexual warfare? And I would like to know what business it is of *yours,* when you seem to sleep with anyone who looks at you, whom I may or may not have slept with."

That was, unfortunately, very fair. He folded his arms as tight as he could over his chest, regretting the fact that he had let Sylvain get away without at least smashing his fist into that beautiful, arrogant nose of his.

He glanced across the parking lot to the Marquis van, where the men from the warehouse had finished loading *Dominique's supplies,* but Sylvain hadn't yet climbed in to drive away. He stood leaning against the driver door, his arms folded and one ankle crossed over the other, as if he had all the time in the world to watch this play unfold.

What the hell was he standing there for? In case Jaime needed rescue? It wasn't too late for Dom to cross the parking lot and smash that nose.

"Does Sylvain sleep around, too?" Jaime asked suddenly, cautiously, like someone with a vested interest in knowing.

"I have no idea," Dom said sullenly. He would do just about anything to be able to rebuke that "too." God damn it, that part of his past was his own screwed-up fault. "I think he's engaged now, *en fait*," he added stiffly. *So . . . off limits. Stay away from him.*

That information didn't seem to hit her any great, rocking blow. She nodded slightly, satisfied.

"To some billionaire," he added for good measure. "Who produces this mass-market *merde* they call chocolate. I don't know how Sylvain can still manage to act as if he's the lord of the earth, but of course if anyone were to sell out, it would be him."

Her face grew quite still. She looked at the ground, not at him, her profile a pure, lovely thing, like marble with freckles, and distant, as if it was roped off in a museum.

"Jaime." His fists flexed and unflexed, in hiding behind his biceps. "Are you interested in Sylvain?" *Do you lap him up like the last bit of sauce on your plate, too?*

Jaime gave him an incredulous look. "Are all the women you know nymphomaniacs?"

Probably not all of them. He wouldn't be surprised if there were more than a few certifiable ones in his past, though. He scrubbed a hand over his face. "I don't really know them," he said after a moment, low.

On her face, puzzlement and shock. Why did he have to go and admit the worst details about himself? Did some part of him want her to discover who he really was, so she would flee to safety?

All the anger seemed to drain out of her, leaving her

bleak and exhausted. His heart congealed. *Don't look that way because of me. Please don't.* She glanced toward Sylvain across the lot, and pain froze him. If she chose to ride back with him . . .

She rubbed her eyebrows with weary fingers, but she couldn't get them to smooth out. "It isn't clear where my interest lies?" she asked, low. "What we've done, that's"—her voice broke, and she swallowed and forced it out stronger—"just normal, for you?"

He said nothing, breathing hard, staring at her. It was, in fact, normal for women to act like sex addicts with him. But just sex, addicted to sex and nothing else. So for the rest—he didn't know. It was all new territory to him. No, she wasn't the same. She didn't feel the same. But could she really want *him*?

All of him?

Well, the parts of him he was willing to let her know about?

"You think I might be doing the same thing with Sylvain tomorrow night or maybe I might have been, a few nights ago?"

He dug his fingers into his biceps, wanting to rend things at the images that flashed through him. See, this was what he had been afraid of. That all those years of trying to turn himself into someone worthwhile would fail at the first real test. And they had only been in a relationship two days.

A castle-in-the-sky daydream of a relationship. He hadn't even known her name forty-eight hours ago. "Have you ever been to the beach?" he asked. He had been once. Ridden his bike out to Brittany, which was only a few hours away. He had been too old to build a sandcastle, which was what he really wanted to do. He had felt lonely and lousy and ridden back the same day.

"Many times," Jaime said stiffly. "Why?"

"I was just thinking about sandcastles." How it must feel to build one. The texture of the sand, the water, the sun, the joy of building, and then in the end the way it all flowed away, nothing to keep, but no harm done. It was not so different from sculpting things out of chocolate, really.

Jaime looked back toward Sylvain, patiently waiting. *Don't leave with him. Don't. But you would be smarter if you did.* "All right, I get it," she said flatly. "They're fun, and they don't last. Don't you need to go check on your vanilla beans or something?"

And give her a chance to slip off with Sylvain? "He can have them," Dom said harshly, shorting his own chocolates in the brutal competition for Paris's best without a second thought. He pushed her helmet onto her head. "I want you."

CHAPTER 14

A motorcycle was a terrible flashback to the era of women's economic and legal dependence, Dom decided. No matter how much a woman might be angry or might want her distance, she had to hold onto you while you took her where you wanted.

As such he was deeply, terribly glad of it and probably needed to buy a car as soon as possible. Where he was going to park a car near his apartment, he had no idea.

It was the height of annoyance that Sylvain followed them all the way back to the city, no matter how painstakingly slowly Dom drove to try to make the other man so frustrated he would give up and pass them. Especially since Dom, had it not been for his priceless passenger with her thighs wrapped around his, could have lost the bastard at any time, given the motorcycle's greater speed and maneuverability. And *that* would have been a hell of a lot more fun.

Sylvain waited until the frequent stoplights and the people filling the sidewalks in the heart of the city gave Jaime the possibility to slip away any time she wanted to, before he headed off in his own direction.

Fool, Dom thought. But he did manage not to make any vulgar gestures at him. Mostly because he didn't want to look worse than he already did.

He stopped the bike in front of Jaime's apartment, before he could yield to the impulse to kidnap her. She slipped out of Célie's helmet and his jacket, her face grave as she glanced from her apartment door back to him. Without a word, she handed both helmet and jacket back to him.

His heart started beating too hard, that panicky desperate feeling. "Keep it." Even if she never let him back in again, she would have that piece of him in her apartment with her. When she packed, she would have to look at its big bulk and figure out what to do with it.

Her brows knit. She pulled the jacket back slowly against her chest, her fingers stroking over the leather.

His panicked heart eased under the stroke of those fingers, as if he was still wearing the jacket, as if those fingers were gliding right there on his back, under his shoulder blade, where that spot of the jacket would fall. Sylvain's voice sounded in his head: *After all the chocolates I made for you. After all the chocolates . . . for you, I made for you.* He strapped her borrowed helmet on to the back of the bike and looked at her again. "Jaime. Are you just using me?"

Like every other woman. To get over Sylvain, maybe, if he was having an affair with her even while engaged to his billionaire?

Her face—all the light left it. His jacket drooped in her hands until it dragged on the ground. "Yes," she said, her face empty. "Yes, I am."

He pressed both open palms on the seat of his bike and stared down at them. Even against that black leather, they looked too big, too hard.

"All right," he said finally. "I'd better get back to work."

He left his bike there and walked. He didn't trust himself to drive.

"I don't know what influence Sylvain expects me to have on your sex life, but I suppose I should tell you that he really doesn't like Dominique," Cade said. They were at a café at the end of the Île Saint-Louis, with a view of Notre-Dame and the river. It was a little too cool still to sit outside, really, but they weren't the only ones who had found the April day too tempting to stay inside. Most of the outdoor tables were full. A blond woman with a pony-tail was playing the violin on a wooden block right at the middle of the bridge that arched between them and the cathedral, the notes soaring over the world and through them, like some great gift.

"I believe it's mutual," Jaime said dryly.

"Also, I should tell you, he really did hit on me. Actu-ally, it was a little too arrogant for 'hit on.' I think it was more like he made it clear he would be happy to scratch my itch if I happened to have one."

"Thank you, Cade." Jaime's voice was ground out of her. "Can you stop now?"

"Do you think he knows who you are? That it's some kind of pissing contest with Sylvain?"

Jaime's jaw clenched. Her eyes and nostrils both stung, but she would be damned if she would let Cade see. "I have no idea. I mean, it would explain some things. Clearly, he couldn't be interested in me." She turned her head away, jaw very hard, staring out over the river.

There was a moment's silence. "Jaime. That's bullshit. Why do you think that?"

Jaime shot her a dry, burning look. "The same reason you and Sylvain do, I assume, but for God's sake, let's not compare notes and make sure."

Cade was silenced. Well, there was an accomplishment. Her boardroom-managing sister, who could handle all kinds of discord, opened her mouth and closed it a couple of times, finding nothing she dared say.

"Besides—" Jaime focused as hard as she could on the violinist, who, standing on her bucket, notes flying so beautifully into the air, reminded her of *La Victoire de Samothrace.* "I told him the truth about me, so I don't think you need to worry about him anymore."

"You *told* him? And he still nearly picked a fight right in front of you?"

Jaime's right hand closed into a slow, hard fist. *"That's not the truth of me, Cade."*

Cade started to speak and paused, then pulled control around her like a cloak, the way she must exude calm when boardroom tempers flew off the handle. "What truth, exactly, did you tell him?"

Jaime looked back at the violinist. The girl looked so happy. So . . . victorious. "That I was just using him. What else could I possibly be doing?"

CHAPTER 15

The knock on the door that evening made her jump; it was the first time anyone had knocked on it. Her sister called her to come down. Dominique had rung the buzzer from below. Her grandfather made her come to him. Her father was in the States right now. No one else even knew where she lived yet. It was a very soft knock, very gentle.

She looked through the peephole and jumped again, her heart pumping madly. She opened it too fast. Dominique leaned with his forearm against the jamb, gazing down at her. His black hair was damp, and the heat and strength of him hit her with an almost physical force. He had come from the gym. She could see it in the extra bulge to his muscles, in his heat. His eyes in the shadow of the hall were all black.

"What for?" he asked.

She looked up at him, uncomprehending. The way his body leaned, she had only to step forward to be in a cave of Dominique.

"What are you using me for?"

Her brows knit harder.

"For sex?" He closed his hands around her waist, and a burn started instantly, spreading through her everywhere from his palms.

"For a distraction? To cure a broken heart?"

"For *you*," she said impatiently. A distraction. "What do you think you are, a magazine in an airport?"

From the flicker of his eyes, it had occurred to him. He walked her back into her apartment, his hands on her waist. Arousal instantly began to seep in and melt her, just from his taking control of her body, just from the door swinging shut behind him. "Why don't you explain that a little bit?"

"The difference between you and a magazine?"

"How you're using me."

"For *you*," she said again, frustrated and helpless. Did he think she wanted to go into her weaknesses? She hated her weaknesses.

His hands flexed on her waist. "What about *me*?"

She didn't even know any other way to tell him that didn't go into the nitty-gritty of how pathetic she was. She put her hand on his chest. "You."

His chest rose and fell in a long, hard breath under her hand. "Maybe you should explain what you mean by 'using.' "

"Maybe you should explain what *you* mean by using. You asked the question."

He was silent for a long time, his hands flexing uneasily into her ribs, in a way that sent little ripples of pleasure through her. "That you're in it for something that's *not* me. That anyone else would do."

"Oh, no," she said involuntarily. "No, I really don't think so." Surely she wasn't that bad? That she would have turned to any other strong man who paid her attention with that same desire to press herself against him and never let herself be pulled away? *I love you,* she thought again, on a great tidal wave, that might wash over her body and spill out of her mouth. She clamped her lips together. Talk about a using thing to say.

His hands tightened on her waist. "Think what?"

"That anyone else would do."

He stared down at her for a long moment. "I don't care," he said abruptly.

She closed her eyes. "Yes. That's what I thought. But you confused me there for a little while."

He looked at her. He spoke the next three words as if he was ripping them out of himself along with a big slice of skin: "I do care. What I mean is—if you're just using me—I'll take that, Jaime. You can use me all you want to."

He turned her against the wall, blocked her in with his arms and his body. "Here. Here's something else to use."

So she did use him. He had said she could. He pushed her up against that wall and lowered his mouth toward hers, and she put both hands on his shoulders and pushed him back. And he went. Falling back before the pressure of her hands as if it was some kind of superior military force, letting her push him into her room, down onto her bed.

He lay back as if she could have made him, yielding her those powerful muscles as an athlete might bend before a princess. The eroticism of that jolted through her. He wore only a fitted, deep gray T-shirt, a soft, fine knit, too little for the cool spring evening. She pushed it off him.

His muscles were still engorged from his workout and tightening ever harder as she looked. He made a little sound when she placed her palm in the center of his chest, like a starving man at the first bite of food.

She stroked him everywhere, the ridged muscles of his abdomen, the soft curling hairs over hard muscle on his chest, across broad shoulders and over tense biceps. He tried to close his hands around her hips, but she pushed them down. "You told me I could use you."

A couple of long breaths that swelled his chest against

her hands. It was still early evening, the sun not yet set, and for the first time while they made love, she could see the true color of his eyes: the brown that lurked, that made them not quite black, like dark, dark water. "All right."

It was a million times better than sitting in his *salon,* soaking up his flavors. She got to soak up him, all over everywhere him, hands running along his body, mouth kissing those gorgeous impossible muscles, all the way down, down, down his arm, over every hard curve and line of tendon and muscle, down to his wrist, to the inside of his wrist, to press a kiss into the center of his palm, to curve her face into that big hand, stroking it back and forth against the calluses, wallowing in him.

"Jaime." His voice sounded broken, all rough and harsh, with none of that veil of gentleness she was used to.

She rubbed her face the same way over his stomach, his chest, like an animal seeking comfort, and the hand in which she had nestled followed her, riding on her skull, the nape of her neck, gripping her shoulder in a sudden spasm. She didn't like having her nape exposed, but it didn't feel breakable or fragile with his big hand curved over it. It felt utterly enveloped and protected.

God, the warmth of him, the strength of him, she could bury herself in it and never come out. "You're so beautiful," she whispered against his stomach, in English, all her French having left her.

And, "So beautiful," against the bone and muscle of his hip as she pressed his jeans down.

And, "So beautiful," as she slid back up him, dragging her body against his the way one might drag a finger down a plate to lick that last little bit of deliciousness, to get every taste she could.

His hands scraped up and down her back, trying not to hold her, but occasionally the stroke tightened into a grip, despite himself. He shuddered under her. "Jaime."

Her name in his mouth was always such a shock. It made her dream all kinds of things.

She laid her body the length of him, all her weight on him, framed his face in her hands, and kissed his mouth. Taking her time. Feeling the flex and yield of his lips to her, the strength of his response, the taste of him, the way her hands could sink into his overlong hair, all silk, while the heel of her palms rubbed against the roughness of his jaw. She sank deeper and deeper into his mouth, unable to pull herself away now that she had started, kissing him over and over, angling her mouth, first one way, then another, exploring every fit.

With her every touch, more power seemed to gather in his body, more and more and more until it seemed close to breaking out of him, uncontainable, like lightning from a storm cloud. He dragged one hand over the headboard but found no purchase on its flat surface. She ran her hand up that stretched arm, over the bulge of biceps, and he fisted his hand over the pillow, squeezing one great corner of it into a small ball.

He wrenched his mouth away. "Jaime. Let me." His other hand curled over her bottom, pressing her against his arousal.

She buried her face in his neck and let him push her jeans down, let him part her thighs, let him slide her down on him. She loved the shivering flick that ran through his body when he pulled her onto him, as if he had been touched with a whip. She loved the sound he made. "*Ma chérie*. Let me. Let me."

His hands began to move her in a slow, steady, deep rhythm, while she kissed his shoulders. Her thigh-length sweater fell over his hands, tugged between their bodies. He slid his hands up once to push it off, but she would have none of it, pressing down again, catching it between their skin.

He did not try too hard. His focus now was elsewhere. Condensing into his sex, into the rhythm of their hips. He rolled them over suddenly, and she liked that, liked losing power, liked finding herself in the cave of his body. Caught in a cage formed by his strength. "Jaime." He slipped a hand down the length of her, between their bodies. "Do you like that, *minette*? Do you like it?" He was breathing very hard, the rough words almost soundless. "Ma *chérie*," he breathed as her body fell back into the mattress, all weakness, while her hips arched up. "Mine. Use me. *Oui, minou*. Use me just—like—that."

She convulsed into him. It felt like skydiving into the sun, right into its brilliant heat. The sun surged back at her, his heat driving into her deeply, his hands hardening in one last bruising second as they both came together.

Later, Dom lay on his back, with one arm behind his head and the other around her, curling her into his side. She felt damp, lax, entirely his. "It's funny," he said softly. "I don't feel used."

She must have thought he was making fun, for she pinched his ribs. He caught her hand and closed it in his so she couldn't repeat the gesture.

He turned his head to look down at her, not joking at all. "I don't know if you're very good at it, using people."

CHAPTER 16

"Guillemette," Dom said to his *maîtresse de salle,* whose skill in English had been one of the reasons he'd hired her. They were alone downstairs, making sure the displays were all perfect to start the day. "What does *boo-fool* mean?" Something like that. The funny way English hit some syllables hard and swallowed the others made it difficult for him to pick them all out. Especially when they were mouthed against his skin.

Guillemette concentrated a moment. "Byoo-ti-fool?" she said finally. She flipped open one of their English-language brochures and pointed to its description of his *salon.* Oh, he knew that word. English had the strangest pronunciation.

"*Beau,*" Guillemette said, and tilted her head. "More really than *beau. Beautiful* is a much stronger word in English."

He felt hands run all over his skin, a soft silken stroke.

Unlike his above-stairs team, Guillemette was far too elegant and well-mannered to make fun of him, but she busied herself quite briskly with organizing sacks and displays for the day, sneaking glances at him. On her subtly made-up cheekbones, a little blush showed. Suggesting she was guessing fairly accurately at contexts in which he might have heard that word recently.

Blushing himself, he ran up the stairs.

*   *   *

"Are you using me for a romantic fling with a French-
man that you can write about in your travel journal?"
Dom asked that evening, as they walked. She had come
late in the afternoon, when he was ready to leave the *salon* in the capable hands of his evening *responsable,* and he
had sat with her while she ate his newest *tarte,* taking great
and erotic delight in every morsel he watched her lips
close over. Then he had walked with her past the Place
République up to the Canal St. Martin. He liked this
neighborhood, on the border between upscale tranquility
and energetic protest and diversity. He liked the iron footbridges and the dark water and how the bars spilled directly onto its banks, the life of the street so much closer
to the water here than by the Seine. Nineteenth-century
buildings lined the canal, built for laborers and occupied
now by people like him, who had snagged an apartment
just before prices went out of the stratosphere. He liked to
think he and the area had something in common, built for
labor and now revealing their beauty to everyone who had
underestimated them.

A romantic fling was the height he had been aiming for,
at first, and he should be satisfied with having qualified.
But, as with most of his ambitions, a part of him was already reaching for bigger and better things. And a part of
him was trying to slap his hand for reaching for them, but
given his past history, he was particularly impervious to
being kept down by slaps. Even his own.

Jaime gave him an annoyed look. "You're rather aggressively persistent, aren't you?"

Dom tried not to look smug. If she was only just now
figuring that out, he had been disguising himself pretty
well.

She rolled her eyes at whatever she saw in his face, but
her mouth curved. She looked at the brown-black water

of the canal again. They were leaning on the rail of one of the lower footbridges, in the rustling shelter of the spring-green trees to either side of the canal. "I've been here three months already, Dominique. I'm not souvenir hunting."

Three months? She had only shown up in his life two weeks ago. "So whose chocolates were you eating before?" he asked jealously. *After all those chocolates I made for you,* Sylvain had said. Sylvain didn't even have a *salon.* If he was feeding her his chocolates, it was somewhere private.

"I like La Maison des Sorcières," she volunteered.

The place Philippe's fiancée Magalie and her aunts had. Where they made *chocolat chaud* and dark chocolate witches and pretended to themselves they could ensorcel anyone who walked by. Which felt disturbingly like it might be true, sometimes; he could never understand why Magalie's hot chocolate tempted him so much when he was the person who made the best damn hot chocolate in Paris.

Yes, he could see Jaime there, soaking up that witch-house atmosphere with the same concentration with which she had sat soaking up his. Drinking their chocolate. Nibbling on their witches. Damn it, now he was jealous of a lesbian couple in their sixties and their niece. He slanted Jaime a glance. "You're not attracted to women, are you?"

"What?"

"I was just checking!"

"Good lord." She sounded resigned, a little wary or tired. "Have most of the women you've dated been ambisexual gymnasts, or what?"

Kind of, yes. He considered the length of the canal for a moment, the little bridges marching away under the glow of the old lamps, such a tighter and more intimate chain of bridges than those over the glorious sweep of the Seine. "I haven't actually dated them." He kept his tone as neutral as he could.

She curled her hands around the metal rail. She didn't

give him a shocked, uncomprehending look again. She didn't look at him at all. She just stood there, staring into almost-black water, digesting the information. "It's almost the same color as your eyes," she said finally, her tone a little dry, self-mocking.

He looked down at the still, deep water. Over on the far bridge from them, someone imitating the film *Amélie* tried to ricochet a stone, and the water trembled a little. Just like him.

"I don't understand what you're getting out of this," she said suddenly, and he looked up to find her watching him sideways.

"Getting out of this?" Maybe something was being lost in translation.

She made a bleak gesture between herself and him.

"You," he said, uncomprehending. And realized he sounded exactly like her the night before.

Her eyebrows flexed deeply. Her head stayed tucked down and away from him, but her eyes tracked up his body. She opened her mouth, closed it hard, and finally opened it again. "That makes no sense."

His hands itched to close around slim shoulders, to trace her with his palms, even here in public, claiming every shape of her body with his touch. "How can't it make sense?"

There was something she was not telling him, her face severe and frustrated. Something she could not stand to say. He, of all people, could recognize that. "Why not the brunette?" she finally said, brusquely, an obvious red herring. She pressed those full lips of hers together hard. "Because you already had her?"

He stiffened. It was true, he had. And it had been good sex, too. Rough and wild, the kind of sex that seemed to require a mutual tip shoved into each other's pockets before they parted. The thought of Jaime imagining him that way—imagining herself used in that way—made him feel sick. *Putain,* was there nothing of him beneath the surface he presented to her, and the chocolates and pastries he fed her, that was good enough to deserve her?

He wished he could make himself *table rase,* erase everything of him up until the point he had met her, the way he swept an eraser across the whiteboard in his office at the start of a new week.

He was trying so hard to be different for her, to not be the man he had been before. And she couldn't even tell. To her, he was still—a sordid, rough user of a man. He looked down at his hands, closing around the railing, half expecting to see them chapped from cold, bloody work.

No. Cocoa butter softened everything. The morning he had woken up, after a week working chocolate in the pastry kitchens, to discover how soft his hands were had been the morning that decided his future career path. But no matter how much he drowned them in chocolate, the scars and the size weren't something he could ever change. And he kept the calluses on the palms on purpose. In case he needed them.

"I just want you," he said, low. "I'm sorry." That pissed him off, to hear himself apologizing for wanting her. Couldn't it be just a little bit a compliment to her?

She looked as taken aback as if he had thrown cold water into her face. "Did you just *apologize*?"

He shook his head. Wishing desperately that he hadn't.

"Why?" She searched his face, and he struggled to get his gentlemanly mask back in place. He had slipped up, there. She had spotted something. She was trying hard to see behind it.

"Why would you be sorry?" she persisted, probingly, a dog after a bone.

Putain d'imbécile, he apostrophized himself. What was

the point of trying to convince her she should put herself in his hands if he was going to confess the truth at the first most casual interrogation?

His damn better half had seen a chance to warn her. Better *half*? Who was he kidding? A feeble ten percent, at best.

He threw himself back into the refuge of his more dominant selfish ninety percent as hard as he could. "For not having better words for it. You asked what I'm getting out of this. You. That's all I want."

All. And maybe a serving of moon and stars while he was at it. What a stupid thing to say.

"Why?" she asked incredulously.

He gave a funny little shrug, trying to slide this moment toward safer territory. "You still haven't let me count all your freckles."

She had an uncomfortably penetrating look when she wasn't lost in a romantic daze. It boded ill for a long-term relationship. "So once you have, you'll be ready to move on?"

His heart pounded too hard, that sick feeling resurging. He turned back to the canal abruptly, gripping the rail, staring down at the brown water. "Do you *want* me to move on?" Shit, why had he asked her that? She might say yes.

"I would understand it, if you did," she said slowly, reluctantly.

His hands gripped harder. "Why? Because you want to, yourself?"

She gave him one of those incredulous looks. "No. Because I'm the one getting everything out of this."

His lips parted in shock. Maybe his disguise as a nice guy was too good. He snuck a glance at her. If he told her what an idiotic thing that was to say, might her illusions shatter too quickly?

"You only get me, as you said." There was a grim downward set to her mouth, her gaze internal. "What there is of me."

She sounded like his own internal voice. As if herself wasn't that much to offer. But *his* internal voice was justified. He tried a smile. "I like that. You."

She studied him in puzzled frustration. "Not that this is the most important thing in the world, *obviously,* but that brunette was nearly as gorgeous as you."

She thought he was gorgeous? A silly, pleased grin grew over his face, even as he flushed. No wonder his team couldn't stop making fun of him. This was pathetic.

Gorgeous. He tucked his hands into his back jeans pockets, just to make sure they didn't spoil the picture. "I like you," he repeated. That had to be obvious by now. Surely he didn't have to dig his entire dirty soul up and spread it at her feet right this second to prove it to her?

"Why?" she said again.

He looked at her, all freckles and bones that should be softer, and that tsunami of arousal and warmth flooded through him yet again. He was almost getting used to how very helpless he felt in its waves. "Every time I look at you, I want to lick you all over," he breathed.

She blushed over every visible centimeter of skin, and he glanced involuntarily up the street to his apartment. She didn't know how close it was, and he couldn't decide if he should tell her. What if he let her more deeply into him and she didn't like what she saw? But if he could get her up there before the sun finished setting, even she couldn't make him turn off the sun so she could hide. He would be able to see how far she blushed.

He slipped one hand out of his jeans pocket and curled it over hers on the bridge railing, almost forgetting the scars. "So how are you using me?"

"Not again." He liked her exasperation. He had never

been at a point in a relationship where the woman could roll her eyes and let him hold her hand at the same time. He wondered if she could roll her eyes and still let him make love to her, too.

"You're married. Is that it?" Oh, God, that would be the most horrible thing anyone had ever done to him.

"*No,* I'm not married. Have you *ever* dated anyone with any morals or sense?"

He slanted her a dark, rueful glance and decided not to point out the obvious about his sexual history to her again. "I am right now, I take it?" he asked hopefully.

Her smile burst up like the sun coming up on a planet that had never felt a sunrise.

What?

Whatever he had said, it made her slip closer to him, tucking herself up in the arm he immediately, obligingly curved around her.

"So *how* are you using me again?" he asked, puzzled.

"Oh, for—" She let out a huff of breath. But didn't pull away. He loved that. The not pulling away.

"I have to say, being used by you is a much nicer experience than you seem to think." *Keep using me. I could stay like this forever.*

The terrible seizing of his heart when he even tried to believe he could have forever. The memory of that shocking free-fall terror when he realized his mother was *gone.* The freefall had seemed to go on forever, that whole next school year at the very least. And on. For *years* he would wake up with that sickening lurch in his heart.

Jaime knocked her head against the nearest immovable object, his chest. Clearly talking her into something wasn't his best skill. He shoved consideration of his heart away into a dark, abandoned space, the way he always had to, and leaned his body into hers a little, angling her back against the railing of the bridge. She looked up as she felt his weight press, hint, hover just short of actually making her carry it. Her lips softened right away. Oh, yes, how he loved the way her lips now softened the instant he looked at her a certain way. He dipped his head and kissed those lips, taking his time, consigning that suitcase of hers to perdition, giving them all the time in the world.

She made a little sound and slipped her hands in under his jacket, climbing up his back.

He teased her lips, kept his voice so low you could almost think he wasn't aggressively persistent. "Tell me, Jaime. How are you using me?"

She yanked her head away, pulling back so far to glare at him that he had to catch her, alarmed at her angle over the railing and the water. "Like—like a plant uses the sun, all right? Or . . . or a sponge uses water. Satisfied now? Don't you *ever* let anything go?"

He let people go all the time. But his hands flexed into her bottom, in a strong message. Not her. *No, I won't let her go, and you can't make me,* his hungry, childish devil told his better half. His better ten percent.

"The sun." As the words sank in, they seemed to replace oxygen. He forgot to breathe normal air. The sun? She used him like the sun? He was *the sun.* Him.

Her mouth twisted. "The sun and the water don't get much out of it."

He could only stare. She had just told him he was the *sun* to her, and she thought he didn't get anything out of it?

What the hell was he doing wrong? Hadn't she even noticed the gooey melted marshmallow of him all over her hands? Did he need to be bringing her flowers or something? Presents? Should he be getting jewelry?

He couldn't imagine jewelry on her. She didn't even wear a watch. It was as if the pure, clean lines of her needed to stay uncluttered of anything but the fairy dust freckles. But, whatever, it was his day off Monday, maybe he should take her down the Faubourg Saint-Honoré and see if anything in the glitzy windows made her eyes sparkle.

"I think the sun analogy only goes so far," he said very dryly. Not that he wanted to refuse it. It bathed through him, healing all kinds of old bruises, to be her sun. "How could you possibly think I'm not getting anything out of it?" Every time he touched her, he had to restrain himself from squeezing her like *she* was a sponge in the desert from which he could suck the last drop of water.

Now she pulled away from him. He wanted to fight that, to overpower her, because always there was a part of him that knew he *could,* but once again he managed to remind his instincts what decent men did and let her go.

She put a body width between them, slipping her hands into the opposite wide sleeves of her light loose sweater. She turned her back to the water she said looked like his eyes, but she didn't quite face him, either. She pressed her butt back into the rail and gazed across the bridge up the canal the other way, to the group spilled out from the bar around the next bridge, their plastic cups of beer in the slow-gathering dusk gleaming like fireflies caught on the edge of the street lamps.

"I don't have anything to offer anyone right now," she said.

He gave an incredulous laugh. Nothing to *offer?* When she made him feel so happy, what was that to her? Nothing? "What are you talking about?"

"My worth—the things I've been good at—I can't do right now. I don't want to. I might never do them again. And that's—that's what is good about me. Without it . . . there's only me."

His eyebrows drew together. "That sounds like a good place to start over. With only you. *Putain,* I would love to have a base like that."

Her eyes widened. Her mouth softened. She looked at him as if she thought about easing back toward him, but she bent her head and thought worse of it. "I do have money," she said harshly, as if it was forced out of her. "If . . . it's needed. I do have that."

He stared at her, as betrayed as if she had knifed him in the back after thirty other senators. She had money? She thought he cared? She thought he *might* care? She thought . . . what? That he was going to scrounge after her money, like some boy crawling out of a scrapheap? Not the boy who had beaten his bloody way to the top of the hill and could claim its kingship?

She had money. She was some kind of privileged princess. Fuck. Doing what? Crawling in the muck? Playing Lady Chatterley? Was that how she was using him?

You didn't think the sun could be bought with money.

His hand closed slowly into a fist over the rail, bruising his hard palm. "What the fuck do you think I care about that?" he asked, low and far more harshly than she knew how to say anything.

Her eyes flared and she flinched, like someone who had known she was making a mistake before she ever made it.

"Why the hell did you just flinch from me? Do you think I'll hurt you if I'm angry?"

Now she blinked, confused. "Wh—?"

"Fuck you," he said, unbearably hurt. He had bared his all for her. He had tried to lay cloaks over mud puddles. Any day now, he would have let her know that he read *poetry*. He would have been sprawling on his stomach on the bed beside her, reading her the pieces that reminded him of her. *"Va te faire foutre."*

He turned and strode away.

CHAPTER 17

He got as far as the next bridge before his frantic heart managed to beat so fast that he could barely walk anymore and he had to clutch at the post at the corner. He looked back.

She was standing still where he had left her, looking at the water. Not at him.

He turned and ran. Ran back to her as fast as he could. "I'm sorry," he said before he even reached her. "I'm sorry."

He stopped in front of her, trying to take her hands. She fisted them and looked up at him, her jaw very hard and a sheen of tears in her eyes. "*Putain,* I'm sorry, I'm so sorry. Please don't, Jaime." He sounded like his father, in the early days, when his father still felt horrified at himself after he hit his little boy or his wife. "I'm sorry, Jaime." He squeezed her hands frantically, trying to make them relax to his hold. God, he hated how he sounded so much like his father. *Merde,* worse, he sounded like *himself,* when he was young enough to try to apologize his way out of a beating, before he set himself against his father in pure hatred.

He seemed to be making it worse. That full mouth that had set so hard against him trembled now, and the sheen grew until it shivered on the edge of her lashes, ready to fall. "But why did you *say* that to me?" he asked desperately. "As if I'm here for money?"

A far more horrible thing to say to him than *fuck you* to her. God, *fuck you*—that was just one of the more polite ways people expressed themselves to each other when he was growing up. It didn't *hurt,* like reaching into a man with nasty claws when he was trying so hard to be a prince for you and suggesting he was just some poor, desperate butcher who could be bought.

"I wasn't even talking about you," she said angrily. "I was saying something important about me. So fuck you."

His eyes widened at that, and then involuntarily he grinned, desperately relieved to have his own given back to him again.

He dragged her hand up to his mouth, and it stayed balled in a fist as his lips brushed it, as if she wanted to hit him. He bet she felt fine expressing anger by making a fist. He bet where she grew up, people didn't actually go around hitting each other whenever they got mad. "I'm a self-absorbed bastard," he said, wishing to hell that wasn't so true. "Tell me what you were trying to say."

She wrenched her hand away, and he had to let her do that, because he was trying to be the good guy. It didn't help that even after eleven years on his own, he still had to remind himself over and over what good guys did, to override his own instincts to just hold on. She turned, anger in every line of her body, walking away, but when he fell into step beside her, she didn't try to shove him in the path of an oncoming car or anything. She expected him, she wanted him, to fall into step beside her. So, good, they were just in a fight, like a normal couple, and he was doing the right thing now. He wasn't being too aggressive or too pushy, he was supposed to be following her while she walked her mad off, making amends.

"Tell me," he coaxed again, after a couple of bridges.

She sat down abruptly on the low concrete bank of the canal, where the water was so close she could have trailed her hand in it. It was a more awkward seat for him, with his longer legs, but he joined her. "I have a lot of money that I didn't earn," she said finally. "I think it's safe to say that, right now, that's the most important thing I can offer to most people who meet me."

His eyebrows shot up at that incredible underestimation of herself. "How many people who meet you even know that? You wear jeans and sweaters." He understood, vaguely, that there were all kinds of prices for jeans, but hers looked ordinary to him. He was pretty sure Guillemette, whom he didn't exactly pay a fortune, wore higher-end clothes than Jaime did.

Jaime gave him an odd, dry look but didn't answer his question. "I had this idea of *contributing* to people, of helping them rather than making money off of them, when I was pretty young. And I've been doing that. God, I had value; I changed thousands of lives. But—I *know* there are so many people who are still suffering, who still need help. And yet—it's like I've hit a wall."

She looked away toward the cobblestones, her back to the water. He had this sense of not being told something. "What kind of wall?" She wanted to save *everybody*?

As far as ambitions went, that certainly put becoming one of the best chocolatiers in the world into a different perspective, didn't it?

She flexed her hands around that something she was not saying. "This wall between me and—going back to it. I can't think my way through to *do* it anymore, and here I am, stuck. I'm such a damn baby." She sounded so angry, suddenly, as if she despised herself.

Did that make him the mud in which her wheels were churning? He frowned, deeply disturbed by the possibility, but forced himself to focus on *her* self-contempt. "What kind of work did you do, exactly?"

A glance to his face that skittered away. She seemed to choose her words. "Labor practices and sustainability. It ended up more and more being work against child labor, particularly child slave labor."

Her words shook him, profoundly. He stared at his scarred, ugly hands, the forearms pressed against his knees, remembering the first day in that abattoir at age twelve. He hadn't realized it then, but at least, if he had known anything about his own country's legal system, he would have had some kind of choice. If you called a terrifying leap from the familiar situation he knew he could survive into the foster care system a choice.

"I had a lot of backing," she said very dryly. "Don't imagine me a hero, because I very clearly am not. But, with that backing, I did manage to do a lot of good."

He didn't think he was *imagining* a hero at all. A hero. He was dating a hero. Him. "Then why did you stop?"

"I told you." A hard twist to her lips. "Because I'm a spoiled baby and can't face it anymore."

It must be a terribly hard thing to do. He wondered if she would ever be ready to talk about the details with him, to go beyond her vague "development work," or if talking about it was just too difficult. He had read once that many emergency room nurses or doctors quit because, even though they might do so much good, they just could not stand to face the badness of the world another day.

"You wore yourself out." A light clicked on. Her face as she sat in his *salon,* soaking up the taste and the moment. He reached out and closed those rough hands of his around her slim, heroine hands. "Are you using me to— to fill yourself back up again?"

Her eyes met his. For a moment, her face was naked. "Yes," she whispered, as if ashamed.

Oh. Not mud then. Him. As renewable energy for a heroine. He pulled her in tight to him, despite the public place. He seized her too hard and had to force his hold to relax. "And you thought that was a problem?"

He had always insisted he made chocolate that could nourish the gods. It was about damn time he found a goddess.

CHAPTER 18

"You're looking great," Cade told Jaime as they sat at the café in the Tuileries again. As the spring grew balmier, it was almost impossible to stay inside. Jaime, used to equatorial climes and still too skinny to have any insulation, shivered a little but forced herself to tough it out. "A sense of empowerment from dumping Dominique Richard, by any chance?"

Jaime rubbed her arm. Its muscles *were* getting stronger, the bones less prominent. "A sense of empowerment from keeping him, maybe. I'm pretty sure he's the source of any strength and power I currently have." Just sitting in his *salon,* she felt stronger. He was that *salon's* source, and the closer she got to him, the safer, and warmer, and more beautiful she felt, until, when he had her in his arms, nothing in the world could ever be ugly again.

Cade worried the inside of her lip, watching her. "I doubt it," she said finally, dryly. "Maybe you need to draw up a little CV of your own achievements. I'm pretty sure most of that strength and power comes from you."

"I'm working on it," Jaime said wryly. She glanced fleetingly at her sister and then away. "I feel a little—crumpled." She made a can-crushing gesture with her hand and something flinched across Cade's face. "Like I can't stand on my own two feet."

"I believe that's *normal* right now," Cade said between her teeth. "It's called convalescence. Can't you cut yourself some slack?"

"That's what I'm doing right now, cutting myself some slack."

"Oh, is that what you call slack?" Cade pressed her fingertips together and studied her sister. "And Dominique Richard is your crutch?"

"Maybe." He didn't feel awkward like a crutch. His strength both filled her and wrapped around her, warm and whole. A sun with muscles to hold onto her.

Cade's expression was both intrigued and wary. "Dominique Richard. You have no idea how strange the idea is. Jamie—it worries me that you might depend on him."

"Why?" Jaime's mouth twisted. "Do you think it broke me, Cade? That now I'm one of those clinging vine women who can't stand on her own two feet?"

Cade stared at her, her face whitening. After a moment, she spoke grimly. "By 'broke,' do you mean that literally or figuratively?"

"Oh, let's leave the literal side out of this." Jaime made a shoving motion with one hand, as if she was trying to scrape a big load of manure off the table. "I'm perfectly fi—"

"I know," Cade interrupted sharply. "I know you're fine. Let's just take that as a given, that you're perfectly fine. So you don't have to say it anymore."

"Well, why *do* I have to say it? Is that all I'll be for the rest of my life, some broken body, too stupid to keep out of trouble?"

"It was *three months ago,* Jaime. *Three months* and *the rest of your life* aren't exactly the same thing."

"Right. Right." Jaime scrubbed a hand over her face and gazed at a giant, black, twisted metal sculpture of a mother spider that loomed over the tulips and well-tended grass. Lucky her, the Tuileries were hosting a nightmare as a temporary exhibit. She shifted her chair away from the lurid vision and focused on a classical, green-tinted statue of a fleeing nymph. Casting a terrified look back over her shoulder.

For God's sake. She focused hard on the table instead. "You know, I'm just fine, until I think about going back there. And then—" She repeated that crumpling motion with her fist, illustrative of her soul collapsing like an empty can.

Cade knit her fingers, her problem-solving mode. Jaime wondered if her sister's boardroom adversaries knew Cade's tells like that, the way she pressed just the tips of her fingers together in a haughty peak to assert her control over a situation, the way more and more fingers would thread as the problem got more complex, requiring ever greater care to resolve. They were all threaded now. "Have you actually caught yourself up on the political situation since you've been in the hospital? I would argue against personally going back there anytime soon."

"That might be a stronger argument if you and Dad and Grandpa hadn't *always* argued that I shouldn't be going to these places."

Cade bit something back, but Jaime knew exactly what it was: *And Dad and Grandpa and I were always right.*

"You weren't right," Jaime said out loud. "I did a lot of good."

Cade rubbed a hand over her face. "I'm not arguing that, Jaime."

"I could do more. I was supposed to be organizing a Round Table on the Cocoa Economy in Abidjan. You remember? I mentioned the idea to you just before . . ."

Cade was silent. Thoughtful. Cade, who could reorganize the world in the space of a boardroom meeting, but who had never managed to re-organize her sister. "Well, if you'll take my advice," Cade said finally, proving that she could no more stop trying than Jaime could, "if you want to have the people who can make a difference actually come, you'll organize it in Paris. Because until the political situation calms in Côte d'Ivoire, none of the chocolate manufacturers will send someone down there. But you could probably fly farming cooperative representatives up here. And government officials, if it's settled by then who they're going to be."

Jaime frowned. "I want to get those CEOs out on the farms, so they can see something when this is discussed besides how much more sustainable cocoa costs."

Cade made a low, deeply annoyed sound. "Damn it. Why do I always have to be the pragmatist? Sure, personal, one-on-one visits from the billionaires of the world might be *better.* But here's a thought: rather than killing yourself over an ideal, why don't you find what's doable and get it done."

Two pairs of blue eyes locked, an old battle of strong wills.

"I'm on board for the Round Table, by the way," Cade said. "As you should know. Just say the word, and I'll start leveraging every other person in the chocolate industry I can into it. But that will be a lot more people if it's in Paris."

A Round Table like the one she had in mind could take six months or more to set in motion. At it, she could develop long-term, three- and five-year projects. Work with Cade, their father, their grandfather, to muscle and persuade all the great chocolate companies to get on board.

Was that even—fair? To do all this without leaving Paris? Was it a cop-out?

"Or in Washington or New York or London," Cade added. "If it would facilitate a break-up. God knows, when I said I would love for you to date a Parisian, I didn't have an arrogant, womanizing brute in mind."

Dom stood in the tiny waiting room, the only person there and that was probably a good thing because he dwarfed the small space. He glanced at the magazines on a table. *What do you think you are, a magazine in an airport?* He pulled a book out of his jacket pocket and leaned back against a wall, because he wasn't good at sitting and waiting. Then he stroked his new jacket, despite his best intentions. He couldn't stop himself. The soft leather, the elegant, edgy style of it. It wasn't that he couldn't afford something like this, but he didn't pay much attention to clothes, and so this was the nicest thing he had ever worn.

He couldn't stop petting it. Ever since Jaime had shown up with it in its designer shopping bag, tilting her head down as she handed it to him, blushing a little as he pulled it out, until he had to lay his hand over the nape of her neck, so deliciously exposed and vulnerable to him. She had stilled under his hand on her nape, a profound intense quiet, and then looked up at him under the weight of it.

It melted him into helpless nothing when she looked at him like that. As if she couldn't believe how wonderful he was. But at the same time, he had to fight himself to keep from tightening his hand on her nape, from nudging her: *Go ahead and believe. Believe in me.*

Selfish bastard that he was. But if he could make himself into someone she really could believe in, that didn't count as luring her under false pretenses, did it?

He couldn't stop wearing the jacket, even though Célie chortled things like, "It's so *sweet*. Isn't he *adorable*?" whenever she could pretend she thought he was out of earshot.

In fact, he was going to have a really hard time in July when he was sweating like a pig but couldn't bear to take it off.

She could have given him back his own jacket.

But she had kept it for herself.

Rubbing the edge of its replacement between his fingers, he tried to concentrate on his book. He had only read a few verses when Pierre Paulin came out.

"I like the beard." Dom sat across from him in his office.

The older man touched the neat gray beard at his chin and grinned. "Isn't it perfect? You can always trust a man with a gray beard to know the answer to your life. I might have had to start dying it, if it hadn't come in naturally. So. It's been a long time—five years?"

He knew better than Dom did, since he had his records right there in front of him, but that was about right. When Dom was twenty-three he'd worried about how he could run his own business the way a normal man did; he'd needed help figuring out what a *good* person did with frustrations and anger and impulses to punch something. The gym was already a lifeline by then, but it turned out Pierre had a few other tips, too.

"Still like Prévert?" Pierre nodded to the book in his hand.

Dom slipped it back into his pocket. "I do. Still hate poetry?"

"Sorry," Pierre said apologetically. "I'm an uncivilized barbarian, I know."

Dominique, who had seen his last school at twelve, grinned wryly at the man with multiple degrees sitting across from him. Maybe Pierre had gotten too much of education and Dom had never gotten enough. His apartment was walled with books. "So you remember how you wanted to work with me on my inability to handle a deeper, significant relationship?"

Pierre glanced at his notes from that last meeting five years ago. "And you told me your lack of deeper relationships was working for you just fine."

Dom nodded and settled back into his chair, pressing into it to make sure it formed a firm wall at his back. This hour was going to be a really long one, and he might as well be braced. Plus, when you were in a terrifying freefall, it was nice to have something hard to hold onto. "I think I'm ready for the lessons."

CHAPTER 19

D om turned a small oval fève of couverture chocolate in his fingers against the marble counter. It started so hard, but never as hard or cold as the marble. His fingers had already started to melt it. Near his hand lay a small pile of them. Smooth, dense, dark perfection. How could he put that in the center of a ganache? How could he make a chocolate whose last bite denied all the ease of the first, refusing to melt on the tongue?

He could call it *J'aime,* and only a tiny few in the world would ever understand the reference. But they would be the people who mattered.

If he made her the perfect chocolate, would she trust him? Would she let him strip her naked in the daylight? Would she press her face into his chest and confide some detail of that life she could not return to? *And what are you thinking of doing with that knowledge, you bastard? Feeding the fear, so you can keep her safe in your arms?*

Speaking of trust. He rubbed the nape of his neck.

"Monsieur," Guillemette said from the top of the stairs. "There's a James Corey below to see you."

He blinked, disoriented. Between *James* and *Jaime,* pronounced correctly the way Guillemette could manage, there was not that much difference, and the Corey name after it threw him completely off.

"Oh." He figured it out. "Are the Coreys *still* trying to buy my name to put on their chocolates? Why, did Cade ditch Sylvain?" he asked hopefully.

No, wait, did he hope for that? He liked seeing the other man suffer, but if Sylvain turned his attentions back to Jaime—

"He didn't say, *Monsieur*."

Dom rolled his eyes. "Well, send him up." Might as well get it over with. Besides, he liked being sought after so much he could pick and choose and turn people down. It was so different from the way he had started his life.

"He isn't very young," Guillemette hinted.

What? Oh, the stairs. Dom sighed and touched his hard little ovals of chocolate. "I'll come down."

The white-haired man inspecting his displays had to be in his late seventies, but he seemed spry, with no cane or limp. Although considerably shorter than Dom, he carried himself as if he could buy and sell Dom with the snap of his fingers. The resemblance to Cade Corey was striking.

He could hardly come onto the old man so aggressively that he would drive him off, as he had with Cade, so he extended his hand courteously instead. *"Je peux vous aider, monsieur?"*

Blue eyes met his, and a ripple ran through Dom, almost of recognition. Something about the eyes. Their energy? Their age, surrounded by heavy wrinkles? *"Je ne sais pas."* The old Corey's French was rusty, wielded with a heavy accent, each word pulled out carefully. "I wanted to get a look at you."

Dom raised his eyebrows, not sure why he should let this man or anyone else inspect him. Except, damn it, the man was close to three times his age.

"See what you were made of." The older man got a crafty look in his eye. "I don't suppose you would let me look around your kitchens, would you?"

"I'll even let you buy a sample of everything in the store to take home and run tests on," Dom said cordially. "Every other chocolatier-pâtissier in Paris does it all the time."

"Don't have anything of value to hide, is that it?" the old man said.

Dom showed him the sharp edge of his teeth. "It's all in here." He tapped himself on the chest.

James Corey gave a snort of laughter. "Good place to keep it." He went to the base of the stairs and placed an age-freckled hand on the banister. " 'Course, it could be a danger; hearts get stolen, too." He gave Dominique a sharp look.

Dom laughed. "I don't keep mine on me anymore."

The old man studied Dominique with a long, steady, oddly familiar look. "Feel pretty secure about where you got it stored, do you?"

Dom stopped smiling.

"You're positive the person who's got it isn't going to run off with it to some foreign clime?"

That bastard. Anxiety closed around his lungs and squeezed. Dom fought it with all the arrogance in him, forcing himself to sound unassailable: "Well, I doubt she'll try to steal my name and *savoir-faire* with it." His name. *Jaime Richard* passed through his mind with sudden cruel beauty, a ray of light lined with shards of glass.

He drew a breath, riding it out. He had ridden out crueler pains than a pipe dream, that was for sure.

The old man's eyebrows went up. He started slowly up the stairs. It was a lousy view, compared to Jaime's butt, but Dom should probably walk behind an old man up the stairs, too. And keep a hand ready.

He didn't have to grab the old billionaire's butt, thank God. James Corey mounted the stairs with no sign of faltering.

And smiled with pure delight when he walked into the

wide, luminous space, its great windows open to the spring and its marble counters gleaming. *"Beau,"* he said with that intense drawling accent of his. *"Très, très beau.* You can't make any real money off of it, but I can see how you wouldn't mind."

"I get by," Dominique said with some asperity. Not billions, and not even millions, not in his personal income, but he was doing just fine, thank you. And he had barely gotten started. He got e-mails every single day begging him to open a shop in Tokyo or New York.

"Are you going to show me around?" the billionaire asked, proving that just like his granddaughter Cade, he was completely *gonflé.* If the man had been thirty years younger, Dom could have refused that presumption. But given his age, what could he say?

"Si vous voulez. Do you know anything about making chocolate?"

The retired head of the largest chocolate-making company on the planet gave him a narrow look. "You Parisian chocolatiers can be a little hard to stand sometimes."

"I mean real chocolate," Dom corrected apologetically, not having intended the insult.

The blue eyes got narrower.

Dom coughed. "Chocolate that tastes good?"

The old man huffed and muttered something about his granddaughter's lack of sense.

Dom grinned. "You can't really blame Cade for choosing Sylvain. She asked me, and I wouldn't stoop."

The old man's gaze sharpened. A spark of unholy glee lit his eyes. "Wouldn't stoop to a Corey?"

"Have a taste," Dom said kindly, proffering him a chocolate. "Then you'll understand."

The old man gave the chocolate—his *Paris Brûlée*—an annoyed look. But he bit into it, and his annoyance faded, his gaze softening, growing hungry. "Smoke," he murmured. "Smoke in chocolate. You know, I might like you, kid."

Dom pulled the tray of chocolates back, annoyed. *Might like* him? "There's an épicerie down the street that sells *bonbons,* if you're desperate for crap."

"And then again, I might not," the old Corey said, giving Dom a nice jolt of satisfaction. He did love to piss people off, especially people who thought they got to make some kind of assessment of his worth. The old man ate the second half of his *Paris Brûlée* and licked the trace of chocolate off his thumb.

So Dominique might be able to tolerate him, after all.

"What's this?" James Corey stopped before the great half-carved block of chocolate. "You give up?" That sharp glance again.

Dom bared his teeth just a little. "I don't give up. But the expo isn't for another week, and I do have other things to do with my time, besides carving sculptures." Plus, that block of chocolate kept scaring him to death with the statement it was trying to make. Every time he tried to work on it, he became convinced he was jinxing himself and had to go do something less terrifying.

The old man scanned the rough-hewn folds of the block of chocolate, trying to see what it would become. "We've got a lot of money, we Coreys," he mentioned.

"Yes, and you know what would be wonderful? If you spent some of it putting Sylvain Marquis's name all over some crappy bar you sell in supermarkets all over the world." Joy shot through him just at the thought. "*That* would be beautiful."

James Corey was starting to look both thoughtful and amused. "You don't want any of the money yourself?"

Seriously, what was it with people trying to buy him recently? First Cade Corey, then Jaime, now this guy. Did he *look* affordable? "Why don't you go ahead and tell me what you want to buy from me, and I'll let you know if I want your money."

The old man's penetrating straight look was so oddly familiar, with, underlying it, a deep amusement. That was all he needed, some billionaire too old for him to sock hanging around his *laboratoire* acting as if Dom was the butt of some private joke. "I hear you like to play with very wild flavors," James Corey said, so extremely casually that Dom braced himself. Here came the pitch. A few million for his name on something that probably had peanuts in it. Dom had gone pretty far, but even he would never put peanuts in chocolate.

"Have you ever thought about spinach?"

"Spinach?" At least the peanuts would have been a *challenge.* "You want to pay me to put spinach in chocolate? That's boring! Go pay some chemist to do it."

"Boring?" James Corey looked offended. "You mean you can't do it."

"I mean why would I *want* to do it? It's the blandest flavor out there. I don't use chocolate to hide flavors, I use other flavors to bring the chocolate out."

"I have paid chemists to do it." James Corey folded his arms. "And they can't." His growing annoyance made Dom feel better already. "I don't think much of people who claim they *could* do something impossible if only they wanted to bother."

Dom gave him an incredulous look. "Trust me, on the list of impossible things I'm working on right now, spinach doesn't even make the first page. For one thing, it's not impossible, and even if it were, I don't see why I have to go do every impossible thing that crosses *your* mind."

"So what are the other impossible things?" the old man asked craftily.

"None of your business." Be someone's sun. Be perfect for her.

"Are they worth more than twenty million dollars?" The blue eyes gleamed.

"Hell, yes. But if you want to pay me twenty million dollars to blend spinach and chocolate for you, I'll squeeze it in." It would probably only take him an hour or two and would be *les doigts dans le nez* compared to the other tasks, a piece of cake. Jaime might even get a kick out of watching him. "But don't you ever put my name on it."

James Corey's eyebrows rose. "Twenty million and not even the right to use your name. You think a lot of yourself, don't you?"

He tried to. "You're the one who started the bidding." What was Dom supposed to do, bargain him down to what it was really worth? People who had too much money were very strange.

"What if I wanted something else for the twenty million?" The old man had the oddest glint in his eye, like Satan in a desert. "What if I asked you to seduce my granddaughter away from Sylvain Marquis?"

Dominique stared and then grinned. Someone else who hated Sylvain. Nice to know the man was marrying into the family from hell. "Well, I'm sorry I can't help you, but it's a nice idea. Good luck with it." He was going to need it, if he was going to try to get something out of Cade's steel grasp.

"Why can't you help me?" A snide look. "Impossible?"

This old man was starting to seriously piss him off. "I think maybe you have me mistaken for someone else. I'm Dominique Richard, not your prostitute. I work with chocolate. I've got a girlfriend." He started to hyperventilate, just claiming it. A girlfriend suggested something permanent, solid. Not someone who could disappear on him if he blinked too hard. "And your twenty million isn't worth either one of those things."

James Corey rested a hand on one of Dom's marble counters as if *he* owned it, and studied him a long moment.

Dominique showed him his teeth. "Must be hell, not having anything worth more than money."

"Oh, I've got a couple of things worth more than money," the old man said. "Two or three. But I always like to make sure. It's really lousy when my treasure gets treated by someone else like trash."

"You ever thought about settling down?" Grandpa Jack asked.

Jaime nearly jumped out of her skin. Which was saying a lot, since she had just finished her weekly physical therapy session, and even her skin was exhausted. They were sitting in the ultra-luxury Hôtel de Leucé off the Elysées, eating something from the Leucé's Michelin three-star pastry chef Luc Leroi that melted like snow over her hot, tired tongue. She would have liked to be sitting in Dominique's *salon* instead, but didn't dare meet her grandfather there. So they were on the opposite side of Paris, eating desserts in which ice kissed fire and birthed spring. And that cost over fifty euros each, which would not even be a decimal point in her grandfather's budget, but which made him roll his eyes anyway.

"Settling—down?"

"Yes! You know, get married, have kids, stop running around the world."

Jaime gaped at him. Both her father and her grandfather treated all men who approached Jaime and Cade as if they needed to be tested for rabies.

"Your sister's doing it," Grandpa Jack said, as if Jaime had ever imitated a damn thing Cade did in her entire life.

"I thought you wanted me to run Corey," Jaime said dryly.

"I do want you to run Corey. But given how stubborn you are, it's good to have other options."

"I have another option." Jaime took a bite of the ice hidden under the lava flow of raspberry and caramel *coulis.* "I'm supposed to be organizing a Round Table in Abidjan. When I . . . get out of physical therapy."

Fortunately, Jaime paid her PT quite a lot. Too much for the woman to be in any hurry to say Jaime didn't need her anymore.

"I recommend you organize that Round Table in Paris."

Oh, for God's sake, Cade had talked to him about that, too.

"Pretty sure we can make it really hard for you to get a visa to Côte d'Ivoire. Something about being responsible for thirty percent of their GNP."

"I doubt it." *Please, Grandpa. Close the borders to me. Let me stay here . . .* nice and safe, with that hot, hot mouth taking hers, arms holding her like he would never let her go . . . She shivered with longing every time she thought about being caught by him. "You'd be surprised how much political capital I have down there. An amazing number of people think my work stopping exploitation and improving cacao farm sustainability is quite valuable to them."

Grandpa Jack grunted, clearly contemplating the battle of influences, which government officials each could pull into play.

"Cade has been gossiping, hasn't she? Is that why you flew back over here?"

Her grandfather looked indignant. "Because you think I can't afford my own spies?"

Jaime narrowed her eyes. "Do you really have spies on me, or are you just trying not to incriminate Cade?"

Grandpa Jack just sniffed. "You keep yourself out of trouble for, let's say, a good ten years, and I'll consider taking my eye back off you."

Jaime gritted her teeth on a flash of rage. Grandpa Jack, Cade, her father, they all acted as if that one incident had reduced her to a five-year-old: too small to walk down the street by herself. And the worst of it was, they had almost been right. She could barely convince herself to walk down the street, those first few days. She was doing better now. Paris was a good place to fight your demons. The streets were so tempting to explore, the gritty realism of their dirt and crowds tempered by that element of fairytale inherent to the city.

"Hate to see you get involved with a guy who is even more trouble. But I wouldn't mind seeing you with someone who would beat the crap out of trouble and make you happy. 'Course, if you're going to settle down with someone, you wouldn't want to be running around to the ends of the earth all the time. Might have to learn how to delegate."

Jaime gazed down at her arms, resting on the little table in the pillared hall. In her grandfather's company, she had her sleeves pushed up: no point in hiding her scars from him. Goose bumps had risen all up and down her skin. She tried to pretend it was from the snow-melt dessert and not that shiver of longing to never regain her backbone so she could more easily tuck her life into someone else's. "Grandpa. Did I ever mention to you that my *sex life* is my own business?"

Grandpa Jack scowled. "That's just indecent. Your sex life. You can't date like a normal person?"

"I think you're picturing a normal person in the fifties."

Her grandfather glared at her a long moment, with bright blue eyes and a steady, penetrating gaze she and

Cade had both inherited from him. "Just tell me one thing, snippy: do you have a boyfriend here in Paris or not?"

Jaime stared at her arms while the hair on them rose straight up. She swallowed, rubbing it down, missing the stroke of a hard, big hand that could make all her shivers disappear instantly. He had said something about them dating, but from there to claiming he was her boyfriend was one hell of a jump. Presumptuous as anything on the part of a woman who kept living out of her suitcase on the off chance she would get up the courage to zip it closed and go back to being someone she could respect again. Presumptuous about a man she had known three nights and who had never once stayed through till morning.

"Not," she said low, but her fingertips rubbed up and down her forearm, and her stomach rose up in protest at the denial. She felt like Judas.

Settle down. Stay in Paris. Have a boyfriend. Have a boyfriend who held her in his big, hard hands as if she were precious. When *he* was the one who was precious. Was it really because she was broken, that that sounded so beautifully enticing, like a whirlpool she wanted to be sucked down into so she could never drag herself back out to her old life? Or was it just because—he was the most enticing man she had ever met?

Her grandfather sat back, his gaze very sharp. "Interesting. You know, I was just talking to someone earlier today about one person's treasure being another person's trash. Any way you look at it, it's a real sad thing to see."

CHAPTER 20

Dom was waiting for the dawn.

Jaime had forgotten it was his day off, or maybe she didn't know. He hadn't warned her, last night. So she curled up against him naked, trusting him to slip off in the darkness.

But today, he could stay in bed as long as he liked. Long enough to see the light fill this room and to count her freckles.

Long enough to see where she blushed to.

He still felt sulky about her refusal to leave the light on the first times they had made love, when her blush must have covered every millimeter of her body. Now he would probably have to do something extra special to bring out the full blush.

His gaze slid down her body, which was slowly growing clearer in the light, and he grinned a slow, wicked grin.

His fingers stroked her head absently. He hated that short, feathered haircut of hers. He didn't think it suited her, and she used so much hairspray to hold it in place, it fought his hands off like a scratchy hedgehog. But the night had worn some of that scratchiness off, and he slipped his fingertips under the remaining mat of it, rubbing them gently back and forth against her skull, watching the colors of her body grow clearer.

Just when he was able to confirm that her nipples were, indeed, a dusky pink like her blush and not a golden-brown like her freckles, his fingertips slid over something.

A little irregularity. He had probably dragged his hands over it many times in the heat of passion and never noticed before. But now, it caught his attention. He followed the crooked line of it, short, just a few centimeters, under the feathering of her hair. That was a scar.

As if he had touched off some alert in her security system, she came awake, her body stiffening against his. "What happened here?" he asked softly. His mind flashed over different possibilities, from a childhood fall to a brain tumor operation.

Her body flinched, but she said easily, "Nothing. A bump on my head not too long ago. It didn't do much damage, but they had to stitch it up and shave the hair around it. That's why my hair is so short right now."

His whole being froze. The lie of it. So exactly like his mother's voice. God, he himself had probably sounded like that, too, when he was younger, when he still defended his father—or himself? See, I don't really deserve to be beaten!—to teachers with a lie.

"Who gave you the bump?" He twisted to sit on the edge of the bed with his back to her, feeling sick. Feeling revulsion. He could not, he would not, get involved with a woman who defended the man who beat her. *Strong women, only strong women, only the absolute strongest women ever.* Strong enough to kick him out, if he turned into his father.

And at the same time it was breaking his heart to think she had been abused. To imagine it . . . he could imagine it all too well. He curled deeper over himself, stomach churning.

She didn't say anything.

All at once, she sprang out of the bed. He watched her,

from the corners of his eyes, fists clenched together between his knees. She pulled on a heavy bathrobe, cinch-
ing the belt in mad, hard yanks.

He lunged suddenly, yanking the bathrobe apart. She
fought him with all the tightness she could put into her
folded arms, but he forced the sleeve down. So easy to
override her strength. And expose the jagged fresh scar.
"Did you break your arm when you fell down, too?
Maybe some ribs?" He hated the sound of his own voice,
harsh, accusing.

Her eyes narrowed. She jerked the bathrobe out of his
hands and tied it again, in hard yanks. "What business is it
of yours?"

His head jerked to the side as if the words were a blow
across his cheek. He took a step back.

"God damn it," she said in English, and strode into the
other room. He heard her banging a glass on the counter
in the kitchen area.

He followed her as far as the living room but couldn't
bring himself to follow her farther.

After a moment, she came back into the room, so small
and anodyne in its rented ideal-Paris coziness, with its red
curtains and scuffed hardwood floors and tall windows
with their wrought iron railing.

"I got the crap beaten out of me, all right? Are you
happy?"

"Oh, fuck." He folded in on himself. His butt glanced
against the edge of the couch, and he slid on down to the
floor, wrapping his arms around his knees. Like he used to
sit when his parents fought, after he had given up on trying to stop it.

"Is that why you're in Paris?" he asked harshly. "To get
away from him?"

"They've been arrested," she said flatly. "It was stupid
for them to go after me, but then, people are stupid. I'm

here because I was airlifted here, and my sister is here, and . . . I like your *salon*."

"My God." He didn't know if he could take this. He was about to vomit. "*They've* been arrested? You had to be airlifted here? Oh, fuck. Fuck. Fuck."

Was there nothing precious in his life that could be kept safe? Not himself, not his family, and not even *her*.

"Just tell me," he said to his knees. "Tell me what the hell happened."

Jaime looked down at his masochistic grip on his black hair, knowing she sounded cruel, but furious with him for forcing this out of her, for dragging it into their relationship, which was supposed to be all gold and sunlight. That *nothing else* could touch.

She didn't know what she was to him, but she didn't want to be someone even smaller, a victim to be pitied or taken care of.

"Just a trafficker in Côte d'Ivoire who hired some thugs to pay me back for my interference." She shrugged, as if it didn't matter at all. It was what she wanted, for it not to matter at all to her life. Not at *all*. "There were four of them. They seemed to—like teaching women lessons." The *pleasure* they had taken in beating her, in the way her body wrapped around itself, her hands clasping over her nape and head . . . It had hurt something in her even worse than the two months in the hospital, that thrill in her suffering. She was such a wimp. She wanted to save those who suffered, but she folded like a wuss when she suffered herself.

"Were you raped, too?" Dominique asked harshly.

She flinched and shook her head. She wrote checks to charitable organizations in places like Darfur every day, to appease her guilt over the women who suffered so much worse and had no choice but to survive it.

Jesus, Dominique was intrusive. What kind of question was that to ask, anyway?

"What happened?" Dominique's voice was *so harsh*. It was rubbing her raw with its harshness. She wanted him to go away.

"I was found. I'm vague on the details, but my sister must have had me airlifted here as one of the nearest top medical facilities."

Blurred memories of her sister's strained face whenever she opened her eyes, of the tears streaming down it at least once. Maybe she should go a little easier on Cade about that anxious hovering.

"That's why you were so thin when you first started coming," Dominique breathed. *"When was this?"*

"A little over three months ago."

Dominique scrubbed his face in his hands.

"I got out of the hospital over a month ago," Jaime said impatiently. "I only go see a physical therapist once a week now. I'm perfectly fine."

"You had to spend nearly two months in the hospital." His tone had gone flat, as if it couldn't sustain anymore.

"Yes, but hospitals always keep people twice as long here as they do in the U.S. I'm perfectly—"

"Shut up. Just—don't say that again. Give me a second."

What a crappy way to start the morning. Jaime strode into her bathroom, slamming the door. In the mirror over the sink, her freckles stood out more than usual, that grim determined look not at all an expression that favored her. It seemed sullen and defiant in the beveled elegant frame of the mirror, her hair a spiky mess. The blow hadn't been too bad, a glancing cut and a mild concussion rather than real brain damage, but they had shaved around the area so they could stitch it up, and of course that had left few options for a haircut afterward. The scar would fade, and as her hair grew longer, it would make it easier to conceal without so much stupid hairspray. Thus the array of hair vitamins hiding behind the beveled mirror.

She stepped under the shower, rubbing soap over and over the scar on her forearm, where the broken bone had pushed through the skin, as if she could wash away the whole incident.

She tilted her head back, letting the water stream down over her face.

A current of air brought goose bumps to her skin. Dominique stepped in naked under the shower and just picked her up.

Before she could even brace herself in stubborn refusal to be pitied. Just picked her up and wrapped her tight against his body, like a child might clutch a teddy bear, leaning back against the wall and letting the water stream over her back, his face.

He didn't say anything at all. She couldn't see his face, his hold was so tight. Her pride demanded she wriggle free. It was not very comfortable to be clutched like a teddy bear during a child's nightmare. But it was oddly *comforting*.

She subsided into him, tension slowly draining out of her until she was as boneless as that same teddy bear, her focus filled with him. The strength of the arms that seemed not to tire of her weight. His heartbeat, too hard and fast under her ear. The way his head arched back from her, pressed into the wall, face into the spray. How complete she felt, as if he would never let her go.

He never said anything at all. He didn't try to make love to her. He didn't let her go until the hot water ran out and she started shivering from the cold spray on her back. Then he dried her off and took her over to his empty kitchens, where he made her *chocolat chaud* and a totally extravagant *millefeuille au chocolat noir* for breakfast and watched intently until she ate every bite.

It might not be what the doctor had ordered for her, *mille-feuilles* for breakfast. But the golden flakiness sandwiching intense chocolate cream, fed to her by a rough, wild man who watched her every bite with absorption . . . it filled her with his *caring,* as if he could stuff her so full of golden warmth and rich, sweet reassurance that she could be healed down to the marrow of her bones.

CHAPTER 21

"You're dating someone who survived a traumatic beating recently?" Pierre asked, disturbed. "It makes sense that you would end up with someone like that, but . . ."

Dominique pressed his heels against the floor, driving himself harder against the back of his seat. "I'm not repeating any *putain de cycle*."

"It would only be natural if you were attracted to someone like your mother," Pierre said gently.

"I'm not."

Pierre hesitated.

"She was attacked while doing development work by people who were hired to do it, which is hardly the same thing as someone who remains in an abusive relationship," he said between his teeth. What kind of development work? *Putain,* what was her last name? Was he some kind of animal, that he didn't know those things about her already?

Pierre maintained a neutral expression. "How do you feel about it?"

"She's strong." Dom met the psychologist's eyes for a moment. "She's strong enough to kick me out." To zip that suitcase up and leave him. The day before, his day off, which should have been a day of pure bliss, strolling through Paris with her, had been awkward, delicate, and rather horrible. He had felt as if everything he did, from taking her hand too carefully to letting it go when her jaw set and she snapped something about not being fragile, was breaking something between them.

He glanced uneasily at his phone. Jaime hadn't shown up today. She knew he left around four, didn't she? And Guillemette was smart enough to text him if she did show up?

Pierre looked thoughtful, which was one of his tricks of the trade, and glanced down at his notes. "Is eighteen still the last time you hit someone?"

"Yes," Dom said wistfully. There had been three of them and one of him, and all four of them had wound up bloody and bruised. There had been something gloriously satisfying about it, and if one of his opponents hadn't pulled a knife and gotten Dom a night's stay in the emergency room and all four of them arrested—he might right this minute be his own father, instead of the man he had decided to become.

Pierre glanced at his birth date and did the math. "Ten years. That's a pretty long run, Dominique."

He had always respected this about Pierre: the man didn't try to make you sit on a couch. He let you have a nice, hard chair to push yourself back into. "I've never been in a relationship with anyone who was vulnerable to me. And you have no idea how much I would like to beat the fuck out of someone right now."

"But you're not," Pierre said approvingly. "That's the important part."

"They're in prison on another continent, Pierre. And I hope their prison is one of those horrendous hellholes you hear about, too. What, did you think it was my *self-control* that was stopping me?"

"Ah." Pierre, the intellectual who believed in using his

words to resolve things, let one corner of his mouth kick up wryly. "Well. We're going to hold you excused on that one. But when you say you've never been in a relationship with anyone vulnerable to you, I'm not sure I agree. When you first came to see me, it was for your employees . . . ? Who, I believe, have in several cases come from very problematic backgrounds and would therefore be considered a vulnerable and dependent group . . ."

"You don't *hit* your employees. You might yell at them or in some psychological way be a bastard—"

"But you don't," Pierre said. "You don't yell at them or psychologically abuse them."

"No, they walk all over me," Dom said, aggrieved. Sylvain and Philippe probably got to yell at their team once in a while to keep them in line, without suffering mountains of angst over it.

"They don't abuse *you*?"

Dom's eyebrows went up. It had been sixteen years since anyone had been able to get away with abusing him. "No, I think it's a pretty happy place to work for everyone, to tell the truth." He could feel light coming out of his *salon* and kitchens from blocks away. It was a heaven to hell contrast with the abattoir where he had started his working life. He loved it, the contrast. Every single day he walked into his *salon,* he loved it.

"That's an amazing accomplishment in and of itself, Dominique. All your work is amazing." A diehard fan, Pierre came in at least once a week.

Dom couldn't stop a pleased smile. But he said, "Those are employees. The relationship is different. There's been no real test of me, ever. I've never allowed one." How the hell could he be so selfish as to make Jaime his guinea pig? He needed to let her go.

But she said he was her sun. If he let her go . . . she

might be cold and empty. And who would destroy anyone who tried to hurt her?

"Hmm."

Dom had forgotten how annoying Pierre's *hmms* were.

"You said once a long time ago that you had never hit anyone smaller than you."

"No."

"Not ever. Not even young on the playground."

"I got in a lot of fights, but I think they were with boys pretty much my size." He had been a big child, but it wasn't until his teenage growth spurt that he had turned into such a bruiser. He hadn't really had anything against any of the younger, smaller kids, anyway. It had been the bigger ones, the ones who tried to bully him or others, who drove him into a rage.

"You know, Dominique, I tried to tell you once before, and you left and never came back, but I'm going to say it again. I think you might be selling yourself short in relationships. I don't think you'll let yourself ever do what your father did."

His *hmms* were annoying, but fundamentally, Pierre was such a damned good guy. "How can you be so sure?"

"I can't be *sure.*"

Dom's heart sank. He wanted sure.

"But I have much greater hope in you than you seem to in yourself, Dominique. You're not so good at hope, but I've never seen anyone to match you in determination. You just go and do what you decide you want yourself to do. If you don't know how, you find out how. Like now." Pierre nodded at him.

Dominique stared at his big taut hands, trying not to admit something. That maybe, he was focusing on the question of whether he should let her go because it was easier than the real fear: when and how she would leave him. He took a deep breath, concentrated on it, let it slowly out. "So . . . how? How do I do this deeper relationship thing?"

"Have you considered that both of you could come see me together?"

Dominique shook his head, repelled. "*She* doesn't need it."

Pierre's eyebrows rose a little bit. "Someone who was traumatically beaten just a few months ago? Are you sure?"

"She's very strong," Dominique said stubbornly. He saw her sitting in his *salon,* the still, absorbed focus of her. She had him. He was her healing. Thinking about it that way made him a little uneasy. He could feed her senses and her body, he could warm her, he could let her soak up everything she wanted from him. But . . . he wasn't a doctor.

"It might help you two to understand each other. Given her past experience and yours—you're going to have some issues you need to communicate about."

Dominique gave him an appalled look. "No. I mean, she can communicate about whatever she needs to, but she doesn't need to know *anything* about my past." Drag her into that ugly period of worthlessness? She thought he was her *sun.* Not some dirty mongrel that had heaved itself out of the mud.

If Pierre raised his eyebrows one more time, he might glue the things in place. "Do I take it that this woman doesn't, in fact, know anything?"

Dominique shook his head vehemently.

"All she knows about you is that you're one of the world's top chocolatiers, and she has no idea what you climbed up from to get there?"

Dominique knew he was looking unbearably smug. But, come on, it was quite a disguise to pull off.

"Well. You asked how to work on having a deeper relationship. Honesty might be a good place to start."

Was his psychologist *crazy*? "Pierre. She *trusts* me. You want me to be honest with her and ruin that?"

Pierre gave him a very wry look and waited.

"Fuck that." She let his hands curve around her skull. She let him lock her body under all his size and muscle, and she wrapped her arms around him and kissed him while he did. He was never, never, never going to let her find out that no woman in her right mind would trust him with herself. "Pierre—you're a good man, and I respect your advice. But I would lie *comme un arracheur de dents* for this woman." Lie like the lowest worm there was.

No *texto* from Guillemette. He swung back by his *salon,* but Jaime hadn't come by.

She hated his knowledge of the attack. He could tell.

Pierre would probably say he should let her see one of his wounds, let her know that he knew what it was like, to have someone hurt you, to keep on doing it after you were on the ground and not fighting anymore and not even conscious to receive it, to do it when all you had done was want to love them.

But everybody knew that boys raised violently became violent men. *He* knew it. He rode that violence inside him like a wild beast all the time, trying not to let it buck him off. He couldn't tell her that she should leave him.

She thought he was her sun. She thought she wanted to soak him into her soul, that he was that beautiful. When they used the chocolate in the enrobing machines to coat something with nuts or fruit in it, they had to purify it afterward: pour it all through stretched women's pantyhose, let the sieve catch even the finest bits that corrupted the chocolate's purity, then return the chocolate to the cleaned *enrobeuse,* maybe temper it again, as if all its past use and abuse had never been. He wished he could do that to himself for her.

He didn't want her to realize he wasn't a sun.

He hated it when she didn't come. He got that cold, desperate feeling in his stomach, the fear trying to push out of the shell he locked it into. But she hadn't come once before, right? When she was feeling exposed and vulnerable.

So he went to the gym, and she wasn't there, and he cut his workout short and went to her apartment. She wasn't there, either, and he kept trying to tell himself not to be an idiot, not to squeeze all the breath out of her by grabbing onto her too tight. She didn't have to be glued to him.

He had stepped back out onto the street—lecturing himself that he couldn't hang out there waiting for her to show up, that was too *louche,* too creepy, something his father would probably have done—when he saw her. Coming up the street with her hands empty, no shopping, a tiny backpack of a purse. Her steps fractured when she saw him, and the man striding briskly behind her flowed off to the street around her and back to the sidewalk without even breaking pace, still talking on his phone.

Dom let him pass and looked back at her. Her eyes were wide, somber. *Merde.*

He left her door and met her halfway. Three quarters of the way. It took her a while to start moving toward him.

"I missed you." He smiled down at her, while his heart pounded sickeningly.

Her face softened into a shy smile. His heart eased a little. "You must get tired of me sitting in your *salon* all day."

"Ah, non," he said involuntarily. *"Non. Non."* It bathed his whole body in warmth to know she was sitting there. Soaking him up. Sometimes he still stood in the little corner of glass and stone, smearing chocolate prints against the glass as he watched her, the poor child outside the candy shop he couldn't quite believe he had the right to

enter. The size of his chocolate prints, compared to the little foggy ones they often had to wipe off the front of his *own* windows, was . . . humiliating. Like his insides should really have grown at the same rate as his outsides.

He reached out and stroked the tips of his fingers along the line between her hair and cheek, to prove to himself that he could. That she would like it. "I like feeding you."

Her smile bloomed.

"Come for a walk?" he coaxed. "I know a restaurant you will love." Thank God for his city. He had a thousand restaurants she would love. That was three years of nightly temptation.

But her smile faded. She bit her lip. "I can't."

His heart clutched with panic again. *Normal,* he tried to tell himself. *Normal that she would sometimes have other plans. Don't, don't do something stupid or clingy or creepy. Don't you dare ask her what they are.* "All right," he said easily. Easily. God. He trailed his fingers over her shoulder, down her arm, lifting the tips of her fingers in the tips of his. For all the world as if he was confident and normal. "Come by tomorrow and I'll make you something special."

Her smile kicked back up. Her eyes clung to his. "All right."

He looped his arm around her, turned them both into the nearest doorway, and kissed her. She pressed herself instantly against him, as if she liked the feel of him along the length of her body. He smiled down at her, deeply relieved. "I'll miss you tonight."

Her hands flexed into his shirt, grabbing fistfuls. "Me, too."

So . . . he tried to feel like a completely normal person when he left her, and not like he wanted to throw his arms around her legs so that she had to drag him with her every step.

CHAPTER 22

"Jamie. I'm just trying to tell you. He's a total bastard." Sylvain stood at his granite kitchen counter, running a knife through shallots with blurred speed as if they were Dominique's fingers. Sylvain in a kitchen, the murderous poet.

Cade toasted Jaime silently with her wine and wandered out into the living room area as if this subject had nothing to do with her. Lying traitor. She had invited Jaime to facilitate this lecture.

"You know, I had other offers for this evening," Jaime said coldly. Strolling around Paris hand in hand with Dominique. She *hated* proving she was strong again and not a clinging vine. It made those hours of brutal physical therapy look like a piece of cake.

Next time you're trying not to cling, go take in a show. They're dancing Firebird *and* The Rite of Spring *at the Opéra Garnier. You might find it motivating. You can decide whether you want to be the sacrificial virgin or the bird that rises from the ashes.* Instead of defending her sex life to her family.

Someday she had to tell Dominique her last name, so she could make him join her for these cozy dinners. But for now, it was nice to be anonymous. He couldn't Google her and find the five pages of results that suggested she had done nothing with her life but get beat up.

Although seeing Sylvain's face if she arrived with Dominique Richard in tow as his dinner guest would have been priceless. Not worth adding one more possible blow to her relationship with Dominique, but otherwise hilarious.

Dominique's face, though, when she had said she was busy that evening. That hard, guarded look. Her whole right side felt empty, as if it should be pressed against something. That broad swath of skin over her shoulders and down over her biceps, where his arm would have draped, was cold . . .

"I'm just—I'm worried about you." Sylvain studied her, a man whose very first acquaintance with her had been when she was a battered pulp being hauled around on a hospital bed, and who was never going to get over it. "You're vulnerable right now. *Et il s'en fout.*" He doesn't give a damn.

Jaime remembered the shower, being held like a teddy bear. "That's not true, Sylvain."

He gave her a frustrated look. "He's a very good flirt. You wouldn't necessarily know *qu'il s'en fout.*"

"He's not, really." Cade drifted back from the living room. "A good flirt. I mean, he is in a direct way, but the long, elaborate, sensual seduction—not his thing." Her gaze lingered a subtle moment on Sylvain, giving Jaime far more insight into her sister's sex life than she was at all comfortable with.

Why the hell did Cade feel so comfortable barging into hers? "Cade, can you call up a picture on your phone of the man you think is Dominique Richard? Because I'm really not sure we know the same person."

Cade's eyebrows went up, and then *she* looked uncomfortable. Oh, great, Jaime had given her a visual. This was ghastly.

"I don't mean to be any ruder than the two of you are, but my personal life is none of your business."

And God knew, comparing the way Dominique Richard had flirted with each sister was *not* her idea of fun.

Sylvain gave her a blankly uncomprehending look. "We're your family. How in the world could you say that?"

Cade grinned at her smugly. "He's got a little sister of his own."

It pissed her off beyond belief, the way Cade always thought of her as the little sister who needed guidance. "Is she all grown up, too?"

"Oh, no, she's only twenty-one." Sylvain sounded appalled.

"Sylvain, didn't you start your own business at twenty-one?"

He dumped all the shallots in a pan and gave her a long, steady, disgruntled look.

"Look, I am in exactly the situation I want to be in, and if you would give me the respect of believing I wouldn't let myself be in any other type of situation, I would appreciate that."

"Oh, yeah, I forgot to tell you," Cade informed her fiancé ironically. "She's using *him.*"

"*Oh, pour l'amour de Dieu.*" Sylvain attacked some mushrooms far more viciously than the weak little fungi merited. He stopped after a moment to give Jaime a hard look. "He's not violent, is he?"

"*Violent?*"

"You can just feel it simmering in him all the time, violence."

"You're just saying that because he's so big and he looks so . . . rough." Rough-edged, hard, bad-boy, leathers . . .

trying to hide that soft ganache center of his. He was so *gentle* with her.

"No," Sylvain said impatiently. "*Putain,* Jamie, I grew up in the *banlieue,* too. Not as bad a one as his, but I know the difference between bravado violence and the real thing. He's got it in him."

"Maybe with *you!* You're not exactly his friend and ally."

"How many times did you say he got arrested?" Sylvain asked Cade.

"*Sylvain!*" Cade hissed. She gave Jaime an awkward look.

Jaime's blood boiled. "Did you have him investigated *more* after you heard I was going out with him? What the hell, Cade? Did I do that to you with Sylvain?"

"You didn't even know about Sylvain or care," Cade said impatiently and with an old anger. "You were off in Papua New Guinea at the time. And, to answer the question, once. He got arrested once, when he was eighteen. A knife fight, but he didn't have the knife. The times before that were calls to *la D. D. A. S. S.* when he was a lot younger."

Jaime absolutely refused to take advantage of Cade's continued prying into other people's private lives, but . . . "What's *la D. D. A. S. S.*?"

Cade raised her eyebrows at Sylvain.

"They check on family issues," he said reluctantly. "And some other things."

Jaime's eyebrows plummeted. She walked away through the living room to stand at Sylvain's great balcony windows, open to the spring night.

"Don't start getting *le coeur tendre!*" Sylvain called after her, frustrated. "Have some sense!"

"Jamie? Sense?" Cade asked incredulously, and Jaime's head almost exploded. How could her family honestly believe that she had reformed cacao farm labor practices in difficult parts of the world without at least some sense being involved? Did they think it was all wild-eyed activism and pure luck?

Yeah, they did, didn't they?

"What were the calls for?" Jaime asked stiffly, looking back.

Cade shook her head. "You know those kinds of records are sealed. I don't know how my team managed to find out they even happened. His mother left when he was pretty young. It could have been teachers trying to make sure he was being cared for properly."

If his teachers were trying to make sure he was all right, then he must have been showing some pretty obvious signs of not being all right. No mother and—what kind of father sent his son to work in a slaughterhouse? She flinched at the possibilities, her heart curling in her in pity for a little boy, in awe of a grown man. Was there nothing he couldn't rise above, to become that big, rough, gentle man proffering her wild chocolates with a coaxing smile?

Damn it, how could she ask him to stick himself with a woman who couldn't rise above *anything*?

"I don't want to talk about him anymore," Jaime said abruptly, harshly. "We can talk about something else, or I'm leaving."

Cade sighed. Sylvain looked frustrated, biting his tongue.

But they talked about something else.

After dinner, Cade nestled against Sylvain on the couch, while Jaime curled against the lonely edge of an armchair, trying not to feel miserable. They didn't mean to rub her isolation in her face. But at that moment, she wanted nothing so much as to spend the rest of her life exactly like them: in Paris, in some simple, quiet apartment, curled up against . . .

She looked down at her hands. Feeling a wash of need that terrified her. Couldn't she stand on her own anymore?

The irony. She had spent so much of her life wanting *not* to be like Cade or their family. She had been the independent one, the one who was wild and free. And now she was just begging for a nice, safe cage.

Begging for it from a man who had never had a cage in his life, who had broken through every bar that held him.

"Dad's coming back in this weekend," Cade said suddenly. Their father had installed himself in Paris for the first month of Jaime's hospitalization, but then, when it was clear she was stable and mending, had had to start flying back and forth to Corey headquarters. "What do you think about having Dominique join us for dinner?"

"Isn't that a bit like dragging a gladiator into the emperor's arena? None of you have the right to give him your thumb up or down."

Cade raised her eyebrows and exchanged an incredulous look with Sylvain. "See, this is what I have to put up with. She honestly thinks that," Cade told her fiancé.

"My thumb's down," Sylvain said. "I have absolutely no need to see him again to make up my mind."

"Then you don't have to," Jaime said sharply. "Trust me, he won't be the first man I've dated whom I never introduced to the family."

"And he won't be the last?" Cade suggested.

"Oh, are you just using him as a healing process?" Sylvain brightened. "*That* would be fine."

Jaime pressed her lips so tight together, it was a wonder her rage didn't implode them. "You know what? Why don't we talk about you two instead of me? Like all Sylvain's defects. I never really got a chance to not welcome him to the family."

Sylvain grinned at her, entirely unfazed. "Go ahead, figure out a way to blame me for the fact that your sister broke into my *laboratoire* and stole from me."

Damn it, it was hard to insult a man when her first memory of him was the anxious, carved lines of his sculpted face softening into a smile as he offered her one of the best chocolates in the world to tempt her appetite awake after weeks of IVs. All while telling her stories in that low, elegant, melted chocolate voice of his: who he was, what he was doing there, how he had met her sister.

It had been one hell of a story, too, how he had met her sister. Jaime hadn't known Cade had it in her. "So how is it working out for you?" she asked him maliciously. "Having Cade as an 'apprentice.' "

Cade, who, like Jeanne d'Arc, could go boss around the King, the Pope, and probably multiple presidents while she was at it, and consider it all in a day's work.

Sylvain laughed. "It's not so much that she can't take direction, it's that she keeps trying to take charge of the business. And it's my business."

Cade pressed her lips together and shifted restlessly, and Jaime felt a tiny twinge of guilt for stirring up trouble. She did want her sister to be happy.

"Plus"—Sylvain slid a sidelong glance at his fiancée— "I think she's bored." Something he clearly didn't take as a compliment.

Jaime raised her eyebrows. Cade got to spend her days having a hottie like Sylvain Marquis lean over her and show her how to temper chocolate. It sounded like most women's idea of Happy Ever After.

"I'm not bored. I love it." A smile softened Cade's mouth. "It's like a dream come true."

Well, good. Her sister wasn't insane, then.

"But," Cade admitted, and Jaime felt a strong desire to strangle her. Cade had spent her entire life focused on run-

ning a major business. Couldn't she just enjoy her free-
dom?

Her brain hiccupped, trying to draw attention to an in-
consistency in her thinking. Something about enjoying
things without a guilt trip about what one wasn't doing instead . . .

". . . I love being around fine chocolate, I love being—
immersed in someone who's immersed in it."

Jaime blushed at that window into her sister's heart. But
Sylvain tilted his head toward Cade, sitting beside him on
the couch, and squeezed her shoulders. Cade wasn't really
talking to Jaime, was she?

"I love doing it. But maybe . . . doing it as a hobby. It's
true what Sylvain says that I keep trying to take over every
business I even notice and make it run ten times better. I
think the *fromager* is going to stop letting me buy cheese
there."

"You're giving him a permanent migraine. He doesn't
want to have a website and export his products to the
world," Sylvain said.

"At the same time, it's not as if I can be a Corey vice
president *part-time.* I don't know. I'm not sure what I
should be sinking my teeth into."

If she added, *Besides Sylvain, of course,* Jaime was going
to have to leave. But Cade spared her, being far too elegant to actually say such a thing, even if a tiny grin flitted
across her face that was worth a thousand words.

"I really like the idea of helping you get this Round
Table going, to be honest," Cade told her.

"I'm trying to walk *without* crutches, Cade."

A frustrated press of Cade's lips. "I worry about whether
I'm giving enough back to the world, too, Jamie. Especially now, when I'm living purely for my own pleasure."

Sylvain smirked at that *purely for my own pleasure.*

"I've been interested in this ever since you raised our awareness of the issues, and I do think it's time to take this beyond Corey Chocolate, to bring in a large consortium of chocolate producers and really stamp out the problem for once and for all."

Sylvain tried not to frown. "In Abidjan?"

"My vote's for Paris, but I believe Jaime thinks that a reluctance to put herself into an unstable political situation in a country where she just nearly got killed indicates weakness."

Sylvain drew supple, gorgeous eyebrows together. "You know, Jamie, just because you feel weak doesn't mean that every action you take *is* weak."

Cade smiled approvingly and snuggled a little closer to him on the couch.

Sylvain had the lousiest taste in armchairs, Jaime thought glumly. She might as well have been trying to snuggle up to a rock on Mars. Her sister and Sylvain looked so sure of each other. Cade might be restless and Sylvain might be balking at some of her efforts to take charge, but neither of these things threatened their relationship. Their love seemed to be a given, and everything else was just adjustments to make around that happy, immutable center.

Leaving the apartment, she struggled against need and loneliness. Cade had called her a taxi, but she paid off the driver at the edge of the Seine and got out, slowly crossing the bridge. Notre-Dame gleamed to her right, the Louvre down the river to her left, and far away the Eiffel Tower, glowing pristinely, emitted no sparkles at the moment. A group of men heckled her, trying to get her to sit with them, and her skin tightened in uncontrollable overreaction, her pace quick as they called after her, laughing and contemptuous both: *Miss, miss.*

Once she reached the Marais, people left her alone, same-sex couples mixed generously with the heterosexual ones on the sidewalks, beautifully or daringly dressed people strolling between bars and cafés along the seventeenth-century streets.

If she had had his number, she might have called him. If she had known where he lived, she might have shown up at his door, unable to spend a night apart. Hoping he didn't have someone else there, that he was glad to see her.

But she didn't know any of those things.

She recalled his brush-off of that brunette: *She's not going to call me later. She doesn't even have my number.*

She stopped at a bar and got hit on by a pretty blonde with curly hair, which she found infinitely easier to tolerate than being hit on by men in the street. She laughed and shook her head, and regretfully informed the blonde that she was traitorously dating a *man,* and was told with a wink that one night could change her mind. Finally, she couldn't draw out her single drink any longer or field the advances with any more deftness, and she had to go back to her dark, empty apartment.

She tried a couple of things, to be strong. She took a shower. She answered a voicemail from her father, talking for a while. She tried to open a book. And still, she found herself pulling her comforter over her head and sobbing into its darkness. Just sobbing and sobbing, because she was so lonely and so cold and for all those other reasons that cruelly struck her like a rain of fists.

CHAPTER 23

On Wednesdays, Dom usually had lunch with the wine-seller down the street, a friendly relationship that had developed despite Dom's lack of interest in the other man's products. Dom enjoyed it. He didn't have many people approximating friends, and the others were all kitchen friendships, people he had gotten to know working his way up, busy, ambitious workaholics like himself, with few windows for socializing.

This Wednesday, he was bad company, falling out of the conversation over and over without realizing it, his face growing grim. A whole day and night without seeing her except for that moment in the street made for a too-long stretch that uncurled fear in him, from that tight, hard knot where he always carried it.

When he walked into his shop after lunch and saw her sitting there, relief hit him so hard it left him shaky, and he had to practice breathing calmly as he walked over to her table.

After one quick glance up, she didn't look at him. Her hands closed tightly around her cup of chocolate, and she focused on it as if she was trying desperately not to do something. Her sweater sleeves had fallen back to expose the goose bumps on the lower part of her forearms.

He flipped a chair around to sit beside her and forced

himself not to pull her straight into his lap and wrap her up. Damn public places. Even his own. He laid his big hand over that goose bump–ridden forearm—one good thing about the size of his hand, he could wrap it around the whole exposed area of skin and have plenty left over to slide his fingers up under the sleeve and cover more. His fingertips brushed against the scar she liked to hide high on her forearm. Probably from a broken bone jutting through the skin. Oh, God, try not to think about it. He curled his hand around her head and kissed her. Too long, too intimately for the middle of his own *salon*.

All the tension drained off him. When her lips parted, the fear slunk back into its huddle in his middle.

The hand not caught under his hold slipped to clutch a fistful of his shirt. Again, he felt her fighting not to do something.

"It's all right," he whispered, pulling back enough to study her face. She looked like she was coming down with something: circles under her eyes, a hint of red around the rims. "Go ahead and do it."

Her hand flexed in his shirt. "Do what?"

"Whatever it is you're trying not to do. You can do it to me."

He had survived everything else, after all.

She shook her head, her mouth a bitter twist as she forced her gaze back to her chocolate. "You don't know what you're asking."

"Then why don't you tell me?"

Blue eyes locked with his in one moment of naked honesty. "If I could, I would crawl into you and never come out."

It shook his whole body, like the crash of a demolished building. He had to wait until the shock waves settled down. Then he stood, pulling her up with him.

"Guillemette." He managed to keep his blush down to

the barest hint of heat on his cheekbones. "Could you tell them upstairs I'll be out for a while?"

He took her to his apartment because it was closer. In the end, that decided him, and if it hadn't been what decided him with quite a few other women in the past, he would have felt much less like the *merde* he was when he brought her there, too. He saw her eyes flicker and her face close when she realized they had been standing just beneath it the other day and he had never told her.

She closed back into that steel center of hers where he could never reach.

But he could lure her out of it, into his hands.

He could.

"Crawl into me." He pushed his apartment door closed behind him, pulling her in against his body. "It's all right." He yanked his half-buttoned shirt and T-shirt over his head in one gesture, and wrapped her up, lifting her, his bare back against the door. "Go ahead."

"I love you," she said into his chest, and pure terror washed over him.

"Oh, God, don't say that." He carried her into his bedroom, pulling off her clothes as he went. "Don't—are you going to leave me?" He buried them under his comforter, wrenched her clothes off, pressed his mouth into the join of her shoulder, his hands too hard on her hips. "Please don't say that," he begged almost inaudibly against her skin.

She froze against him.

"No, don't. Don't freeze. I'll do anything, Jaime." He dragged his hands over her roughly, everywhere over her, trying to mark her as his so they could both remember it. Even if she was gone. "Tell me what's wrong. I can fix it."

He sounded so much like himself as a child, the first few times his mother had thought about leaving, it was horrible. Damn it, he had put that all behind him.

"I know," she said into his skin. "I know. You fix everything. Everything about me. I'm sorry. I'm sorry to say it. I didn't mean to. I just—" She shivered all over and tried to bury herself deeper into him, as if he was the only heat source in a blizzard. He could feel her lips press together against his skin, the way she folded them in, trying so hard not to say something; she couldn't even kiss him. "I can't get enough of you. I'm like some vampire, I'll suck you dry."

"No." He stroked her body urgently. "You said I was the sun, and you can't suck that dry. I promise I won't run out. I promise. You make me feel—" *like I can give out heat and love forever. And never, ever falter.*

He rolled onto his back, pulling her on top of him, so that his hands could move more freely, so that she could feel all the hard, big strength of his body, how her entire weight could lie on it and he could hold it easily. He knew the value of strength, that was one thing he knew very well.

It was to make himself unassailable. And now to make her unassailable, too. At last somebody *needed* his strength.

He had suddenly the clearest understanding he had ever had of the way his father had gone so wrong. A man's strength was supposed to be against the *outside* world: to fight it back from himself and those he took under his protection: his wife, his children, and for a man strong enough, more people still, people like his employees. To turn it *inward,* against the very people you had been given that strength to protect, because you couldn't deal with the outward fight, was the ultimate weakness.

I love you, she mouthed against his skin. Even he knew that much English. His body flicked as if at the impact of a fist. His hands tightened on her, but he said nothing. He didn't try to stop her again. He had told her he could take anything she wanted to do to him; he had to take this, too. *I love you.* Her lips brushed across him, telling his body a secret his mind wasn't supposed to know. This time it hurt less like a fist and more like the pressure of a massage, his muscles slowly relaxing to it, no longer flinching but soaking it up.

He raked a hand through that short hair of hers, nuzzling along her scar through the veil of her hair. She shook her head, trying to knock his mouth away. He kissed it anyway, firm, one last time, then let himself be shooed down over her face, her throat. He tricked her. Tracing over her shoulder and down her arm, kissing every centimeter of her scar there before she realized what he was doing.

"Stop it," she said in English, pushing at his chest. But he had tricked her there, too. She couldn't push him away, because he was the one underneath, pressed against the bed. She could get away herself, but she couldn't force him back no matter what she did. Let her push him. He liked the pressure of her hands against his muscles.

"Mmm." He let her know it. Caught her other hand and pressed it against his chest, too, let her know how much pushing he could take. "I like that. Even harder, if you want. I'm a little sore."

The heels of her palms ground in instantly, a sweet, intense ache in his overworked muscles, with the force of someone who had been on the receiving end of physical therapy. "Why?" she whispered.

He shrugged, and her hands rode over the muscles that rippled with the movement. "I work out too much when I . . . need to deal with things."

He had gone back to the gym, the night before, when he left her in the street because she had "other plans."

"What things?"

It would probably not be reassuring to her to know that she couldn't do something else for an evening without driving him to extremes. His hands found a scar he hadn't seen the day before. Neat and surgical, on her belly. They must have had to operate. Which could only have been because she had received so many blows to the belly that . . . "*Mon coeur.*" He squeezed her too tightly to him again, fighting the need to interrupt his lovemaking to go throw up. Sexy.

He rolled them over, putting himself between her and the rest of the world. "*Jaime,*" he whispered, combing her hair back, kissing her again. "I love *you,*" he whispered in the shadow of the comforter.

Her body jerked under his. Her eyes went very wide, staring up at him. He shrugged the comforter off them enough so that he could see their color. Fall forever blue. "You can't possibly," she protested. Why was her voice so afraid and so hungry, as if he was holding out something delicious to taunt a starving woman but was planning to snatch it away?

He shrugged. "That's what people once thought about me becoming *Meilleur Ouvrier de France.* That I couldn't possibly. But I did it, just the same."

A little spark of annoyance in her eyes. Jaime did humble the way a convalescing wounded fighter might take occasional naps. "Meaning that it's hard to love me?"

"It's horribly hard," he said, betrayed into honesty. "It's the most gut-wrenching thing I have ever done in my life, and that's saying a lot. But I'm going to do it, nevertheless." He kissed her, delving into her mouth, taking his time about it, proving to her that there was at least one aspect of loving her he knew exactly how to do.

When he lifted his head at last, she stared up at him, her lips parted but her eyebrows flexed, caught between softness and perplexity. "You can't mean it," she said finally. "How could you? It doesn't make sense."

Oh, he knew *that.* For him to crumble so completely and utterly at her feet, just from her sitting so quietly at his table, eating him bite by little bite? *He,* who had spent his entire adult life keeping women as far away from his heart as he possibly could? No, it probably didn't count as anyone's idea of normal.

"I'll make it make sense," he promised the tender space where the muscles of her shoulder stretched under pale freckled skin toward her breasts. "Just give me time." *Don't leave me.*

She tucked her arms up between them as if she wanted every last centimeter of herself to be in the shelter of his body. Who knew that having her under his protection could be so utterly arousing? "Why do you get to say it, if I'm not supposed to?" she challenged.

Because he didn't say it as if he was about to wrench himself away from her. He wanted to keep her safe from him—she must maintain her independence—but if he could manage that safety, he would never leave her. His worst, most sickening fear was that even if he couldn't manage to keep her safe, he probably wouldn't have the strength to leave her. That would be up to her. His father had clung desperately to his mother, despite his violence. "Because I mean it," he made the mistake of saying.

It was like watching half-melted chocolate get hit with water. That luscious warmth seized, catching her between pleasure and a terrible mess. "*You* mean it? What am I doing, joking? Or just too weak to know what I'm feeling?"

Merde, Dom. You, of all people, know that you can ruin the shiniest, most beautiful thing you ever saw with one careless drop of water. Don't screw up! "Have you ever said it to anyone else?" he asked, proving that no matter how great the treasure he held in his hands, some part of him could persist in destroying it.

Her eyebrows drew down. Yes, she had come here wanting to crawl into him, and what had he done with that? Managed to piss her off. "I had a boyfriend in college."

It should have been the triumph of his argument, but he

didn't want to win his argument. Jealousy curled in him, sick and thick, at the thought of anyone else tracing his fingers over those pixie-dusted cheekbones. Anyone else curling that body in under his protection. "Had," he forced himself to say. "You told him you loved him, but you aren't still with him."

Her eyes were ice-cold. "He had another girlfriend on the side. The one he was actually attracted to. You know what?" Her body jerked against his arms and for a moment he forgot and held her against her will. "Just let me go. I don't have to defend myself to you. I said it. You don't like it. But it's not an *insult*."

Shit. He lifted an arm enough so she could slide out from under him if she insisted, but he didn't roll away and make it easy. "Jaime." Her name flicked over her and held her, mid-slide, as if he had caught her with silk ribbons. "You said the same thing. You said I couldn't mean it."

She hesitated, arrested, her blue eyes catching his again.

"Why do you think that? That I can't mean it?" How clumsy was he at this? *Get some damn jewelry, Dom.* Although he couldn't imagine what kind of jewelry could convince a woman who had so much money people dated her for that rather than herself. It seemed as if she might want something she couldn't buy, instead.

Her body turned back toward the offered shelter of his, pupils dilating, mouth softening, as if he made her entire being fuzzy. Melted. He fought to control the surge of arousal at the thought.

"Because you're so beautiful," she whispered. Her hands lifted to stroke over his shoulders and arms, shaping the muscles. "You're so wonderful. How could you *possibly*—" She broke off. "For someone everyone thinks is so arrogant, sometimes you ask the *stupidest* questions. As if you have no idea how extraordinary you are."

He felt light-headed. He had to duck his head and start

pressing kisses to her skin almost the way someone might lower his head and breathe through a paper bag. "Can you tell me?" he whispered, hiding his boy's shamed, longing face between her breasts. "Could you give me an idea?"

She sank her fingers into his thick, overlong hair as if it was the most beautiful texture in the world. "Your hair is like *silk,*" she said, and he shivered as she petted it. "It's so black and it's so beautiful, and I love the silk here." Her fingers traced the edge of where his head pressed against her breast. "And the prickles here." Around the other side, the edge of his jaw against her tender skin. "The two of them together drive me *insane.*"

Oh, God. He twisted his head and bit suddenly into the side of her breast, a little too feral, a little too hard, the only thing he could do with the fierce arousal that swept through him. She shuddered and pressed her body up against him.

"And here." Her hands dragged down his shoulders and back. "Your back is *so smooth.* And just under that smoothness, all those muscles. You're so strong. I bet you've had more women dig their hands into those muscles than you can even count."

That was true. He shook his head against her breasts, shaking the memories away. He had worried about bringing her here, but all those sexual encounters didn't lurk nearly as close to ruining this moment as he had thought. She dominated his focus, pushing his sexual past so far away he could barely recall it. "I can count you," he whispered against the soft underside of her breast and licked up it to the nipple.

Her fingernails flexed into his skin. He liked that, that he could make her hurt him just a little, like a caress. He suckled harder, and her fingernails dug harder, and he laughed a little, triumphant and wild, against her skin.

"You're so *strong,*" she said enviously. "I love how

strong you are. But so gentle. You probably take care of kittens."

Not really, no. Vulnerability in others scared him. He matched himself against the strongest people he could find and kept as far away as possible from the others. His employees didn't count, right? It wasn't his fault they kept tucking themselves up under his wing. He might not care for kittens, but he didn't go kicking them into oncoming traffic, either.

Jaime's strange mix of strength and vulnerability terrified him, even while it drew him inexorably. He did want to take care of her, but she didn't remind him of a kitten in the least. She was a very strong person, and yet she had opened her shields and let him in where he could do untold damage. Wouldn't that be amazing, if he could deserve that estimation of his worth?

"You're so disciplined and determined, you don't let *anything* stop you."

Yes, it didn't bear thinking, the life he would have had if he let things stop him. He worked his way downward, teasing with rough jaw and teeth and mouth and tongue across her belly. All that time shaving himself raw, and she *liked* the prickles.

"You're so—I bet every woman you meet craves you."

He lifted his head enough to give her a crinkled, funny look. "It might be that you idealize me *un tout petit peu.*"

Not that he wanted her to realize how much, but he had some kind of conscience. After all, she had suffered a recent blow to the head. Every woman he met craved him, *putain.* He did tend to attract a lot of women who craved a good, hard fu—but anyway. He would bet it was not the kind of craving she was talking about.

"No, I don't." She sounded both surprised and slightly offended. "I don't idealize you at all."

Well, no one could say he hadn't tried. He didn't have

to hammer the point in. He returned to his path down over her belly.

"And I love—Dominique, what are you doing?" She wrapped her hands in his hair again, trying to drag him back up. "Don't—"

"Shhh. Shhh. *I* love to see you blush. God, your freckles go everywhere," he said giddily, nipping across her hip, the curve of bone and the way her body grew softer, so much more vulnerable, between the frame of those bones.

He grabbed a fistful of the comforter and ripped it entirely off them, shoving it onto the floor, so that the light from his window spilled over her, and it was the most beautiful thing he had ever seen. Her body against his white sheet, the fairy dust of freckles that was such a faint pale gold there where her skin rarely saw the sun, but which gilded her everywhere. She was growing less thin, he thought with triumph. Two weeks of his *salon* were filling her up, softening the ribs and wrist bones, while her Paris walking and gym workouts built back her strength.

Braced on his elbows, he lifted his head, centered there above her hips, and just gazed at her for a long time. And under his gaze, she blushed all over, slow, sweeping, ever darkening, a tide of color that made her freckles brighten from her head to her toes. She twisted uncomfortably, but he had outsmarted her: the curtains were open, the comforter now on the floor, and the full bright sun of a spring afternoon shone all over her.

"How could anyone *not* love you?" he asked, puzzled, and bent his head and licked her right up the seam of her sex, finding and tonguing her clitoris.

She yelped, and her hands yanked in his hair. "Domi—" She couldn't get his name out all the way, and she tried to knock him away with a twist of her hips.

"Shhh." He cupped his hands under her buttocks, holding her there, loving his ability to hold her there, tonguing her again. "You'll like it. Shhh. And I *love* to see you blush."

"No. Please, I don't—" She was crimson with embarrassment. As she moaned despite herself, she threw both arms up to hide her face. The scar stood out on the right forearm, a jagged white line against the freckles.

"Of course I won't do anything you don't want me to do," he said soothingly, blowing gently the length of her sex, watching the petals open helplessly to the stream of air. A faint, acutely victorious smile crinkled his eyes as he lingered just above the nub of her sex, letting the stream of air play over her, and her whole body shuddered in his hold. "Can you tell me what you don't want me to do, *minette*?"

"I—don't—" She bit into her own forearm as he rubbed his rough jaw against her, her hands flexing helplessly open and closed on empty air. "Domi—" She broke off with a moan again.

"*Vas-y, minette,*" he told her reassuringly, drawing his jaw over the tender inner skin of her thighs, just shy of her sex, ostensibly giving her time to collect herself. "What don't you want me to do? You can tell me. It's not this, is it?" He licked her again, taking his time. Her body shook, her thighs clenching around his shoulders, so that he had to let go of her bottom and force them apart with his hands. He pinned her to the bed with his forearms. "No, it couldn't be that. Was it this you didn't want?" Her hips kept trying to arch up, and he kept controlling them, so that the movement transferred to the rest of her body, her back arching, her arms locked over her face in pure desperation. "*Non, ça va aussi?* And this?"

She just moaned, her body shaking in sharp pants.

He laughed in uncontrollable joy and triumph. "*Minette,* you are so red. *Tiens, bébé.*" He pressed his mouth to her in earnest, and laughed out loud when she screamed as she came.

CHAPTER 24

Jaime climbed all over him afterward, dragging him into her, pulling him on top of her, taking each of his hard thrusts as if it was the deepest and most intimate of caresses. He was going to curdle her soul with embarrassment, but he felt so very, very good.

She liked even the way he laughed softly afterward, as if he was very, very happy, lying with her tucked into his shoulder, lazily stroking her back. She rather liked the fact that making love to her made him feel exultantly victorious.

She had forgotten to tell him how much she loved his hands. She drew the one that was stroking her up to her face and curved it around her cheek, so that she vanished in it, kissing it. And she must have fallen briefly asleep.

When she woke, it was at the slight tugs against her of Dominique's body, a brush of denim. He must have caught his jeans somehow with his toe without slipping out from under her, because they were now draped partly across his body, and he had the phone that had been in his pocket in one hand, texting. She blinked sleepily, focusing with increasing interest on the books that filled the whole wall beyond his hand, row after row, primarily of the discreet white *livres de poche* favored by Gallimard for its classics of great literature and poetry. She stirred, trying to make out the titles.

"Pardon," he said, when he saw he had woken her. "I was just letting them know I wouldn't be back in this afternoon."

He dropped the phone on top of a book on the nightstand and went back to stroking her gently, lost in thought. After a little while, he took her hand from his chest and kissed the palm and then tucked it back against him.

Could he really love her? How was it even possible? She wasn't beautiful, and her days of doing things more valuable than beauty seemed to be at a dead halt. All she had ever done was take from him, take everything he had to give.

He acted as if *that* was a reason to love her.

Something flickered in her brain, an instant of almost comprehension. But then it was gone.

"Can you do that?" she asked. "Just disappear for the afternoon?" She didn't want to be a detriment to his work on top of everything else.

"Not regularly, no. But I don't do it regularly."

So those other women, the ones he "didn't date," had to wait until after hours. She sighed a little, imagining him working his chocolate, knowing some gorgeous woman was waiting for him, and gazed at her still too-thin freckled arm lying across his perfectly sculpted chest, wondering what in the world it was doing there.

"Do you even like jewelry?" he asked suddenly, and she jumped.

"No."

His brows lifted at her vehemence. *"Une aversion?"*

"I don't like things in general, except sometimes when they're special, when people give them to me." She was thinking of the little treasures grandmothers might weave for her to say thank you, the miniature dugout canoe carved by a grateful father . . .

He held her eyes in a long, steady look. He didn't say anything.

She started to flush, delicately, her eyes widening. "I'm not—collecting souvenirs here."

"Souvenirs." Just like that, the bliss was gone. "Something you could pack up in your luggage when you leave?"

Her heart began to pound sickeningly. *I don't want to leave. I don't want to leave. Please don't let me leave you.*

"When your solar panels are fully charged, so to speak," Dominique said grimly. "What are you going to do? How long do you think it will take before you'll have to come back and charge up some more? Or do you seek out different suns each time?"

From the cuddling bliss of a few moments ago to this was a stark, spiraling plunge. Something ugly raged in his voice, trying to break free. *Don't leave me,* he had said, when she told him she loved him. *Oh, God, don't say that, don't leave me.*

She looked at the slim freckled arm that she thought had no force. And that was pretty scrawny and unattractive right now, to tell the truth. She tightened it around him, and he almost didn't breathe. What if the worst thing she could possibly do to him was get strong enough to leave him?

"I was—I was actually thinking about ways I might be able to continue to accomplish some good from Paris," she said carefully.

"Oh, fuck." He left the bed so fast, his watch left a long scratch on her back as he yanked his arm out from under her. He moved naked to the casement window, pressing one elbow into its frame above his head, staring out. His other arm was wrapped around his middle.

Jaime tried hard to breathe. Her eyes were stinging. *Think. Think. This doesn't make sense.*

"*You're* not married, are you?" she said suddenly. Why

would he beg her not to leave him and then react like that when she suggested she might stay?

He jerked. As if the question was the slap that kept someone from fainting. "What?" He shook himself, managed to turn his head enough to look at her. One corner of his mouth turned up reluctantly. "Have *you* ever dated anyone with morals and sense?"

Her own mouth curved with almost the same reluctance. "I take it I am now?"

"No." He dropped his arm and turned to face her, back pressed against the window frame now, both arms folded over his middle. "No. You're not."

The blow took her in the belly. *Don't be ridiculous, you know what belly blows feel like. If Cade hadn't found such an amazing surgeon, you would have lost your spleen to them.* "Not dating you?"

"Not dating someone with morals and sense. But I'm not married, no. *Merde,* Jaime."

It was true, she should never have had that moment of doubt. Cade would definitely have told her if he was married. As a statement of faith, mentioning her sister's investigative teams might lack something, though. "You asked *me.*"

He shook his head, that shaggy hair of his even wilder than usual after her hands had been all through it. "I was just trying to figure out how you were using me. I never said I was using you."

They stared at each other for a moment, in what seemed to be mutual terror of something. Dominique looked so big, so hard, so dangerous. What could scare him?

"I won't leave *you,*" he said suddenly, the words so hard they could have chopped through the air and split some great ancient oak stump. Even he could hear it resonate, echoing in the air between them while he drew a breath and stared at her.

Her brows crinkled. "That's—I've never heard anyone promise not to leave a woman like a warning before."

Dom said nothing for a moment, very grim. "I've never heard anyone promise not to leave me. So it may be I've got the tone wrong." He forced himself to hold her gaze. "You need to be aware of that, Jaime. I'm not going to be able to leave you, even if I should, so if you need to get away from me, you're going to have to do it yourself."

Liar that he was, Dom thought. He had intended a warning, he just hadn't been able to carry it through. *Please let me keep her.* How could he do anything but take the most precious care of her?

But God knew for a long time his father had acted like they were precious between bouts of violence, until he just started blaming them all the time so he could avoid the guilt. Dom wouldn't hurt her. He *knew* he wouldn't. He could be everything she needed him to be. But . . . he kept feeling he should warn her what she was dealing with.

Her brow grew deep furrows. "I don't want to leave you," she said carefully.

He lowered his head back against the window frame, light shining over his face. Not wanting to wasn't the same as promising not to.

Not at all.

He had thought he might faint a second ago, when she had started talking about staying with him. From the complete inability to believe it, the frantic, terrified longing for it to be true. He had wanted to claw at her, to hold onto her so tightly she couldn't rip herself away. She had *no* idea, this woman who had been hurt once, just once, no matter how badly, who had never been hurt by people who claimed to love her.

"But I don't want to leech on you," she said.

"Let me see if I follow." He spoke precisely, carefully. Not clawing. "You are extremely rich, and yet by the time

you were *sixteen,* you were spending your summers working with programs in developing countries. As soon as you
finished university, you devoted your career to reforming
labor practices in those countries. Three months ago, some
people"—his voice darkened—"beat the fucking crap out
of you, proving that the fact that you were helping people
did not make everyone love you. You spent two months
establishing a minimal physical recovery, and by that I
mean, where you only need to go to physical therapy once
a week and most people, looking at you, wouldn't know
you had been hurt. You seem to have given yourself *no*
tolerance whatsoever about how long it takes you to re-
cover emotionally. And you're already worried that you
haven't found a new focus, that you don't know what to
do, that you're *going to be a leech on me?* Have I summed
it up?"

She looked as if she didn't entirely appreciate his tone,
but . . . "I guess."

He laughed harshly. "I'm not nearly as worried about
you spending the rest of your life as a *leech* as you are,
Jaime. Let's put it that way. And even if you spent the
whole rest of your life sitting in my *salon* drinking chocolate . . . you don't leech off me. You don't—you've spent
your *whole life* trying to be the best person you can possibly be, and you make me feel like *I'm* the sun. You have *no*
idea what that does for me." He moved forward abruptly,
taking both her hands. "Jaime. I've never been so happy in
my entire life. I've never even thought about being this
happy. And every time you talk about being a leech and
how you have to find something better to do . . . I'm sure
there are plenty of better things to do with your life than
make me feel like the sun. But you don't need to keep
telling me about them. Just, please, shut the hell up."

CHAPTER 25

"You know, to keep her," Pierre said, "you might at least have to believe it's possible to keep her."

Wonderful. In the five years since he had last seen him regularly, his therapist had turned into Peter Pan. Just believe you can fly and add some pixie dust.

A whimsical thought flashed through his brain, an image of pixie dust freckles spilled like gold flecks across pale skin.

"How long have you known her?"

"Three weeks." It wasn't entirely a lie. You could learn a lot about a woman, watching the way she absorbed your chocolate. "We've been going out for one," he admitted, after a moment, since there wasn't any point forcing himself through this therapy session if he wasn't going to tell the truth about at least some things. It was like going to the gym and lifting an empty bar.

"And you want to change your life for her?"

He had started changing the instant he saw her. He tried to maintain a neutral expression.

"That's . . . sweet," Pierre said, half-charmed and mostly wary, the way any intelligent psychologist would be.

It wasn't sweet, it was completely selfish. It was the way to get what he wanted.

Pierre sighed. "I really wish I could meet her to know

whether I'm giving you good advice. It would be terrible if she was just us—"

He broke off but not before Dom caught the idea. *Just using you.*

"She is," he said firmly. "We've got that figured out. It turns out I really like it, being used the way she does it." He just didn't want his use to wear out. On the other hand, it seemed a terrible thing, to wish a woman would stay weak and in need of his strength so he could keep her. Why else did he *have* so much strength, though, if it wasn't so he could cover her with it, too? Surely it could go to some better purpose than just protecting himself? "She thinks I'm wonderful," he admitted finally, trying to say it as offhandedly as he could. He wasn't going to put the whole *sun* business out there where someone else could mock it. It was too fragile and too precious. His breathing was short enough as it was.

Pierre's gaze was so gentle it pissed him off immediately. He did *not* need the man's compassion. Maybe his smelling salts, if he fainted from his attempts to talk about this thing with Jaime, but *not* his pity. "And you're afraid she'll learn the truth and leave you?"

Dom shook his head, ignoring the sick feeling in the pit of his stomach. It had been about ten years since he had had to ignore sick feelings in his stomach quite so diligently, but he still had the way of it. "That's what I'm paying you for, Pierre. So you can teach me how to be perfect in these deep relationships you were always pushing before. You had better know something about them, considering how adamant you were I needed one."

"Do you think you're so sure she'll leave because your mother did?" Pierre suggested.

Dom barely avoided growling at him. "I told you. I don't want to be analyzed. I just want techniques."

"Techniques for making her think you're perfect, entirely secure."

Dom gave him an approving nod. Finally they were getting somewhere.

Pierre raised those *putain de sourcils* of his. "Let me see if I understand. Your real purpose in coming here is to learn how to pretend you are absolutely perfect—"

"Not pretend," Dom said hurriedly. He had always thought his father must have pretended. Why else had his mother ended up with him?

"Is to learn how to *be* absolutely perfect, the ideal man for a long-term relationship."

Dom smiled. "Exactly."

Pierre folded *his* arms and shook his head firmly. "It's hopeless. You'll have a much better chance if you'll be your real self."

Being himself was ridiculous advice, but pretending to be perfect was working pretty well for him. Despite his own therapist's refusal to help. If only he could get over the guilt at selling her fool's gold instead of the real thing.

Even he could be perfect on the first of May, with Jaime beside him. It was a soft day, balmy and gentle, with clouds that hinted at rain but never quite delivered. The fresh lemon scent of lilies-of-the-valley was everywhere, as vendors wandered the streets or stationed themselves at prominent corners with buckets full of them, culled from the woods outside of Paris. Florists sold more formally acquired bunches of the *muguets,* in pots or bouquets, the little white bells dangling sweetly everywhere they looked.

Dom had bought Jaime several bouquets already, after surviving having his heart broken into tiny pieces by the bouquet that she had snuck into the bathroom while he was showering. No one ever, in his whole life, had given him a little bouquet of lilies-of-the-valley on May 1 to wish him fortune and happiness.

"*Ça porte bonheur, oui?*" she had asked shyly.

And it did bring happiness. Oh, it did.

It was amazing how much sweeter the *muguets* on every street corner smelled when someone had given some to you, too. It made his whole heart feel lighter, soaring almost like that *Victoire de Samothrace,* to have her beside him, wishing him happiness. He kept yielding to the impulse to buy just one more simple cluster of the flowers for her, until after the third one he realized the impracticality of trying to bury her in happiness right there in the street. It made for a lot of flowers to carry on a stroll.

So she laughed up at him, her eyes sparkling, and gave one of the bouquets to an old woman sitting quiet and still on a bench, watching the world move by, and another to a scowling teenager who looked considerably startled, her mouth relaxing. One she kept for herself. Dominique resolved to buy her as many as he could carry on the way back to her apartment that afternoon and fill the entire place with them.

They ended up on the end of the Île de la Cité, Notre-Dame's island, descending from the centuries-old Pont Neuf to the lower quay, where tourists gathered to climb onto the *Vedettes* boats that would bear them up and down the Seine. Dom and Jaime headed up the paving stones of the quay to the tip of the island, far away from the milling flock of boaters, sitting with their backs to the stone wall of the garden that rose just behind them. Other couples sat at intervals along the quay, rivals for one of this city's most romantic spots.

Dom sat with one leg drawn up, greasy-headed sparrows and pigeons coming up to inspect them, hoping for food. He twitched one toe and waved the bouquet he had ended up carrying to discourage them, but like him, they weren't that easy to discourage.

Jaime was playing with his other hand. Her weight resting against his side, she used both her hands to do it, pressing palm against palm, linking and unlinking fingers, using her other hand to stroke over the back of his, to trace his scarred knuckles as if they were some fascinating formation, to draw her fingertips down the length of one of his thick, blunt fingers, taking her time, lingering and rubbing over the calluses.

He slid a wary glance at her but couldn't see much more than the top of her head. She seemed utterly absorbed in her task, a little dreamy at it, no purpose to her explorations but pleasure.

His heart didn't know whether to bask in the treatment or curl into a nervous ball. Surely at some point, some shadow of reality would cast itself over even her dreamy golden state, and she would think about what his hands meant.

She tried to close her hands entirely over his, which was completely futile. Even if he closed his hand into a fist, she wouldn't be able to encase it in both of hers, and he didn't want her to see his hand fisted. He stared down at her slim, freckled hand, the way her fingertips ended at his middle knuckle, the sight of his darker skin with the little nicks and scars visible all around hers like an ugly spot no slender, beautiful work of art could ever hide.

"I love your hands," she murmured.

For a moment, he froze. Then, contrarily, he felt as if his entire being was dependent for support on some ice structure that was suddenly melting. "You *what?*"

She flushed a little, the part of her face he could see. Her hands tightened on his, as if someone had tried to wrench it away from her. "You—have no idea. I just . . . I really love them." Her flush darkened a vulnerable crimson. Her hands caressed a little over his and tightened again, as if she couldn't help it.

He stared at their hands together, tried and completely failed to see his as something she could love. "*How* much of those witches' potions did you drink?"

"What?"

"La Maison des Sorcières. You said you drank some of Magalie's chocolate before you met me?"

He tried not to believe Magalie and her aunts could do actual magic, but he couldn't figure out any other explanation. It was like one of those Shakespeare plays he had read in translation last winter, the one where the Fairy Queen was drugged to fall in love with a rude laborer with the head of an ass.

He hated thinking of himself as the ass-headed laborer after he had beaten his way to the top and defied anyone to take him on any other terms than as the best, but . . . she did that to him. The fact that she held in her hands the ability to render him extraordinary or render him nothing was the most terrifying thing about her.

She laughed a little, not taking him seriously. "Oh, no, it was well after I met you. I drank *your* chocolate before I met you. If you want to blame my feelings on a potion, I think that's a far more likely culprit."

He relaxed. Whatever else he might or might not manage, he could always make good chocolate. Forever.

So she rested against his side, cuddling his hand as if it were her special treasure, and he squinted at the light reflecting off the small waves made by a *pompiers* boat, feeling mushy, but trying to appear at least strong enough to scare off the pigeons. He might very well associate the scent of *muguets,* for the rest of his life, with pure, terrified happiness.

"What's an abattoir like here?" she asked.

His hand jerked and spasmed so hard on hers that her

knuckles ground in his grasp and she protested. His big, damned butcher's hand. He let her go. "Who the hell told you about that?"

She hesitated.

"Sylvain," he said bitterly. The stems of the *muguets* crushed in his fist. The damn gossiping kitchen teams. Of course someone on his who had found out about it would have let it slip to someone on Sylvain's. *Bordel de cul,* Sylvain and her gossiping about him, talking over all the ugliest details Sylvain could find about his *life—*

"Is it a secret?" she asked, surprised.

He stiffened. "No." His voice sounded harsh even to his own ears. He had known all his efforts to be gentle with her would eventually fail him. "Why should it be?"*And he had thought he could be perfect. Just for a minute there, he had thought he could be perfect.*

"I don't know," she said slowly, pulling away from her resting place against him to watch his face carefully. Damn it, he didn't want her watching him as if he was a wild animal that might bite. "I can't think of any reason. Unless you just don't like talking about it, in which case I'm sorry."

"Don't apologize to me," he said shortly. Because he was a bastard with a short temper, she should try to soothe him? Like what, before he lashed out at her? "Don't ever apologize to me."

Her eyebrows drew together. She regarded him very straightly with those dusk-blue eyes of hers. "I'll do what I want."

A few of his muscles relaxed, the way they always did when she wouldn't take his shit. He even smiled at her just a little.

"Why did your father send you there?" she asked. "Did he need the money? Did you have trouble in school?"

He had loved school. He had been a passionate reader

and, in any case, would have done anything to make his teachers look at him with approval. He had done extremely well at school, despite his home life, until his mother left, and then . . . he supposed some part of him had hoped the teachers whose pet he had been would hear the cry for help. Instead they had shrugged, mentally dropping him down among the *nuls,* and turned their attention to a new pet, which . . . life lesson learned.

"You have the wrong information. My father didn't send me to work there. *I* went. I got the job. He had to approve it"—to agree that his only son was a total waste and not worth more—"but I got it. And I did it damn well. It gave me a really good excuse to hack at things, at meat and blood and bone."

She stared at him. He couldn't stand the expression on her face.

"It didn't hurt them," he said quickly. "They were already dead. That's why it was so perfect."

"Perfect."

He set his mouth grimly, all his muscles bunched as tight as they could, and that was pretty tight. He waited for her to pity him and tried to brace himself to bear it, not to fight her off like a raging, wounded bull.

She unfolded one of his hands again, pushing against the involuntary resistance of his tightened muscles. He forced them to yield. He always let her do whatever she wanted to him. She tucked her little fist inside his, and then folded his own around it, until his hand engulfed hers, all the freckles consumed by the big, scarred hand. All you could see was something big, and brutal, falsely softened by cocoa butter, but all the scars still there.

"That's what I call perfect," she said, and rested her head against his shoulder again. Under her cheek, his heart gave a big thump like a white wishing fish leaping out of the water. "You are the most amazing person I have ever met.

I should probably be the one giving you the warning: I won't leave *you*. I'm still figuring out how to be strong again, but I've made up my mind about one thing: if you're not willing to leave me, I'm more than happy to return the favor."

CHAPTER 26

om saw the old man waiting for him in the dark, silent street, a huge bag in one hand, before he even got to the door. "Not you again," he said in exasperation. He very definitely needed some time on his own right now, just him, his *salon,* and his chocolate. The things he could count on. This tendency of his heart to start believing that Jaime might actually not leave him was scaring the hell out of him. God, her body tucked so trustingly against his on the quay . . .

"Missed you the other day." James Corey sounded very put out about it, too. "You get to take off work often that way? To spend the afternoon carousing?"

Dom raised his eyebrows at the old man's ire. "Been a while since you spent the afternoon carousing?"

The old billionaire muttered something angrily under his breath.

Dom just glared back at him. "It's five thirty in the morning. Do you think I got up early so I could enjoy someone else's company?" He wanted to work on his sculpture. He could almost believe in it, this morning. Almost not flinch in fear as its form revealed itself under his hands. The Chocolatiers' Expo was that weekend; he couldn't keep putting it off forever, until he could actually believe in himself. He never would have gotten anywhere, if he did that.

"If you already get up this early at your age, just see how much you can sleep when you're mine," James Corey told him. "And this way, I don't run into anyone I don't want to."

"*I* do," Dom said indignantly.

"Yes, well, I have a feeling one of your customers might be even ruder to me than you are."

He had some snobby customers, all right, but he was pretty sure the old man was more than a match for them. Rolling his eyes, he let James Corey follow him inside, primarily because he felt uncomfortable leaving an old man on a dark, empty street to be mugged. He locked the door behind them and flicked on the staircase light, because he loved that, coming into work with the shop all dark, only that spiral staircase gleaming like Joseph's Ladder into heaven.

"I have to say, you have a really nice spot here," the old man allowed.

Dom sighed. He loved being the first person to walk up that glowing staircase in the morning, no one else in the world but him. But . . . old man . . . all that. He sighed a second time, extra heavily to make sure it was audible, and gestured for James Corey to precede him. "But don't come back in the morning again. *Putain,* for this, I should have stayed in bed." His arm over Jaime, her fingers curling sleep-loose to hold that arm to her. Promising not to leave him, until he wanted just for a while to forget his fear, to sink into her and believe her.

"We're still negotiating that spinach deal," James Corey said.

"Oh, am I supposed to be bargaining you up from the twenty million?"

The old man snorted. "I admit, I had some ulterior motives with the twenty-million offer. But seriously, for you to create me a chocolate spinach bar, what would it cost?"

"I think you misunderstood. It's *Sylvain's* name I want to see plastered all over some cheap bar in the supermarket."

"Listen, our bars are good enough for *my* name to be on them," the old man said dangerously.

Dom shrugged. "Everyone has his standards."

"You're just so convinced you're too good for the Coreys, aren't you?"

Dom laughed involuntarily. "Just my chocolate."

James Corey gave him one of those sharp glances of his. "Oh, really? Don't have too high an opinion of *yourself*?"

"Why don't we say twenty-five million? Is that a high enough opinion of myself for you?"

"Selling yourself?"

Dom groaned. "Can I call you a taxi or something? I was really looking forward to coming to work today." Well, he had been at first. Striding through the pre-dawn empty streets, the scent of Jaime still on him, ready to turn that block of chocolate into something so beautiful, so perfect. The closer he got to facing that statue, the more fear had stolen into him, the way it did when he caught himself believing Jaime might not leave him. It was like facing a very big gorge and trying to walk across it on a bridge made out of one very thin piece of paper.

"I brought you some spinach." The old man set the huge bag down on the counter, right at the base of that half-formed chocolate sculpture, as if the damn green leaves were naturally more important.

Dom grinned wryly. He had to like someone who was that annoying. And, well, it was easier than facing his fears. He yanked up the bag of spinach with a great show of impatience and stomped back to his *cuisine.* "Did you bring a contract that spells out the payment schedule and that you can't use my name?"

"Why don't we talk more about the payment later?"

"Ouais," he said dryly. "That's what I thought would happen to that twenty-five million." He poured some cream into a pot and picked through the spinach leaves, tossing in only the freshest. Then he went back into the other room and considered his range of Valrhona for a moment and finally selected a blend of Trinitarios and Criollo, a 72 percent with a powerfully bitter base. "This ought to do it."

He slammed the bag a few good hard knocks against the edge of a counter, breaking the block inside into smaller chunks, then emptied it into a great metal bowl, while the cream infused. He hadn't bothered to turn on a light in the *cuisine,* so that the illumination came only from the stairwell end of the main room of the *laboratoire.* As the old man hovered over him in the dark, they could have been two alchemists concocting the elixir of life. "There." Feeling that the cream had infused with about as much of the bland green flavor as he could take, he sieved the leaves out, pouring the not-quite-boiling now-green cream over the chocolate.

James Corey gaped at him as he dropped the dirty sieve full of leaves into the nearest sink and started stirring the chocolate-cream. "Wh—you threw out the spinach! That's not nutritious!"

Dom stopped stirring. *"Nutritious?"*

"Yes! You know, something moms can feel proud to feed to their kids."

"American moms can feel proud to feed spinach-chocolate bars to their kids? Are you sure that even your country is that crazy?"

The old man folded his arms, outraged. "D-day mean anything to you?"

What? "Were you there?" he asked, his tone shifting into respect despite himself.

"Two years too young," James Corey said reluctantly. "And my dad had had polio, so he couldn't join up, either. But we *did* make the ration bars. Chocolate base, but as packed full of nutrition as we could get them."

Dom gaped at him, for a moment too outraged even to speak. "You are trying to get me to imitate *World War Two ration bars*?"

"Better," the old man said stubbornly. "I want something gourmet."

"Oh, go away," Dom said in complete disgust. Waste of a whole pack of chocolate, some good cream, and his nice, quiet morning by himself working with his sculpture in the dark. Which was the only way he could really work on her anymore. He was afraid if he stood up there carving on her with the lights on, somebody—the block of chocolate maybe—might see too much of his soul. "You know, I could have slept in with my girlfriend this morning, if I had known you were going to be stalking me."

There. He had said the word again. And he was going to keep saying it, *girlfriend,* until he stopped feeling as if he had accidentally thrown himself off a cliff.

James Corey pressed his lips together tightly. "I really don't think you need to describe your sleeping arrangements to me. That's rude, even for you."

"Thanks. She's really cute, too, have I mentioned?"

James Corey gritted his teeth and muttered something under his breath about "granddaughters" and "these damned Parisians."

A flicker of a memory went through Dom's brain. His team gossiping about the delay in Cade and Sylvain's wedding. "How's your other granddaughter, by the way?"

James Corey stiffened, gazing at him with oddly bright eyes.

"I heard she was in the hosp—" Dom stopped. And stared into those familiar blue eyes.

For a moment, no one said anything, Dominique grow-ing whiter and whiter and James Corey smugger and smugger, as if he had been caught red-handed and that was exactly his favorite way to be caught.

Without a word, feeling as if he was walking through solid ice, Dom turned and strode into his office. It took him a second to boot up his computer. But the image re-sults for *Jaime Corey* came back instantly. There she was with an Ivorian man in a T-shirt, standing in front of a blackboard nailed to two posts stuck in the ground, a thatched roof offering it shelter from the sun. The man had one arm slung around her much smaller shoulders and was grinning for the camera. Her hair was long, caught up in a ponytail from which red-caramel wisps were escaping around her fuller, younger face, her nose shiny from the heat and humidity. She wore a huge hat and a tunic of thin, long-sleeved brightly patterned cotton, to protect that fair freckled skin. She looked so confident, so sure of herself, as if nothing in the world could touch her.

There she was—*putain,* a body on a stretcher sur-rounded by emergency professionals, being shifted into a helicopter. Then another with a forced smile for the camera, her face so very thin and two-months-in-the-hospital pale, her hair barely an inch long. That must have been just before she started showing up in his *salon.*

There was no chronological order to the search results. There was one of a very young boy carrying on his head a huge burlap bag that looked as if it must weigh far more than he did. Beside him was another figure, fallen to one knee under a similar huge sack, her head twisted under it awkwardly, a tangled ponytail forced across her face by the burlap. *Putain,* he had even seen that one before, it had been all over the media at the time.

There was another one, the same boy a few years older. It was hard to tell who was prouder, him or Jaime, as he stood beside her with a diploma in his hands. He was looking very serious; Jaime looked as if she had been caught crying.

Jaime Corey.

She had told him she was wealthy.

She had told him she worked with labor practices and against exploitation of children.

And now it was suddenly—all true. He could *see* it.

See that when she made a choice between leaving him or not, who he was asking her to abandon. The child in him uncurled sulkily from its fetal position, wanting to tell that boy in the photo to buzz off. That he needed her, too.

As if he needed any more proof of what a bastard he was.

As if she had ever had any real intention of giving herself to him.

Corey. That was no minor last name to not mention. He didn't know it because she hadn't wanted him to know it. She had wanted to keep part of herself separate. Safe.

He supposed he was lucky she had told him her real first name.

"She never liked to be a parasite, our Jamie," her *fucking namesake* said from the door behind him. "She always had a thing about it, even when she was very young. Stupid school. Some left wing professor got hold of her, and we never got her back."

"Get out." Dom spoke flat, low. "Get out of my place."

The billionaire shrugged at the order. "Has she told you about the dinner invitation yet?"

"Get the hell out."

"Tonight. Her dad's flying in, too. That would be Mack Corey, current president of Corey Chocolate."

"He can go fuck himself, too."

"I'll pass on the message. Meanwhile, it's a real family get-together. And we would like you as our guest of honor."

CHAPTER 27

Something was wrong with Dominique, Jaime thought. He had barely spoken to her when she came in after her gym workout that morning, his lips a flat, hard, non-responsive line when she kissed him. A bitter fury seemed to simmer in him, like that first time she had seen him, staring at her across Philippe Lyonnais's *salon*. Like, and yet far, far worse. He was riding it hard, that fury. He was not letting it buck him off. But he wasn't letting it go, either. She couldn't get near him.

She stood beneath the great chocolate sculpture. Carving tools lay all around the counter at its base, as well as chocolate shavings, some of which had melted in Dominique's hair. Her lips curled. He was so big, so hard, he made her feel so safe, and yet sometimes, there were those little moments, when she wanted to squeeze him to her like a little boy. Her hand had started to lift toward him, still out of sight behind the counter he kept between them as he worked on the sculpture's hem, when he lifted his gaze and speared her with it across the folds of chocolate, black and hard.

Her hand dropped. She rocked back a step, taking a careful breath. "Is this—that question about leaving you again?" It was the closest thing they had had to a fight in the past two days.

His mouth hardened still further. "I guess so."

"Would it—" She drew a breath. It was kind of hard to ask a man if he would be willing to marry you when he was acting so hostile. The idea had come to her while she was struggling to lift far too much weight in the gym. It was a strange idea, maybe. They had known each other so short a time, and yet she felt she knew everything she needed to know about him. Maybe she had known all she needed to know before she even met him, from his rosebuds and rough stone and the taste of his wild, dark, passionate soul on her tongue. But certainly she knew now, his strength and his hunger, and the way he held her hand as if he would lose an arm before he would lose his grip on it.

She had spent so much time basking in his warmth and strength, not realizing he was getting so much he needed back from her. She'd been turned in on herself, healing, taking. Not *thinking,* because he seemed so willing to be used by her. He was so hungry to keep giving more.

She still didn't quite understand what he was getting from her. But he was getting *something.* Something he was desperate not to lose.

She thought of that ten-year-old boy realizing his mother was gone. That it was just him, and the father who would send him to work in a slaughterhouse two years later.

And thought that no matter how premature it was, maybe the ability to count on long-term was the very thing they needed. And that maybe *her* asking *him* would heal about five thousand wounds in his soul. And him saying yes would wipe her fresh and new and whole again, a slate ready for a brand-new day.

Maybe she would only work at the organizational level, work from Paris. Cade claimed she could end up doing even more good that way. Maybe Jaime couldn't get herself back in the field again. She didn't know yet. She had assumed that growing strong meant leaving Dominique.

But . . . there, in the gym, she had kept seeing Sylvain and Cade cuddled together on the couch, an image that seemed to flash across her retina with every single press up from that bench, Atlas lifting the world. When the two got engaged, they had thought they had it figured out—Cade would give up her life and choose Sylvain's. Now they weren't sure that would always work. But they were sure *they* would work, whatever they did about their professional lives.

She watched Dominique chisel with grim care, as if, no matter how badly he wanted to hack the hell out of something, he was going to *force* this statue to be beautiful.

Maybe if she could get him to *smile* at her again, she could do something. Dominique *always* smiled at her. From the very first time he had introduced himself, when he saw her, his eyes warmed like sunlight on that deep, dark water.

She stroked an uneasy finger across the counter, picking up chiseled fragments of chocolate on it, and nibbled them.

His eyes flickered to that movement. Maybe for a second his mouth almost thought about softening.

Suddenly he set his chisel down and leaned all the way across the counter, his hands gripping the edge closest to her. He leaned in close, his eyes glittering bleakly, his private whisper cutting like glass: "You had no right."

She flinched, not even knowing what she had no right to do.

"To sit there and eat my chocolate like you couldn't get enough of me," he whispered fiercely. "I *love* you. And you *always* meant to leave." His hands gripped the edge of the counter so tightly, if it hadn't been marble, it would have broken. *That was why he was gripping it, and not her,* she realized.

She slipped her arms between his, sliding them forward through his chocolate shavings until their faces were only inches apart. "I never thought you would want me to stay. Not at first. You're so much bigger than I am. In every way."

He shook his head, their faces so close his lips almost brushed hers with the movement. Except he looked feral enough to bite her, if they did. "I've never understood it when you say that. I've told you already, you idealize me more than you should, Jaime."

"No. I don't idealize you at all," she repeated.

He released the edge of the marble, with a hard glance around. But any possible audience had already crowded into the other rooms, stretching indefinitely their "need" to find something elsewhere. The enrobing machines, abandoned, let chocolate cascade over nothing, an endless empty fall. "Come into my office," he said abruptly.

Dominique's office was—minute. It was impossible to get the door closed without brushing against each other, and even once it was closed, with him leaning back against his desk, it was only possible to keep about a foot between them. *"He would have been happy to have sex with me in his office,"* Jaime remembered Cade saying, with a sudden, white rage. *"How* many women have you made love to in here?" she asked.

Dominique winced, closed his hands around the edge of his desk, and tilted his head back. For a second he looked—shamed, defeated. Then his face hardened with determination again.

She put her hand on his arm. She could never resist laying claim to that strength. And she wanted him to know he didn't feel dirty to her touch.

He gave her hand a bitter, wary look, as if she had pulled out a whip and he was braced for the beating.

Jaime frowned, searching his face. She stroked her hand slowly down his arm, over the tough texture of the chef's jacket until she came to his skin and could curl her fingers partway around his thick wrist and slide over the back of his hand.

Her mat of freckles against all those tiny scars over his knuckles. Her eyebrows crinkled together. She had worked with teenagers who had been abandoned by their parents or sold into slavery by someone they trusted, who had been beaten and exploited, who had grown into manhood doing brutal, hard work. But she had worked with them— more distantly, in group situations. Solving the problem, not trying to live with them one on one. Still, if she could *quit being so weak and self-absorbed* . . . she might realize that Dominique Richard—rough, gentle, wild, beautiful, overachieving Dominique Richard—had issues.

A lot of issues.

One of the reasons he loved her might be . . . how much she loved him. One of the reasons he might be terrified of her was . . . he was afraid to count on that love.

She studied his tense face again. His hand lay taut under hers as if he both wanted to yank it away and couldn't bear to.

"I don't suppose you would be interested in indulging me in a little fantasy, would you?" she asked.

His face hardened even further. "I'm not having sex with you in this office. Not ever."

Damn it, how many women *had* he screwed in this office?

"That's not the fantasy I had in mind. This one would be after dark, when everyone is gone."

His hand jerked under hers. "No. I'm not your fantasy."

Her eyebrows rose a little. "I think most men *like* being a woman's fantasy."

"Well, *I don't*."

She frowned at him and tried to think of another approach. "So I'm not your groupie?"

His eyebrows flexed. "What the hell are you even talking about?"

"Why don't you ever stay the night with me? Only *one* time, since we started dating, have you stayed until I woke up. It's confusing, the way you're always gone in the morning."

"I've always stayed the whole night," he said, startled. "I leave for work." Still pressed back against his desk, he stared at her. "You didn't know that?"

She shook her head.

"So when you wake up and I'm not there, you've been thinking—what?"

"That it's understandable you would need space. That I need to let you breathe."

There was a silence. "No," was all he said, the word packed tight with meaning. "No. I—breathe better when you're right here."

With a little sigh, she stepped forward and sank into him, letting all her tension leave her. Her face rubbed against the chef's jacket, wishing it gone.

One of his hands unlocked from the edge of the desk, flexing to restore circulation. He brought it warily to press between her shoulder blades. "And you? Do you need space to breathe?"

He smelled of rich deep chocolate and something green underneath it, some experiment perhaps. "I breathe better here, too," she said quite honestly. She drew a breath. "I have an unusual question for you."

"Me, too."

She hesitated. Maybe he was going to ask the same thing? Did she want him to? Her heart squeezed quite tightly at the possibility that he might be thinking along the same lines. "Go ahead," she whispered.

"What's your last name?"

CHAPTER 28

Jaime seethed when she found out what had happened. Dom found it vastly reassuring. She snapped at him for jumping to negative conclusions; she growled about her interfering family. It was all so stable. Safe. Apparently you could annoy the people you loved without provoking a wild rage or driving them away. It was just something that happened sometimes. "What's wrong with you, anyway?" she snapped.

A list of the first dozen or so major things wrong with him flashed through his mind, but he snuck a glance and saw with relief that this was a rhetorical question.

"Couldn't you have just told me my grandfather was being an interfering old—was doing his usual thing? Instead of brooding and imagining things. I don't see why my last name has to make such a big difference." She set her mouth in the closest thing to a sulk he had ever seen her manage, as they approached the elegant old building on the edge of the Jardins du Luxembourg. Sacks loaded the arm he didn't have around her. Jaime had been to the Belleville market while he was working.

"Because it's not the kind of last name you forget to mention, that's why. You didn't want me to know it."

"Dominique. How long have we known each other?"

"A month."

She looked confused.

"Two weeks," he corrected himself reluctantly. Didn't she realize that those two weeks she'd sat in his *salon* counted as knowing him? "In another three days."

His attempts to grab onto long-term were so pathetic.

"And you made it clear what you thought of the Coreys and Sylvain. I wasn't exactly dying to let you know I was one of them."

Dominique stopped dead. "Sylvain. Oh, *putain,* he's going to be my brother-in-law."

Jaime stubbed her toe on the edge of the sidewalk. He held onto her as she hopped, cursing, and only when she finally put her foot back down and gazed up at him with wide eyes did he realize what a presumptuous thing he had just said. He flushed. "In a manner of speaking."

Jaime flushed, too, and looked away. "You're invited to the wedding, by the way," she mentioned as he opened the apartment building door for her. They stepped into rich elegance, red velvet carpet going up the sweeping stairs, a gold-framed glass-doored elevator waiting beside them, a well-dressed security guard nodding a respectful, *Bonsoir, Mademoiselle Corey, Monsieur.*

Just in case he needed any clearer sign that in going to this dinner, he was going to war. Alien territory, filled with hostiles. He was already getting hungry for their blood.

"I'm going to Sylvain Marquis's wedding," he repeated, with flat horror. *Sylvain Marquis, putain.* He tried to keep his voice neutral. "When is it?"

"In June."

June. He forced his lungs to keep working properly when they seemed to have swollen up like big yellow balloons. *June.* That was another month away. *One more month, at least.*

Yes, it was official. His attempts to believe in long-term

were pathetic. No matter what Jaime said about not leaving, he was almost grateful to have to go to Sylvain's damn wedding just because it guaranteed another month.

They stepped into the elegant glass–and–gold elevator, a disappointment as Parisian elevators went. The first time he was in an elevator with her, and it turned out to be a spacious one that left them in public view the whole time. Just another unexpected drawback of dating someone with more money than God.

He frowned suddenly. "What the hell was Sylvain doing making chocolates just for you? That's incestuous, even for him."

"Making chocolates for someone isn't always sexual!" Jaime snapped.

He raised his eyebrows. There might not be anything sexual about a huge Corey factory making chocolate, but when he worked . . .

"He was there," Jaime said abruptly. She didn't have to say when. Her tone said it all. "He came with Cade."

Oh, God. "*Minette*." He pulled her in tight against him, involuntarily. God, Sylvain would have seen, then. Seen what Dom dreaded even to imagine, the way Jaime had looked right after the attack.

He wrapped her tighter against him, pressing her face against his chest. Sylvain could make her all the chocolates he wanted, in those circumstances. Dom wished he had been there himself to feed her. But if he had known her already then . . . if that had happened to her under his watch . . . he wasn't sure how he would have survived it. "*Ma minette*," he whispered, stroking her red-caramel hair. It felt softer today. Now that he had discovered her scar, she had stopped trying to weld her hair with hairspray into a mass that would never let it peek out.

Meaning he was the only person whose gaze mattered? The elevator doors slid open directly onto the apartment foyer. The apartment itself clearly took up the entire top floor.

"Dominique." Cade grinned, gave Jaime a quick hug, and then tilted her face up for Dom's *bises.* "I've been really looking forward to this."

Yes, he bet she had.

"Me, too," James Corey said cheerfully, shaking his hand, looking wickedly pleased and speculative all at once. His namesake grandchild glowered at him.

"Dominique," Sylvain said with intense reluctance, extending his hand for the briefest of shakes. He looked as if someone was trying to force a boot down his throat.

Dom grinned, feeling better and better about this dinner. He loved cramming himself down other people's throats and making them like it.

The last man to greet him was the only one of the group he hadn't met: a man in his fifties, with well-cut gray hair and blue eyes, who studied him critically. "Dominique Richard," he said coldly.

Dom gave the man his sharpest-edged smile, the one that made it clear he was capable of going for the jugular. So this was Jaime's father, the current head of the largest chocolate-producing corporation in the world? If you wanted to call it chocolate.

That made it, what, four against one tonight? Good. He liked being able to fight all his enemies at once. Fewer than that, and he felt like a bully picking on people smaller than he was.

"Mack Corey?" Dom retorted in a similar tone. He disliked the man already. He couldn't make sure his own daughter was surrounded by a small armed force while she traveled in danger zones?

Mack Corey narrowed his eyes at the criticism inherent in Dom's tone. Dominique nearly laughed as he extended his hand. *Come looking for a battle with me, did you?*

Mack Corey matched the shake with the experience of a man who had handled a million aggressive business shakes. "I've heard a lot of bad things about you."

Had he? And had he shared them all with his daughter? Probably, the bastard.

Because Jaime was listening, Dom bit back on the urge to tell her father to fuck off. "I've heard plenty of bad things about you, too."

He walked on past him, to set Jaime's sacks in the kitchen. The cooking area was set off from the main living room, but no walls separated it from the rest of the glossy, modern apartment. Floor-to-ceiling windows took up one entire wall, an uninterrupted line without curtains or shades, providing a beautiful view of the Jardins du Luxembourg. These windows continued on to form one wall of the kitchen, so that working there was like working suspended above the city. Four surrealist, metal stools were tucked under the blue-flecked granite kitchen bar. On the other side of it were stovetops and a refrigerator hidden discreetly behind a wood face that blended with the rest of the cabinets. The dining table, set far enough from the kitchen to make it obvious that the people who cooked in it weren't always the same people who ate at the table, was of the same blue-flecked dark granite, suspended from some type of wiring so fine it seemed to be floating, at first look.

A huge black couch in the living area faced the extraordinary view of the gardens. Near it was a suspended fireplace, clean lines, lit, a fine mesh making sure its sparks would not hit the extravagant fall of ferns and plants filling the wall near it. All around the space, similar falls of ferns saved the modern elements from being too harsh, invoked a sense of peace and simplicity.

He had been in apartments as luxurious. It was quite

common for oil sheikhs, for example, to keep apartments far more extravagant than this in Paris, to show up once or twice a year to use them, and to hire a top name like Dominique Richard to make something to awe their guests at parties. But it was surreal to realize this type of environment seemed normal to Jaime, of all people.

When he turned from the counter, Mack Corey was standing on the opposite side of the bar, his arms folded on it as he studied Dom coldly. "You haven't heard I was arrested for a knife fight or am famous for womanizing."

Damn it. So *Jaime* knew about the knife fight? Well, she did now, that was for sure.

"No, but I've heard your company used child slave labor until your own daughter stopped it."

Mack Corey stiffened. Cade and her grandfather froze, Cade in the act of reaching for a bottle and James Corey in the act of bringing a drink to his lips. Sylvain raised an eyebrow, amused and almost impressed. Jaime looked up from the vegetables she was taking out of the totes and glanced back and forth between the two men with an odd curl to one corner of her lip.

"Our cacao is provided by thousands of plantations, and we haven't always been aware of working conditions on all of them," Mack Corey said icily.

"That's convenient," Dom said. "But we can talk about my arrests or my womanizing if you find that an easier focus for your conscience."

Mack Corey shut his mouth hard. James Corey looked from his son to Dominique with lips pursed on a whistle. Cade's eyes were quite wide as she stirred a drink and slid it down the bar neatly into her father's hand. "Dominique, maybe I should get you something?" she suggested pointedly.

"Water. But go ahead, drink up," he told Mack Corey.

"You've had a long flight to get here and rescue your daughter from me, and you probably deal poorly with failure."

There was an instant's silence. "Well!" James Corey said brightly. "This is *fun*. Jamie, is this the cream of the crop, or are the other guys you've dated all like him?"

That eighty-year-old bastard. He had thirty years more practice than his son at pure genius meanness, didn't he?

"The cream of the crop," Jaime said briefly, in a tone that brooked no argument at all, as she folded her cloth grocery bags. The counter was now crowded with plantains, coconuts, small red bananas, papayas, floppy bags of spices tied by hand, and some kind of bean he didn't even recognize, despite his experience in kitchens.

"I'm sure Jaime is the cream of the crop for you, too," Mack Corey told Dominique coldly. "Considering her worth. No wonder you've stuck with her longer than with anyone else."

Jaime fixed her father with a brilliant, hard look.

"That's funny," Dom told him. "That's exactly what I think myself. I'm not sure you and I evaluate worth the same way, though."

James Corey said something to his son in English, grinning. Mack Corey looked surprised and exasperated, but he unfolded his arms and backed off for a little while.

No wonder Jaime went around thinking people might be interested in her for her money. Dom fixed a disgruntled look on Cade, as the nearest family member he could take things out on. "No other reason someone might be interested in her ever occurs to you people?"

Cade looked rueful. "Dominique, you're a notorious womanizing badass, and you latched onto my sister when she was down. What do you expect us to do? Trust you?"

"No, but you might try trusting *her*," Dom said, annoyed, and turned back to the vegetables and spices spilled over the counter.

Trusting her.

Trusting her.

To have picked him because he deserved to be with her?

Sylvain reached across Jaime's body for one of the bags of spices, his arm brushing hers in passing, his eyes sparkling with interest, and Dom took one long step forward and inserted his body between the two of them, bumping both of them in the process. *"Pardon,"* he said to Jaime, even while his big body shifted her a foot farther down the counter. "What are you making?"

"Whatever Jaime tells me to," Sylvain said easily, not reacting to the bumping beyond a slanted, warning glance. Why the hell did Sylvain get blessed with those poet's good looks? He looked like the kind of person women would fight duels over. "She's in charge tonight. You ever had your honor defended by punitive use of spices before?"

Jaime gave a little, smug smirk. "I'll keep it mild for you," she said patronizingly.

"Thank you," Sylvain said. "But it's cruel to give people false hope. Just tell me what this little spice is, and I'll try to forgive you, though."

Dom closed his hand around the bottom of the bag and yanked it deftly out of Sylvain's relaxed grip, hating him for his clear familiarity with Jaime and her cooking. *He* had never tasted Jaime's cooking. "If you've got unusual spices, I want to know about them," he told Jaime. "Don't share them with *him*. He's boring."

"You're melodramatic," Sylvain retorted. "Don't stab me with that knife. I hear it's been a good ten years since the last time you were in jail."

His jaw clenching, Dom stopped with his hand around the butcher knife he had just picked up to help Jaime.

"I'll tell you what—" Jaime deftly inserted herself between the two men. He felt a sudden sympathy for her father. Even after two months in the hospital, did she *still* have no instinct for self-preservation? "Dominique, you chop on this side, and Sylvain on this side, and the next person who says a word gets to chop the onions."

"I prefer the middle," Dom said, scooping up the onions and putting himself back between the two of them. So he couldn't be nudged aside again, he started mincing, not even looking at the onions while he did it. Despite Sylvain's conviction that he had hung the moon, Dom was the one who had actually worked in a three-star kitchen on his path to becoming chocolatier-pâtissier. It was fascinating to watch Jaime while he did her *petit commis* work, how familiar she seemed with the exotic vegetables and how awkward with the kitchen equipment. Where had she learned to cook this dish, in a village hut?

"I wasn't actually the one with the knife," he mentioned to her, softly enough that *le salaud Sylvain* couldn't hear him defending himself. He just wanted her to know—he had some redeeming qualities. He hadn't actually tried to knife anyone in his life.

She smiled far too easily as she slid him the yams to peel and dice next. How comfortable was she with this knife-fight news? What *more* did she already know about him? He moved briskly through the hard vegetables, not really watching the peeler or lethally sharp knife he was using because he was eyeing her. Jaime had no knife skills to speak of, but she knew what she wanted to do with this recipe. She toasted spices in a skillet over the gas flame, the scents rising around him, teasing him like some secret perfume she wore. This was her life. Before that scar on her arm. "Who taught you this recipe?"

"A family. The grandmother and the mother and their little girl, mostly. They were—very happy."

He didn't know what to do about that. He had a deep fear that the more she remembered the happiness she had created, the more driven she would feel to force herself back to make more. For people she thought deserved it more than he did. What was he talking about, for people who *did* deserve it more than he did. Yet despite his rivalry with those happy memories of hers, he loved seeing her face relax into them, instead of tensing as if the only thing she could see of her past life was the way it had ended.

He took a bite of the papaya he had started cutting for her, sweet and soft, and proffered a square to her lips. She smiled against his fingertips and took the papaya from them with a little kiss.

What if he could actually go on being this insanely happy his entire life?

Her father called something to her in English, and she left the kitchen area for a moment, leaving him and Sylvain alone. He had bought some English-language programs the other day, but he hadn't had time to start practicing. Maybe he could find an audio program he could listen to at the gym. Maybe Jaime could get him started by teaching him all the parts of the body. He grinned a little at the vision. And some of the verbs that went with those parts of the body, too.

Meanwhile, instead of getting lost in erotic English lesson fantasies in the middle of a family get-together, there was something he needed to say, and this might be his only chance without an audience.

"Thank you," he said abruptly, stiffly, to Sylvain. There, he had gotten it out, all right?

Sylvain's supple eyebrows went up, his own knife pausing as he sent him a stunned look.

"For"—Dom jerked his chin over his shoulder, in the direction in which he could hear Jaime speaking in English—"the chocolates, when she was . . ." He swallowed hard.

Sylvain's eyes widened, fixed on him, fascinated. *"Putain, mais tu es amour—"* He broke off. It was the first time since they had known each other that Sylvain had ever started to use *tu* with him, and even Sylvain wasn't obnoxious enough to say the whole sentence out loud. *You're in love with her.*

Dom stared at the papaya a long moment, the first time he had ever lowered his gaze in Sylvain's presence. "Was it bad?" he asked despite himself, harsh and low.

"Richard." Sylvain gripped his arm in an instinct of compassion that was stronger even than their enmity. "Don't ever look at the photos."

Merde.

Jaime did punish them with spices. At least she tried, but the plan backfired, as despite watering eyes, most of the table seemed to enjoy it. James Corey grinned, and Dom was utterly fascinated by the masochistic explosion of flavors in his mouth. He wanted to kiss her with his stinging tongue and see if he could transfer heat that way.

"Dad thinks you actually don't care about money," Mack Corey said incredulously a few bites into the meal, glaring at Dom as if he had grown two heads.

"It's a fixation they have," Sylvain apologized blandly from his end of the table. "They've devoted so much of their life to making money, they can't wrap their minds around the possibility that someone else could have found much better things to do with his time."

"Actually, it's her freckles that appeal," Dom told Jaime's father with the sweetest, meanest smile the world had ever seen. "They go everywhere."

Mack Corey flushed crimson and clutched his fists on the table. James Corey gave that whistle he had been holding back for some time. Cade flinched. "Dominique, *franchement.*"

Sylvain looked amused.

Dom didn't dare look at Jaime. He folded his arms on the table, let the muscles stand out. "Also, maybe her courage, her strength, her overdeveloped sense of responsibility toward the defenseless, her taste for the wild and different, and the way she can just stay so still and absorb things." Why did everyone, including Jaime herself, think her *money* was the thing that was the most valuable? Who the hell cared about that? "I can think of a few other qualities that come before money, too, but they're none of your damn business."

Jaime slipped a hand over one of the fists he had lodged in each crook of his arms. He loosened the one she touched enough to turn his hand over and close his fingers around hers.

Across the table, Cade gave him that look she shared with her younger sister: long, steady, evaluating. He couldn't believe he hadn't seen the family resemblance before, except, to be honest, he had never paid that much attention to Cade. She inclined her head slightly to him and raised a silent toast to her sister.

Since his entire concept of family presumed they were the enemy—to Jaime if they were a bad family and to him if they were a good one—this gesture threw him a little.

On his right, James Corey gave a sudden crack of laughter. "You know, Richard, I can't make up my mind, but I actually might like you. At least you're better than that Doctors Without Borders guy she was dating last fall."

Dom slid a glance at Jaime beside him. She had a startled, annoyed look on her face, as if maybe her grandfather's knowledge of the doctor guy had caught her by surprise. "I'm better than someone in the *Médecins sans frontières?*"

"His sense of peace and self-sacrifice extended to his girlfriends," James Corey said with remembered dislike. "He sold himself cheap, too. Why else do you think I get all that junk mail from MSF these days?"

Sylvain rested his chin on his fists and gazed at his future grandfather-in-law with a dumbstruck expression. "It's amazing," he told Dominique. Was Dom the closest thing Sylvain had in the room to a kindred soul at this point? Poor bastard. "It's like money is the only way they know how to process things."

"Did you fly into Ghana and buy Alec off?" Jaime demanded incredulously. "Grandpa, you know, having guys stop calling me after three dates for no reason I can figure is not that great for my self-esteem. Plus, *three dates.* Isn't that a little premature? And you say I waste money."

"Yeah, well, having them think you're worth sacrificing for a cause would be a lot worse for your self-esteem, long-term," her grandfather retorted. "You already have enough complexes about that kind of thing. Besides, he was an idiot. A quarter million." He snorted. "Tax deductible, too."

Jaime looked up at Dominique. "I don't know if I should even ask, but how much did he offer you?"

"To screw up my chances with you? Twenty million. But I thought we were talking about spinach at the time."

Jaime stared at him.

In the background, Sylvain muttered, "I'm begging you, James, stop with the spinach."

"*I* didn't start the bidding that high," Dom told Jaime, feeling oddly defensive. He had no idea why the guy before him had only gotten offered a quarter million in comparison.

"*Twenty million?*" Mack Corey asked his father. "Are

you *crazy*? You'd better not have been planning to sell shares."

"You could tell right away he wasn't going to break for a paltry quarter million," James Corey said impatiently. "There's such a thing as shock value. You know that, Mack. Or you should by now. How long have I been trying to teach you the business?"

Jaime managed to blink a couple of times, staring at Dom. "And you weren't even interested?"

Dom gazed down the table at Sylvain, his palms turning upward in a moment of complete, shared what-the-fuck?

Sylvain shook his head and made a little twisting motion of thumb and forefinger near his temple, indicative of people who were crazy.

"Instead of *you*?" Dom asked Jaime, which was the closest he could come to expressing how utterly self-destructive he would have to be to choose any sum of money over the right to lean his big body over hers and watch her mouth soften in anticipation.

"Very screwed up sense of values, in this family," Sylvain said dryly. "Especially of their own value. You just have to be patient. Sorry about that. I know patience isn't on your very short list of virtues."

CHAPTER 29

Cade and Jaime stood in one of the windows with a long-range view of the Eiffel Tower, Jaime leaning back under one of the huge ferns, so that she seemed to be posed between a jungle and the glowing lights of the epitome of civilization. Dominique, Sylvain, and James Corey were over by the table still, talking about spinach in chocolate, Sylvain with a groan, their grandfather with passion and indignation, and Dominique shaking his head. Their father had moved away to the kitchen counter to handle something over his phone.

"Well, he's impressed Dad," Cade allowed. "He loves men who don't give a damn what he thinks of them."

"He's being a bastard."

Cade's eyebrows went up. "Dad or Dominique?"

"Who do you think?"

"Well, I know who *I* think, but they do say love is blind."

"I was talking about Dad!"

Cade grinned. "I think the two of them are evenly matched."

"I bet he and Grandpa weren't this bad with Sylvain," Jaime said bitterly.

Cade had to admit it was true. She held up a hand to forestall Jaime's protest. "And you're right, of course,

Jaime. It's because they don't trust you to take care of yourself."

Jaime closed her mouth. She hadn't been going to phrase her protest quite like that. She had been going to say it was because they thought she was the goof-off, irresponsible one. That she *didn't take care of herself* had a slightly different focus. Kind of an accurate focus, in fact.

Cade's eyes locked with hers. "And it's true. You don't."

"I am right now. That's about all I *am* doing, is taking care of myself."

"Well, it's about damn time. You know, Jamie, what happened to you would be enough to traumatize anyone—it sure as hell traumatized all of *us* and we didn't have to live it, only observe—but you might have had burnout building from way before that. Even I've been burned out, in my way; that's how I ended up making headline news as a thief. That, and I think I could seriously accuse Sylvain of entrapment."

Jaime frowned uneasily. "If you get burned out, Dad can hire a replacement for your job. If I get burned out . . . there's no one to replace me."

Cade's mouth twisted wryly. "And here I spent so much time thinking *I* was irreplaceable. Actually, Jaime, you might be surprised how many highly qualified people a well-run non-profit could draw to it."

Of course Cade would see it that way, the organizer, the one who instantly knew how to run the world. Jaime was so used to *not* wanting to run the world. The Lone Ranger was more her hero. Someone who got to ride off into the sunset, help without taking on all that desk work. Would the Lone Ranger have been much more effective if he had entered politics and reformed law enforcement in the Wild West, rather than going one silver bullet at a time?

"You know, I would really like to do this with you," Cade said. "Work on developing a plan across corporations, push them to follow through, expand what you've been doing for Corey beyond our own companies, so that *one hundred percent* of the cacao beans in the world come from sustainable practices and fair trade. With my business knowledge and your firsthand awareness of the issues, we could really do something here. We could *eliminate* this problem. I know we could. A three-year plan, maybe a five-year plan . . . we could do it. Jaime—when are you going to have enough of being on the far side of the world from us? Because I would like to know you better again. To work with you. I think we could be a rather interesting team."

"You'd try to boss me around," Jaime said wryly.

Cade made an impatient movement with one hand. "Maybe. I haven't noticed you ever letting me succeed before. Unless you're still thinking about that Monopoly game when I got you to trade the dark blues for the light ones when you were six."

"Bottom line over ethics," Jaime murmured, with the singsong rhythm of an old exchange of insults.

"I was eight. My ethics have improved."

"Oh, *that's* what all the breaking and entering was about. Improved ethics."

Cade ignored that jibe in a resigned way, as someone who had survived quite a few comments on her career as a thief. She left the support of the window and shifted closer to Jaime, pushing persuasion. "Jaime, people do move up from field work. They do shift into administration, as the field work wears them out, as they realize their skills and knowledge can accomplish perhaps even more in a different way. It's not a weakness."

"It feels like a weakness."

Cade pressed a thumb and forefinger to her knit eyebrows, massaging. "You are so hard on yourself."

"Yeah." Jaime's ironic glance took in her sister, her father, her grandfather. "I wonder where I got that habit."

Cade opened her hand, in silent acceptance. "But I think it got worse for you. Maybe from seeing so many people who needed help. You have such a guilt complex."

"Well, I *should* have a guilt complex. The inequality between my luck in the birth draw and that of other people's is . . . there's not even a word for how big it is."

Cade looked a little guilty herself.

Jaime went back to the earlier subject. "Even with the focus on broader organization, I still need to go into the field sometimes, to keep everyone honest. I so hate this 'we didn't know' claim."

"Can I come?" a rough, low voice asked as an arm wedged its way between her and the window frame, forcing a place for itself over her shoulders. She looked up, startled.

"When you visit the farms," Dominique explained. "I've wanted to go to the source for years. Célie has been after me to take her along, too. It's one of the dreams of her life to go visit cacao farms in different parts of the world. I just haven't managed it yet."

For a moment, she couldn't even process the idea. Then a hard little bud deep inside Jaime, that she had been afraid was locked forever by fear, suddenly loosened its green husk, the petals starting to peek through and unfurl.

Dominique gave her a funny little smile, shy and aggressive all at once. As if he was going to impose himself no matter what, but wasn't sure of his reception. "It would be fun," he told her softly. His fingers curled around hers. "A lot of fun."

Fun. Fun to look across a fire at him as the villagers grilled crickets or some other challenge-gift for their palates; she bet he would eat them, too, just like she had, and grin while he did it. Fun to think of curling up in a hut with him, of laughing at some of the discomfort, or sharing fury at some injustice discovered. Fun to watch his bright curiosity at the cacao production, watch him taste all the new flavors, watch the stars that nearly touched her hair cling in his.

She had been concentrating on getting the courage to go back. It felt like a long time since she had been able to think of *fun*. From long before the attack, even. It had been fun once, hadn't it? Not, obviously, when she saw people suffering, but work on labor practices actually let her work with a lot of people who *weren't* suffering, or whose lives were growing exponentially better because of her role in them. It wasn't an instinct for martyrdom that had first drawn her to her work, but the richness of the experience. Her flight from the world of business as a teenager into what she had found so different, and exotic, and rewarding.

"Do you know I've never tasted the fruit?"

"It's sweeter than a mango," both sisters murmured at once.

Dominique looked jealous, his lips shifting subtly as if he was trying to taste something. "See? I'm sure I could do something with that."

Maybe she didn't need to stock up on his strength so she could leave him and brave alone a world that she now knew held terrors. Maybe she could take the source of strength with her. Would it be so weak? Maybe it was all right to let someone hold her through the nightmare, until she got through to morning. She helped people because she needed to help them and they needed the help. Maybe he could help her, if he needed that and so did she.

Eventually she would grow stronger, wouldn't she? The memories of that attack would fade before the present. Could she do it all? Could she base herself here, keep that warm, golden shelter of him that seemed to renew every-thing about her, work on developing a project across cor-porations, and, as her confidence regenerated, take short trips into the field? And come back here, to him?

She linked her fingers through his, which spread her own fingers far too wide, uncomfortably so, but she did it anyway and held on tight.

Her hand was a silly, tiny thing against his, but for the first time in a long time, it looked stronger again.

Sylvain cleared his throat. "I don't suppose *I* could come once in a while?" he suggested wistfully.

Dominique glared at him. "No, you could not. Go to Tahiti or something that costs a million dollars with Cade." He tightened his fingers around Jaime's. "This is *mine*."

"We can go visit some of our cooperatives if you want to," Cade intervened with asperity. "Whenever you want to. Ignore him."

"Yes, but traveling with Dominique sounds like so much fun," Sylvain said acerbically.

"*Cade* travels with bodyguards in those parts of the world," Mack said roughly, coming up to the group. "And Jaime can start doing it, too. Or did you think you could fight any attackers off by yourself?" he asked Dominique contemptuously.

Dominique looked at her father as if he would seriously like to punch him. It appeared he was not destined to start getting along with her family any time soon. "No," he said. "She needs bodyguards, too. *I'm* not an idiot."

Mack Corey went white around the mouth. Even Jaime had to admit that was a very low blow. Her father had sat at her bedside with his face red and rigid, his fists interlocked, his eyes strained until she had thought he might have a stroke or a heart attack with the tears clog-ging his insides. He had regularly insisted on bodyguards for her, from the very first time she had ever set foot in a developing country. She had regularly shrugged in cavalier assurance that she did not need them, *she* knew this world, and left them behind at some hotel. She doubted anyone could beat himself up more than her father about the fact that he had let her get away with it, had taken her word for it that they weren't really necessary.

She studied Dominique curiously. Everyone had told her so often he was a bastard, he was aggressive. She realized she was finally seeing the side of him they saw, all the time. That meeting with Sylvain had not been exceptional, and neither had his encounter with those two men at the *manifestation*. He fought. He fought people back like an enraged pit bull. Dirty, hard, and going straight for the jugular. No wasting time nipping at the ankles.

But his employees walked all over him.

He put rosebuds on his wall.

And that rough, big hand of his ran over her, every time, as gentle as velvet.

"You think she would agree to bodyguards for you?" James Corey asked snarkily.

Dominique rubbed his hand over hers and raised his eyebrows at her, not presuming to speak for her.

She liked that. She liked that he never tried.

"I would," she said. She was not entirely sure she would even be able to get off a plane in Côte d'Ivoire again without having her own personal army waiting for her. That was how sick and panicked she still got at the thought. *Sticks . . . the look in those men's eyes, the pleasure they took in breaking her . . .*

She focused hard on the hand holding hers, riding through the image, getting it to fall back. Something else to remember was that if Dominique was traveling with her, he also would be exposed to any possible attack. And she thought she knew, if they were attacked, where he would put himself. Between her and everyone else. Going down fighting.

The image gave her just a glimpse of what her family must have felt when they'd seen her bludgeoned body. The vision squeezed at her heart like it was a lemon, spilling acid into all her own wounds, burning. She strongly suspected, increasingly all the time, that Dominique had gone down fighting other times in his life, had fought until he was on the ground and couldn't get up.

She lifted their locked hands and pressed a kiss to the scarred knuckles.

Everyone else flushed to varying degrees, except for Sylvain, who smiled and, as if the act were contagious, carried Cade's hand to his lips and kissed it, too.

"I'll have to wait until I see what you can do with spinach, but you know, I really might end up liking you," her grandfather told Dominique. "Don't mind Mack. He's just coming to terms with the fact that he will always be the only white sheep in the family."

Dominique gave her father an incredulous look, clearly not buying that the head of a major international corporation was in any way a white sheep.

"Hold your hope out for grandchildren," James Corey told his son. "They're more likely to turn out the way you wanted than your own kids. Trust me, I know."

Mack Corey gave his father a much put-upon look, Dominique looked as if he had just been hit over the head with a mallet, and Sylvain, Cade, and Jaime all just sighed.

"You really do want to go, don't you?" Jaime whispered to Dominique.

"Minou." His hand lifted and feathered through her hair. "And see real moonlight? And learn what you love? Any time you say the word."

CHAPTER 30

Dom locked his bike just outside his *salon* door and let Jaime into its darkness. His display windows glowed discreetly out onto the street, so that passersby could crave him at all hours and come back when he was open, but inside, only a soft edge of light fell, hushed, on the empty *salon*.

Jaime walked away from him, her heels sounding on the rich wood floor, her hand stroking textures—the rustle of his wrapped caramels, hiding their sun in the darkness; the roughness of the stone arches; the brush of the red velvet curtain; the sleek glass; the tiny exquisite raised form of the white rosebuds.

Dominique tracked her as she moved, his gaze lingering on each spot she had touched, as if her fingerprints glowed gold there. "About this fantasy . . ."

She walked back toward him, still trailing textures, and stopped with her fingertips on the glass that shielded dark, patterned squares framed in metal. Her eyes met and held his, trying for a sultry, promising smile. "I wanted to get a box of chocolates."

In the dark room, he was something wild and dark, a creature called out of the heart of a forest legend. And he came toward her, as if she were the virgin to his mythical beast, as if he could not possibly resist her lure. "Tell me," he murmured, placing his hands on either side of her, leaning in a little, letting her feel the closeness of his body, how big it was, how much it dominated hers, "what flavors do you like?"

Her breath came out in a rush, her brain fogging, chocolate blurring into a background for his mouth held just above hers. "Probably anything of yours," she confessed.

One corner of his mouth kicked up. "Adventurous. I like that in a mouth." His closed over hers then, parting her lips for him, taking his time and taking control, exploring her with heat and slickness and the edge of his teeth until her hands were tangled in the leather jacket she had given him, failing to find the zip.

He pulled his head away and hung over her for a second, breathing hard. Then he reached past her so that his body pressed hers, briefly, hard against the counter, as he stretched to pull open the display case from the opposite side. The pressure on her body eased, to her disappointment. He pulled back enough to proffer a small square to her lips.

"Which one is that?" she asked.

"Why don't you tell me? Tell me what you taste, what you see, what you feel." He slipped it into her mouth. Her lips closed over the tip of his thumb as he drew it away.

"Dark silk," she whispered. "Dark, dark melting silk. That won't let go. It's wrapping around my wrists."

He scraped the overlong cuffs of *his* leather jacket, the one she wore, up to close his hands over her wrists against the counter, rubbing his rough calluses against the sensitive skin. "And do you like it, wrapping around your wrists? Or do you want it to let you go?"

"No, I"—a catch in her voice as his thumb found that sensitive skin inside her wrists and stroked it just right—"like it."

"Which one was it?" His lips brushed hers as he spoke. "I didn't see." His mouth closed over hers again, tasting the flavor that lingered on her tongue.

She lost herself in the kiss, but it was all too elusive. He pulled back, resting his forehead on the top of her head. "You like that one, do you?" There was a tiny smile in his voice, thick with so many other things. He drew a hard breath. "I thought we were doing a fantasy of *yours.*"

"Don't worry, we are."

He pulled off the leather jacket she wore in one yank of the zip and tossed his own over the counter, letting his body press into hers with those barriers gone. Her hands loved the fresh, exposed feel of his torso in the cotton knit. "Did you really fantasize about this, that day here?"

"Oh, yes. And with every single bite I took from that box you made for me."

"Putain." He ran his hands up her body, lifting her to set her on the counter. "I should have put my cell phone number in that box." His mouth took hers again, his hips pressing her thighs apart, settling against her. "I didn't want to scare you away."

"Scare m—?" But his mouth didn't allow hers the leeway to form words.

Still kissing, his body crushed hers again, one arm holding her in a hard grip as he forced her backward, forced her weight to depend on that arm. When he eased her back to stability, he had another chocolate in his hand. "Why would you sc—"

He slipped the chocolate between her parted lips, cutting off the word.

She closed her eyes, at the dark silk that responded so instantly to her body temperature, melting on her tongue. "I thought you said you had never lived anywhere without light."

He shook his head, but his expression said the denial was, in its way, a lie. "I haven't."

"This is a dark that hasn't seen light. It's for secrets."

"Do you like it?" he whispered, with that old, hard-to-hide vulnerability, that eagerness for praise.

"Oh, yes. It's the kind of dark the world was born out of."

"If we want a world to be born, I think we need some sex." He slipped his hands under her tunic and into her leggings, curving them hot against her bottom as he pulled her weight back off the counter onto him, riding his pelvis. "Where do you want me to take you?" he whispered, soft and dark as the center of his chocolate, as he carried her into the center of the room. "In this fantasy of yours."

She drew her hand over the rough, exposed stone of the arch. "Right here."

He held onto her with one hard arm, pressed his own palm against it behind her. "*Minette,* that will hurt your skin."

"That's where I want it," she whispered. "Right here."

He gave a hoarse little laugh. "*I* want it somewhere soft. Where I can take you really hard."

"Next time," she promised into his mouth, her hands threading into his hair. "Next time."

He walked them backward, found his old jacket, and slipped it back on her. With her skin protected, he pressed her back against that stone, dragging his hands between the panels of the jacket, up over her ribs, thumbs sliding over her breasts. "What do you like to tell me? That I'm beautiful? *Minette,* I've never seen anything as beautiful as you."

"Dominique, I have a very good idea how beautiful some of the women you've slept with are—"

He shut her up with his mouth, with his thigh thrusting

between hers. "You don't know what the hell you're talking about." His mouth grew more urgent, his arms trying to shield her from the hardness of the wall as his hips pushed harder. He wasn't kidding, about wanting to take her hard. "Jaime, say I can keep you."

"As a matter of fact, I wanted to talk to you about tha—"

"Just *say it!*" His hands dove into her leggings and dragged them down, panties and all.

The sudden exposure made her pant, the lips of her sex flexing against the air—and then against his thumb as he rubbed them roughly apart.

"Say it."

"You can keep me." She twisted helplessly against his thumb. "Dom—Domini—go slow. Let me just—absorb you."

Another rough, despairing laugh. "I'll try, *minette.* I might need more practice."

He did try. The rock gentled him, the knowledge that he could not thrust too hard while she was literally driven back against stone.

Later, she sat on his lap at that table that had always been hers, studying the backs of his hands. They were scraped raw. While she had been lost in his mesmerizing efforts to go slow, he had been protecting her head and her bottom from the rough stone with the cup of his hands.

"I'm sorry," she said remorsefully, letting one finger glide just above a scrape, not quite touching, just stirring the hairs on the back of his hand.

"It's nothing," he said roughly. "Really. Nothing. I love you." He said it hard, like an order: no arguments accepted. His arms tightened around her.

The most perfect place to be. "Can I stay like this forever?" she asked wistfully.

His arms tucked her in tighter. "Yes," he promised the top of her head.

"I love you," she whispered into his chest. "But I understand why you don't like to hear it."

His hand tightened a little on her skull. "I doubt it."

"It's too clingy," she said, wrapping her arms around as much of him as she could and clinging to him harder.

"Jaime." He tilted her head back, but she only slipped her face into the hollow of his throat and nuzzled there. He smelled delicious, chocolate and her and his own skin, the warm dangerous darkness of it. "It's not clingy enough."

Now she did pull back her head and stare at him in the lights around the edges of his display windows, which were casting zebra lines into the darkness. The great beast lured out of savage woods to lay his horn in her lap. But no unicorn, something far more predatory and wild.

"I want you to promise never to leave me." His fingers flexed tight against her skin and loosened. "But I won't believe you if you do."

"We're so stupid." She felt along his shoulder, over his arm, carefully, learning the shape of the strange beast in the dark. "I want you to promise never to let me go. But it's hard to believe I have the right."

"I know." His hand was rough and gentle on her by turns, as if he kept catching himself stroking her skin too hard and velveted his touch. And then forgot again. "You have to save the youngest first. The people who"—his voice caught oddly—"need it."

She buried herself in him again, folding her arms between his chest and her body, so that she was completely wrapped up in him, no part of her exposed. He recognized her need these days, and his arms obligingly adjusted, helping create that sensation of being wrapped in him.

"I will get stronger than this," she promised him.

"I'm sure you will," he murmured into her hair. "Promise not to leave me when you do. Or promise to come back. If you need to go save people, promise it's me you come back to when you need more strength."

"But you won't believe me. When I promise."

"No," he admitted. "No, I probably never will."

He was facing his worst nightmare, she realized suddenly. For her. The one in which he tried to believe in her when she walked out, tried to believe that she would be back.

And she had to face hers, but in a different way. To set aside its power over her, that vision of men with sticks. To make a choice that was neither focused on fighting back against that vision nor yielding to it, to make a choice that, for once, was . . . *hers.* For her.

"But I might get—stronger." His voice was darker than the shadows around them but wry. "Not as strong as you will, but someday, I might believe you're possible at least some of the time."

She gave a little laugh and twisted her body just for the pleasure of rubbing it against his, of feeling him in every part of her. "It's like Lewis Carroll. *Well, now that we have seen each other, said the unicorn, if you'll believe in me, I'll believe in you.*"

"Am I the Unicorn or Alice?" he asked, surprising her a little, until she thought of his walls of books.

"Oh, you're definitely the fabulous monster." She stroked her hands over his shoulders. Dark and feral and exactly what she needed. A white unicorn would have been too weak. Or too untouched.

He laughed a little, too, and laid the palm of one hand along her face, where, as always, it seemed to caress half her head. "All right. You can be my incredible Alice. So human and so real." He shifted her minutely against him, as if he, too, needed to rub himself with her. "I'll try to believe in you."

Silence fell between them. Maybe they were both trying to believe. Dominique seemed in no hurry to leave. As if he could sit there forever, at that little table in his *salon,* and . . . absorb her.

She swallowed. "About that weird question I wanted to ask."

He said nothing, waited.

She looked up at him in the dark, her body held in the cradle of his hard thighs and chest. "Will you marry me?"

He didn't move. He didn't breathe. Then slowly his hands tightened harder and harder on her thighs until she made a little sound at the pressure. "Oh, God, I think I'm going to be sick."

He shoved her off his lap, striding away from her toward the red velvet curtain. Jaime stumbled and straightened, staring after him, dumbfounded. Her marriage proposal made him *sick*?

He reached out a hand to press it against the white wall of rosebuds, leaning into it. One breath ran through his big body. Another.

He turned his head to look at her over his arm. "Do you *mean* that? You want to—you—Jaime." His eyes were starting to glitter with the most intense emotion. "*Don't* say that unless you're sure—unless you couldn't possibly ever, ever leave me at the altar. What am I saying? How could you be sure? We've only known each other ten days."

"A month," Jaime corrected. "I've known you a month."

The corners of his lips kicked up, involuntarily. He glanced at the little table she had always sat at and then up, to the top of his spiral staircase.

"I'm sure," Jaime said. "Dominique. *Now that we have seen each other. If you'll believe in me . . .*"

"Jaime." He shook his head slowly, as if it hurt every muscle in his body to do it. "I don't know if you should believe in me."

She rocked a step back. Thinking of all the beautiful brunettes and blondes and, yes, probably redheads he must see every day.

"I've been pretending, Jaime." Dom rubbed his hand over the little white rosebuds wistfully. "I've been pretending. So I could keep you. I'm such a bad bet."

Her eyebrows scrunched together. She stared at him as if he was speaking some language she didn't know.

Dom couldn't bring himself to hold her gaze. He let go of his damn rosebuds and walked over to the rough stone. The stone against which they had just made love. He put his palms flat on the warmth there, where the heat of her body pressed there by his had sunk into the stone.

"But you know that, don't you?" he said low. "All this time I thought you thought I was perfect. You knew."

"Perfect?" she said, startled.

"Yeah." His mouth twisted. He hit the side of his fist against the stone. "I guess you never did think that."

"I didn't mean you were *flawless*." She sounded taken aback. "I mean, Jesus, Dominique, you have a really dirty mouth. For example. And in some spots that thick hide of yours turns into such thin skin you can see your whole soul through it. What you are is *wonderful*."

He pressed one hand over his chest, widening his fingers as much as he could to cover himself. "*Don't* look at my soul."

"I'll look at whatever the hell I want. It's *beautiful*."

He looked at her helplessly. Any minute he was going to sink down and just sob into her lap like she was his missing mommy. And she didn't resemble his mother at all . . .

he didn't want her for his mother, it was just . . . she loved him. Every time she looked at him as if he was the moon and the stars, it made every part of him okay. Except he had to remember he wasn't. Okay. "Jaime. I spent six years in a *slaughterhouse*. My father beat the crap out of me and my mother both."

She made a little low sound and flinched. Oh, *merde,* so maybe she hadn't known that. Maybe he could have kept it hidden longer.

He forged on anyway. "My mother didn't even try to take me with her when she left. I don't know how to *do* any of these things, like be calm and reliable and love you; I just *try.* I'm a really, really, really bad bet."

"It depends on what you're betting on. If you want someone bigger than the whole damn world, I would say you're the best bet out there."

She washed over him, every time, like a balm for his soul. "Jaime. How did you ever walk into my life?"

"Let's see." She gestured around her. "Because it's *beautiful.* And strong. And I could just soak all that beauty and strength up into me. I walked into your life because you made it a life anyone would want to be inside. And"—she smiled a little, her gaze drifting over his face, his mouth, his body—"it tastes delicious."

Desire and delight ran through him the way they always did, beyond his control. She thought he was beautiful. She thought his life was beautiful. She thought his damn *soul* was beautiful. And, *putain,* but he could not get enough of her little mouth tasting him, all over. "Jaime. I *want* to believe in you. I want to believe in me. You have no idea how much I want to believe it. It's just so hard."

She shook her head. And walked up to him. Walked right up to him. He didn't think she would ever understand what it did to him when she leaned against him like that, as if she was his. As if she could trust him. As if she needed him.

"I guess you'll just have to try, Dominique," she said softly. "I've seen everything else you've tried at, so if you promise me you'll try, that's good enough for me."

CHAPTER 31

She awoke with a crick in her neck, completely disoriented. Tables. Stone. Red velvet. Leather. Chocolate.
The scent of chocolate. What the heck? She was sleeping
on the little red Second Empire–style *canapé* that formed
one of the voluptuous little seating areas in Dominique's
salon. A pastry chef jacket had been rolled up and tucked
under her head, for a pillow. Because they weren't known
for luxury cushioning, in the Second Empire. Two leather
jackets formed her blanket, the one she had given Dominique over her torso, his old one he had given her over
her legs.

It was early morning, and light was just starting to spill
through the great walls of windows, leaving the patterns
of his chocolate sculptures and displays in shadows on the
floor.

This was a really weird place for Dominique to leave
her asleep. She blinked around, finding him nowhere on
the ground floor, and finally took the spiral staircase.

The light seemed to grow richer as she climbed it, the
sun rising higher somewhere beyond the city horizons,
warming, turning the world golden. She stopped dead just
inside the *laboratoire*.

Dominique, almost completely covered in chocolate,
stood on the counter by what had been the block for his

sculpture. He was drawing a small carving tool very delicately over the edge of the careful feathers in a chocolate wing.

Tears filled her eyes. She couldn't help it.

It was *La Victoire de Samothrace*. All in chocolate. Her wings spread behind her. Her body in motion, that one graceful leg leaving the ground behind her, the cloth of her robe fluttering with that caught-in-time instant of her launch into the air.

Jaime brought her hands up to cover her mouth, unable to breathe for the beauty of it. The joy of it.

Dominique's head came up, as if her presence penetrated his concentration. He must be refining the finishing touches, because to her the statue looked complete. Glorious, courageous, ready to soar.

He straightened away from the wing and let his carving tool fall to his side, staring down at her mutely while she took the sculpture in.

But when one of her tears spilled over her lashes and tracked down her cheek, he leaped down and came up to her. He didn't speak. He didn't have to ask her if she liked it. He just stroked the tear off her cheek.

And then gave a startled look at his fingers. He lifted his other hand toward her cheek and stopped midway, gazing at it ruefully. "*Pardon.* I just got chocolate all down your cheek. And I don't think I'll be able to wipe it off."

"No." She shook her head, a smile starting to sparkle through her tears until she felt like a rainbow. "No, you're completely covered." Shavings of chocolate must have fallen over him as he worked and had melted onto his body as he kept working. All night. To get from the half-formed sculpture it had been to this, he must have worked all night. Chocolate completely coated his hair, his face, his forearms, his hands, his chef's jacket. "Oh, God. Don't take a shower. Don't even wash your hands."

A slow grin grew on his face. "My team's going to be here soon."

"I'll drive the motorcycle. It's not that much harder than a moped, is it?"

"Umm. Maybe a littl—"

"Hush. You just sit behind me and try to stay intact. Or we can walk. My apartment is really close. You're going to look a little silly on the street, but Dominique, you can do this for me. You're like a woman's wildest dream right now."

His grin grew. "If you like me covered in chocolate, you should stick around a long time. It comes with the profession."

"I'm trying to stick around. My marriage proposal still making you feel sick?"

He rubbed his belly, leaving still more chocolate on the front of his jacket. "I think it was the sugar shock. In my career, I'm not used to digesting something so sweet so suddenly." He leaned in and kissed her, touching her with nothing but his mouth. She still tasted chocolate from a shaving that must have melted against his lips. "Jaime." His mouth was so tender, those dark-water eyes of his so bright. "Do you *still* really mean that? That you want to marry me?"

"Surprisingly, one of the things my sister and I learned early in our lives as billionaire heiresses was not to go proposing marriage to anyone unless we meant it. And meant it for the long term."

"Well." He took her hands, forgetting again that his were coated in chocolate. "I have what might be a better proposition."

There he went again. He had a woman ready to marry him, and what did he manage to do with that? Piss her off. Jaime stiffened and pulled at her hands. They slid a little in the chocolaty-ness of his grasp, and he tightened it. "Better than marriage?"

"Just hear me out."

She set her jaw and waited. *La Victoire de Samothrace* soared beside them.

"Would you live with me?" he asked, low. "As much as you can. If you have to travel, I'll come with you as much as I can. I really want to come with you. And you unpack your suitcase, and you live here. With me. For a long time. Three years. A long, long time, until we can see if I can . . . keep this going. If I can be trusted with you. Or four years, maybe four years would be better. Could you do that? If, after four years, I'm still . . . I haven't . . . you think I'm worth marrying, could we do that?"

She stared at him. Her eyes glimmered with tears. *Merde,* he had said the wrong thing. "You want to spend four years proving to me every day you're worth marrying?"

Four would be enough, wouldn't it? If he could manage for four years to be a decent boyfriend, he wouldn't suddenly become his father as soon as they got married, would he? He nodded, hesitantly. For someone who had just proposed marriage to a man she had been dating less than a month, she seemed to find this a weird idea.

She blinked, and one of the tears spilled onto her cheek, trailing down over the chocolate smear from his finger. "Did I ever tell you that being with you—it's like someone just laid me down in the softest, thickest, silkiest comforter?"

Oh, boy, another one. He loved these analogies of hers. They made him feel—silky and thick and hot. Not very soft, though.

"It's so . . . warm. It's so—I feel precious. It's like I could curl up there forever and never, never drag myself out into the cold morning."

It shook his whole soul when she talked like that, opening up doors and windows he didn't even know he had, and spilling parts of his soul out into odd tangles that gleamed like lost treasure. He looked at his big hands, opening and closing involuntarily on hers. He didn't dare say anything, because he didn't want to cry himself.

He glanced up sideways at his *Victoire de Samothrace,* which he didn't know if he had carved more in her honor or in his—it was as if they had blurred together. The sight of it gave him the courage to smile a little, to try to tease. "Did you have a specialist check out that blow to your head?" he asked worriedly.

She burst out laughing. It ran over his skin like a waterfall, fresh and cleansing. "Oh, Dom, what am I going to do with you? The best specialists money could buy. What, did you think Cade went with the public health system?"

He pulled her in against his body, feeling a giddy secret kick of pleasure that he was covering her with his chocolate, that everyone would be able to see where he had held her, and picked up one of her hands, looking at it a moment in his. Chocolate from his hands smeared over her freckles. The same chocolate hid all of his scars, but if he had correctly understood her, she was promising to lick it all off and reveal them again. Not an offer a man could bring himself to refuse, even to protect those old wounds of his. *Merde,* protecting old wounds was what scar tissue was for.

"Yes, if you still want to marry me after four years, I'll marry you," Jaime said. "But I would probably feel more reassured if we got married tomorrow, because I'll have to keep proving myself, too."

"What? No, you won't."

She shrugged, clearly declining to argue with someone so blind.

He gazed down at her, so small in his arms, with that

skin looking as if she were a beignet shaken in a bag of golden sugar. So small, but so steady and strong no matter what she thought, letting him hold her as if she could think of nothing better than to have his arms around her. "If you were only crumbs on a plate, I would pick every last one up with my finger," he said quietly.

Her eyes started glimmering again.

"Could we get engaged?" he asked, rubbing her bare, thin ring finger. "I know you don't like jewelry, and you don't have to wear it when you're visiting plantations, or I could get you something subtle, it doesn't have to be gold, or—" He stopped himself from listing any and every way he would modify what he wanted to suit her, which would have taken days. "I would like that. A promise. Right here." He rubbed the base of her ring finger.

"We could get *married*," she said. "I'm not liking the way this negotiation is going."

"We can't get married, because I might faint." But, surprisingly, he wasn't feeling so light-headed now. The more she said it, the more she stayed in his arms, the more it seemed like something that could actually *happen*. Not like when he had kept trying to find his mother with his *relevé de notes,* his report card, on the off chance that learning he was first in his class would make her come back. And be his mother forever this time. This hope that Jaime had given him was one he was actually starting to *believe* in. "We have to build my strength."

She turned his hand over, studying the base of his own ring finger. It was covered with chocolate. She rubbed a narrow band clear, and he wallowed as he always did in the pleasure of even such a small touch. "Four years."

Maybe three. He wouldn't entirely object if she kept bringing up the marriage proposal regularly until she convinced him. He would completely lavish her with chocolate—or jewelry, flowers, or anything else she might want, like, say, his body covered in chocolate—if she would keep proposing marriage to him.

His heart tightened so hard he was going to kill himself if tears showed in his eyes. "Do you know that if you married me, every time you said your name"—he swallowed, trying to make his voice sound less choked—"you would be saying you loved me?"

"Jaime Richard." She smiled up at him and pushed herself up on tiptoe to kiss him. "And it would be true."

Oh, shit, he had to breathe a minute. His nostrils were stinging.

Maybe two, he thought. Maybe in two years he could say yes. He couldn't wait four years to give her his last name. Or . . . or . . . maybe in one?

She wrapped her finger around the base of his ring finger, like . . . a ring. "I'll make it very, very masculine, titanium or something, and you don't have to wear it while you're working dough or chocolate," she said. "But you damn well better put it on when you go downstairs to talk to your female clients."

She was going to put an engagement ring on him. Oh, that so completely worked for him. He wrapped her up and pulled her against him again, there at the base of his *Victoire de Samothrace,* squeezing her too hard because she held so much of his joy.

AUTHOR'S NOTE

With, as always, my infinite thanks to all the chocolatiers and pâtissiers who have helped me with my research, most particularly in this case Jacques Genin, whose *salon* and *laboratoire* were the inspiration for the setting of Dominique Richard's, and who was very gracious and patient toward me and my many queries, as was his chef chocolatier (or chocolatière) Sophie Vidal. Also, many thanks to Michel Chaudun, another top Paris chocolatier who allowed me to research in his *laboratoire,* with great patience.

The poems on Jaime's and Dominique's placemats in the little *bistro* he takes her to are from the exceptional French poet Jacques Prévert: "Cet amour" and "Je suis comme je suis" from his book *Paroles* (Éditions Gallimard, Paris, 1949). The translations are mine, and Jaime is skipping verses and playing with them in her head as she thinks about them, so these are not direct translations.

LAURA'S RECOMMENDATIONS FOR U.S. ARTISAN CHOCOLATIERS

Looking for good chocolate but can't make it to Paris? Artisan chocolate has seen an extraordinary boom in the United States in the past few years, and it's now possible to taste some amazing chocolate much closer to home. Try these . . .

Miel Bon Bons (www.mielbonbons.com)

Ferrandi- and Le Nôtre–trained chocolatier Bonnie Lau works out of her tiny jewel box of a shop in Durham, North Carolina. Exactly the kind of place you might discover a top chocolatier, thanks to the recent growth in artisan chocolate in the United States. In the past, I've described Bonnie's chocolates as "fanciful, warm, adventurous, and reassuring." Rich, dark ganaches pair with whimsical and sophisticated flavors, and Bonnie's passion for chocolate and what it can do is palpable. My favorite quote from her: "I've saved so many marriages in this shop." And I can guarantee that with her chocolate, she has.

Chocolats Du Calibressan
(www.chococalibressan.com)

My first discovery of Jean-Michel Carré's chocolates was a red-painted caramel-filled chocolate Buddha that, as a surprise gift, had been sitting on my doorstep in mid-July in North Carolina, rising to a melty soft temperature that made it one of the most exquisite flavor-texture combinations I have ever bitten into. I've had an addiction to those Buddhas ever since, and to all the other gorgeous and sumptuously delicious hand-painted chocolates Jean-Michel makes from his place in Carpinteria, California. What is this excellent French chocolatier doing on the American Riviera? It's a love story, of course! His American wife was homesick . . .

Christophe Artisan Chocolatier
(www.christophechocolatier.com)

My family was exasperated at my dragging them through Charleston searching for this chocolatier instead of visiting gardens . . . until they stepped inside. Then they realized it was all worth it. Third-generation French chocolatier Christophe Paume makes his hand-painted chocolates in the heart of historic Charleston, luscious ganaches flavored with everything from tomato-basil to a classic vanilla to . . . gasp . . . peanuts. ("The American market! I had to!"). Check out also his salted caramel chocolate bars, which, out of all the salted caramel chocolate bars I've ever tasted, remain my standout favorite. And what is he doing in Charleston instead of Toulouse, where he was born? It's another love story!

Escazu (www.escazuchocolates.com)

A bean-to-bar microbatch producer that was one of the earliest of its kind to launch in the United States, going full-scale bean-to-bar in 2009. Chef Hallot Parson got pulled into chocolate on a trip to Costa Rica, helping friends track down a cacao farm. He now maintains personal relationships with that same farmer, flying down once a year, as well as with another in Venezuela, and his passion for and investment in every stage of the process shows in the final results: delicious bars with unique notes to their chocolate, for those as passionate about their chocolate as an oenophile is about his wines. This exceptionally good chocolate also gets used for the truffles and confections chocolatier Danielle Centeno makes on the premises, making for an unusually fine texture and flavor. If on the premises, check out also their varieties of hot chocolate, everything from adaptations of half a dozen recipes from the sixteenth and seventeenth centuries to contemporary versions. Check out my website (www.laura florand.com) for some behind-the-scenes glimpses of their bean-to-batch process, including their century-old Spanish grinder and roaster.

John and Kira's (www.johnandkiras.com)

One word: FIGS! The "drunken" figs from John and Kira's are worth a trip in and of themselves. They had the inspiration to stuff delicate dried figs, imported from Spain, with a rich ganache just faintly infused with whiskey, then dip the whole in chocolate again, and the rest is history. For me, anyway. I am now addicted to these figs. Those living in Philadelphia can find John and Kira's chocolates frequently at the small farmer's markets, but they also have an efficient catalog service, having grown from two people to a team of close to a dozen, still continuing to make all their chocolate by hand. And they have a wide variety of other chocolates to taste as well, including adorable ladybugs and bees. Many thanks to Mina de

Caro of the blog Mina's Bookshelf (minadecaro.blogspot
.com) for pointing me in their direction.

Readers Also Recommend

Readers have joined a chocolate hunt to help me find
even more top U.S. artisan chocolates, resulting in more
recommendations than even I have yet had time to taste.
Come check out my website at www.lauraflorand.com to
join the discussion about the best U.S. artisan chocolate or
see whom others have recommended. Here are a few:

In San Francisco, Linda recommends Recchiuti (www
.recchiuti.com) and Xocolate Bar (www.thexocolatebar
.com). I've had Recchiuti's and will concur: Linda knows
her chocolate.

In Atlanta, Chanpreet recommends di Amano (www
.atlantasbestchocolate.com). I'm often in Atlanta, so these
are next on my list. Besides, I like their confidence in buying the web domain "atlantasbestchocolate."

In Kansas, Jan Leyh recommends Christopher Elbow
(www.elbowchocolates.com). I had a chance to try both
his chocolates and his hot chocolate. Both are delicious!
And the chocolates are absolutely beautiful.

In Texas, my own sister Anna recommends Wiseman
House Chocolates (www.wisemanhousechocolates.com).
Dark, rich truffles such as Wild Woman to please the
wildest chocolate hearts. And their hot chocolate (or sip-
ping chocolate or drinking chocolate as artisan chocolatiers often prefer to call it in the U.S.) is delicious. A rich,
full, rounded flavor, just perfect for the whole family on a
winter's evening, from only-eats-plain-pasta small child to
her just-give-me-plain-chocolate father to her gourmet
chocolate snob mother.

And there are many more reader recommendations on our website discussion! This is just a start. Which leaves me with many more chocolates to try—and I hope you, too. If you find something good, please let me know! Readers can contact me at laura@lauraflorand.com, or through Facebook (www.facebook.com/LauraFlorandAuthor) or my website (www.lauraflorand.com).

Laura Florand's *Amour et Chocolat* series continues with *The Chocolate Heart,* coming this December. Read on for a taste . . .

She walked in, blond, small, tanned, smelling of monoï, the tiare-infused coconut oil of the islands. Luc recognized the scent because he smelled and tasted everything that passed through his hands, good or bad.

It wasn't a policy he usually applied to people, but . . . She looked like someone a man wouldn't mind tasting, certainly. A sun goddess you might pick up off a beach, on a tropical escape, feel the sand sticking to her skin when you made love to her, shake it out of the sheets in the morning with a smile on your face.

Or so he imagined. He had never escaped to a tropical island, not ever once, but his ability to imagine—and realize—impossible things was world-famous.

She looked tired, around-the-world-in-eighty-days tired, with a pinch around her eyes that went beyond jet lag. But when she looked up and met his eyes, she pulled out a smile so bright, it was several minutes before Luc realized she had no idea who he was. She hadn't recognized him. She had just seen the symbol of the hotel under his name on his shirt and thrown him the same bright smile she would have given anyone.

So right from the start there was a problem. A conflict, within him, perhaps. Luc knew, with certainty, that she had arrived on the edge of nerves and exhaustion. That she needed tolerance and compassion.

Yet he couldn't quite forgive her for that split second when he had fallen for that bright smile, and it hadn't been for him.

She had probably thought he was the bellboy.

That was one hot bellboy, Summer noticed. Standing near the polished mahogany reception desk, framed by marble columns, light glimmering on his face from a gold chandelier. *Welcome, Madame, to your mausoleum.* Although doubtless *he* thought this place was a gorgeous palace.

Black-haired, probably about thirty, the man curled like a whip around her attention and yanked it to him.

How? She hadn't slept more than ten hours in the past four days, some of which she had spent hanging sick over the side of a cargo ship. How could he wake her up enough to notice him? Even if he was gorgeous—a sculpted, precise elegance, with a perfect, coiled tension in him. Tall and lean and lovely and watching her.

Maybe someone at the hotel had checked out her dating history, figured out her type, and placed him there to keep her distracted and malleable.

How thoughtful of them.

She smiled at him because she was almost never too far gone to smile at someone as if he were special. The gift cost her nothing, certainly not any iota of herself, so why be stingy with it?

The bellboy or whatever he was, stood perfectly still, a hotel logo embroidered on his stylish white shirt, with an open collar and up-to-the-minute cut. For a moment, the power of his presence forced every detail on her: a honed, startlingly handsome face, the copper tone of his skin, the black hair, the black eyes that fixed on her as if he had just spotted water in a desert.

"Monsieur." She put a hand on his wrist, smiling up at him, and a little flick ran up that matte skin. Great. She definitely needed a man who was putty in her hands right now; she didn't have the strength for anyone who could resist her. "Could you show me to my room please?"

Tricky, for a bronze statue to stiffen further, but he managed it. Maybe not such putty after all. Wow, his eyes were so . . . intense. Greed kicked through her, a desire to grab that intensity and wallow in it. *Mine, mine, all mine.* God, she must be out-of-her-mind tired.

"I think you have me mistaken for someone else," Gorgeous said with distinct hauteur. He kept cutting his way through every blurring of her brain, the one clear thing in her fatigue. He looked like a Greek god. A real Greek god, not those heavy-lipped marble things. Born out of Chaos, hardened by fire, ready to go fight some Titans.

"*I'm* Summer Corey," she retorted firmly. Top that, Greek god. "Come on. Here." She dove into her purse and came up with a handful of fifty-euro bills, fresh from the airport distributor, and lowered her voice as she pressed them into his palm. "Just get me to my room before anyone else realizes I'm here, okay? I need a nap."

"A nap."

Preferably in a hammock on the beach, but she wasn't going to get that. She was going to get some opulent bed that gave her hives. "I promise I won't let you get fired for sneaking me in."

Black eyebrows went up. "I promise you I won't be fired."

Oh, for God's sake, couldn't he take extravagant tips for discreet favors to rich clients gracefully? He was working at the top hotel in Paris, for crying out loud. Maybe she was going about this the wrong way. "I *am* Summer Corey." As in, the person who could do the firing, so stop arguing and get moving.

"Congratulations." He left his hand open so that the bills scattered over his feet. "I'm Luc Leroi."

If she had had one iota more energy, she might have gasped and genuflected, just to subvert his arrogant tone. *Le Roi,* the King. She hadn't forgotten any European princes her mom was trying to set her up with, had she? No one came to mind. "So what are you king of?" she asked him with a little grin, which she was pretty proud of. Not everyone could pull out friendly grins for indiscreet bellboys when she felt ready for her own funeral.

His lips parted as if he had taken one to the gut, and his eyes went obsidian.

"Here," he said finally, with an edge to his voice. "Welcome to my kingdom, Summer Corey."

That couldn't be right. According to her father, this was *her* kingdom now. Her parents had always had trouble telling the difference between their daughter's fairy-tale kingdom and her own personal hell.

She curled her hand around his arm and leaned into him confidingly. He took a soft, sudden breath as her body got so close to his. "Here's some advice. When the owner of 'your kingdom' asks to be discreetly shown to her room, it's probably a good idea to help her out, if you want to keep your throne. No matter who you think you are."

His eyes glinted. "That's thoughtful of you. The advice. Can I return the favor?"

Hard arms swept her up against his chest, an iron grip shocking through her. He moved so fast, it took her brain a few seconds to catch up and realize he had just saved her from this cold marble hall. And longer still to remind her that she was probably supposed to be alarmed and not overwhelmed with relief.

"If you think your daddy buying a hotel makes you queen of it, you might want to do some research on your new subjects before you come sweeping into your new queendom. Thierry, Mademoiselle's key."

A young man gaping at them from behind the mahogany desk blinked at the crisp command, fumbled, and finally slipped a card into the two fingers Luc released from her body in order to take it.

Black eyes glittered down at her. "And you might want to know a little bit more about a man before you ask him to escort you to your room."

Her captor strode into the nearest elevator and dipped her enough to press a button without loosening his grip.

Summer stared up into night-black eyes as the doors shut them in. *Never get caught with a strange man by yourself in an elevator.*

Especially if that strange man had literally grabbed you up off the floor and hauled you into it.

Oh, what the hell. It was better than being clawed to shreds by rage and loneliness and anxiety. She laid her head down on his shoulder and went with it.

His fingers spasmed into her, a tiny, quickly controlled pressure. His chest moved in a long breath under her cheek.

A strong shoulder. She curled her face into it, concentrating on the male strength and delicious scent of him. Such a strange, complex mixture of scents, whispers, and promises of the entire world. Her eyes closed, tension draining out of her body.

His fingers flexed into her again, gentler, longer.

Good. He wasn't going to drop her. That was about all she needed to know at this point. She snuggled her face against his muscles, her mouth curving faintly as she drifted toward sleep.

The elevator's stop and his long, smooth stride as he left it nudged her awake again. Why was he walking so fast? Was he really carrying her off?

Her heart beat harder, adrenaline trying to break through her fatigue. She told her adrenaline to shut up. She liked this, plunging into erotic danger just where she had thought to be buried in deadly, merciless elegance. Kidnapped by a gorgeous stranger, you couldn't ask for a better distraction than that . . .